Deep Bay Legacy

(Book Three)

by Kathleen Morris

ISBN 978-1-927828-57-1
2nd edition

This book is dedicated to my veteran brother James, who like the main character, survived in spite of it all, and didn't let PTSD steal his legacy.

TABLE OF CONTENTS

Chapter 1

The waiting room was hot and sticky.

Pip couldn't believe how humid it was for the beginning of June, and the stifling heat made Dinah's pregnancy uncomfortable. Her contractions started by noon yesterday, and gradually got worse throughout the day. By suppertime, he took her to the hospital.

The doctor let Dinah go overdo two weeks, and that annoyed Pip. He was told that wasn't safe. In fact, he was told they would induce after ten days overdue, but it didn't happen. That made him wonder what kind of quack would let her go so long. It was probably why she was having problems.

If something happens to her, or the baby, that doctor will be the one to pay.

Pip wrung his hands as he slumped in a hard orange chair in the waiting room. Every fearful thought ran through his mind. Heart pounding, mouth dry, he could barely breathe as he waited impatiently. Why would they kick him out?

He put his green scrubs on like they told him to, and was prepared for the C-section, but they kicked him out. He understood why she needed surgery, especially with the baby in distress, but why couldn't he be there? She was *his* wife.

Pip bit his nails nervously. No one else was in the waiting room, luckily. Tears streamed down his cheeks, embarrassing for a 25-year-old man. Yet, it was a hospital, and emotional upset was common place, but not for him.

He kept going over details. One minute the monitors were fine, the next they started beeping. Doctors and residents hurried in, nurses bumped into equipment as they rushed around to see what was going on. "The baby's heart rate just took a nose dive!" That's when the doctor ordered him out like he was nobody important. "I'm sorry, Mr. Eaglefeather, we're going to have to ask you to step outside and let us do our work. We need to get the baby out as fast as possible."

At that point, Pip started to feel the bile rising in his throat. How could God bring him this far, and then let everything fall apart? What was going to happen to his wife and baby? Would they be okay, or would he lose everything like when he was a boy? He escaped a childhood of trauma growing up in northern Saskatchewan, witnessing murders, and almost losing his life a few times, living in the bush with his grandfather.

Then, when he met Dinah and found out what kind of childhood she came from, growing up in foster homes, messed up on drugs, getting caught up with the wrong crowd, it was no wonder he found her at the healing lodge.

It was called *Shining Star Lodge*, run by a nice old lady named, Sadie. She helped Dinah become the woman she is today, the future mother of his child. Surely God won't let anything bad happen to them.

Surely!

Pip's stomach grumbled, yet he knew he couldn't eat anything or it would go straight through him as it had done all through the night. His legs were getting cramped, so he decided he'd stretch them and pace the floors again. What else could he do at this point?

Walking toward the window, Pip looked out at the rain, wondering where it had been for so many weeks. Why the long dry spell? Why such heat? Why couldn't the rain have come two weeks ago when Dinah was crying her eyes out with swollen ankles, sweating in their non-air-conditioned apartment? It was the first on his to-do list: Find them a home to live in, instead of a grungy stifling apartment.

They lived there for the first three years of their marriage, and Pip had enough. It was hard to find good accommodations in Saskatoon, and that's where his job was, so moving out of the city wasn't an option. Sure, he wanted to, but he didn't know how. The thought of raising a child in the big city scared him, especially where they lived. The west side was slowly becoming the slums. Homeless people were usually found outside their apartment building, and petty thefts and assaults happened all the time.

God, help me get my family out of here, he prayed, choking back tears. He leaned against the cold damp window, as streams of rain trickled down, and continued to pray in earnest. He prayed for the safety of his wife. He prayed for the safety of his unborn child, and he prayed for the situation to end in a positive way.

Sniffling, Pip realized he should have called people. Having someone to sit with in the waiting room would have been nice, but he couldn't exactly call them now, especially his family. He hadn't heard from them in years. They went their own way after the Deep Bay incident, during his childhood.

After his uncle's death, and the tragic death of one of his older brothers, his middle brother moved to Prince Albert and was usually in and out of the P.A Pen for some drug trafficking violation or another. He didn't want any part of that lifestyle, nor did his brother want anything to do with a *Bible thumper*, he called him. And Grandfather, and Grayling were both dead now. Pip had felt alone for quite some time, but what could he do about it? He didn't have family like everyone else, except maybe co-workers and Facebook friends, and that wasn't the same.

Since Dinah had no family and he had no family, it made him want children all the more. And sure, he kept in touch with those that helped him through his difficult teenage years and the trauma both he and Dinah sustained at Deep Bay, but they had their own lives to live. He promised to call Loretta and Ben as soon as the baby was born, but the baby wasn't born yet, and they were miles away. They had their own grandchildren. And Brian and his wife had moved half across the country. They kept in touch from time to time, usually at Christmas, but that was it.

Since moving to Saskatoon four years ago, he lost touch with most of his friends and acquaintances. He got used to it after a while. Sadie, the old lady who helped Dinah recover as a teenager at *Shining Star Lodge,* is still running the place out there, and gives them a call occasionally, but she's too far away to do any good at all.

"Find a church," Sadie told him. "You need fellowship." But both he and Dinah tried several churches and didn't feel comfortable at any of them. It was just too hard to fit in, especially with him being aboriginal and Dinah being a white woman. They felt like outsiders most of the time.

They just stayed home on Sunday mornings and had their own little Bible study, and sang their own worship songs. Mostly they were just too tired to go anywhere, anyway. After a week of work, including Saturday's, Sunday was really the only day off they had together. It was a shame really. It seemed like the world was getting way too busy for its own good.

Pip's job at Mainway Hardware didn't pay very much but it was all he could get when he first moved to Saskatoon. And without any training or money saved to go to school, it was the best he could get. Sure he moved up the ladder, and was now supervisor in the paint department, but still it didn't pay well. And with a new baby coming, he already started to apply for different jobs. Nobody was hiring. *And while I'm asking, God,* he prayed again, *I need a new job. I need something that's going to pay the bills so Dinah doesn't have to go back to work. And I need a new place for my family so they feel safe.*

Pip brushed away another tear, noticing the rain was really coming down now. The farmers wouldn't be happy, but he was. He loved rain. It rained a lot in northern Saskatchewan where he was from. He missed that very much.

At times, mostly during rush-hour traffic, he longed to go back home to Deep Bay. One time he and Dinah almost moved back there, but it wasn't meant to be. Plans fell through, money ran out, and they had to make a living somehow. Dinah took a job as a librarian at Plainsview Elementary School for a few hours a day. It didn't pay well but it supported her passion; and her passion was writing. She was working on her first book.

In the evening, she worked at the Steakhouse as a waitress. Her tips were good, but Pip advised her to quit when she kept coming home exhausted and swollen every night. She was already six months pregnant and needed to get off her feet. Their income took a nosedive, but he didn't care. His wife and baby were more important.

"Why don't you go to school, Pip?" Sadie always told him whenever she phoned from the Shining Star Lodge. "There's government funding for you. I can send you a list of Aboriginal scholarship programs you can apply for." But he always said no. His excuse was that he didn't want to take a handout, and he felt like that's what it was. He didn't want to fall into the same category as most of the aboriginal students out there, and the assumption that their education was somehow cheapened because it was paid for by the government.

It was bad enough that he had a stigma attached to him, and the only thing people saw was the color of his skin. No, he would not take any government handout. He would make his own way. It was something both grandfather and Grayling drilled into him at a young age. Grandfather used to always say, "We may not have much, and there isn't a lot I can give you, but there is one thing: Dignity, Pipata Eaglefeather. Be proud of who you are and where you came from, and carve your own path as your ancestors did."

And so he had. Life was about making choices, and he knew that when he chose not to go to school. But now, there was a new reason to make a better life. His baby was about to be born and that changed everything. At least he could find a better job, even if he didn't go to school. There was always something out there. Trusting God was what he had done in the past and planned to do for the future. He just needed to get through this.

Pip gave his head a shake. Why was this stuff on his mind right now, anyway? He was too tired to think straight. He raked his shaky fingers through his hair and sat back down on the orange chair. Surely, it wouldn't take much longer for the doctor to let him know what was going on. The not knowing, was killing him.

~~~~

Sadie leafed through her address book looking for Pip's cell phone number. She hadn't heard from him in over a week and the baby was due two weeks ago. She wondered if he had forgotten to call. But surely he wouldn't have forgotten something as important as that. Still, she worried about the two of them. They were not doing very well. If only they would find a church of their own to worship in, they would have the fellowship they needed.

Loneliness was something Sadie knew a great deal about. She wished there was someone else besides her, living at Shining Star Lodge. Sure the guests came and went, but that wasn't the same. She needed companionship as much as Pip and Dinah did.

For the longest time she had been trying to find a way for the board to hire a second maintenance worker. The regular guy wasn't very reliable and when he did show up, he usually didn't do a very good job. It was hard to find reliable workers in the north, and that was exactly her point for hiring a second maintenance worker.

The last time a job was available at Shining Star Lodge, Pip almost moved back, but by the time he decided to take it, the board had already hired someone else: The current lazy maintenance man, Abdul. A decision Sadie wished she could overturn. But perhaps a request for a second full time maintenance man would be approved soon, and she could get Pip and Dinah and their new baby out permanently. Dinah could write all she wanted then. Her little butterfly. Oh how she missed her over the years. It was time to come back home.

But then maybe it wasn't home for them? They were both young, and sometimes when you're young, you want to be as far away from home as possible. Pip especially, he left a lot of pain behind when he moved down south. It wasn't likely he'd want to come back to that. He didn't even have any relatives in the area anymore. The only one he did have, was in prison.

Sadie shook her head and continued to leaf through the address book. Normally she would know the number off the top of her head, but lately she was forgetting things. Perhaps she could chalk it down to old age, but that wasn't the only reason. Mostly she was just unorganized, and running the lodge by herself was a great undertaking. So much so, that it was overwhelming most days.

No, she didn't just need a second maintenance man, she needed a kitchen helper, someone to do the boat work, and housekeeping staff. Trying to do it all on her own was only making her look older, faster. Already her mouse-grey hair was quickly turning white. No man would ever want her now. Sure, when the incident at Shining Star Lodge happened years back, she met a man that took an interest in her. But he was only passing through, and didn't want to stay in such an isolated area, as much as he professed he cared for her.

It wasn't meant to be. No, if God wanted her to find love, He would have to find her someone that would make his home at the lodge with her. Until then, she would have to settle for the many guests that would come and go each month.

It sure would be nice to have familiar faces around, and a baby to dote over. Bring back my butterfly to me! she prayed aloud, then paused, hoping for an audible answer. But God usually wasn't as direct as that. No, she knew the way it worked. Experience told her that God's answers were never, no, but rather, not now, or, I have something else in mind.

When people say God doesn't answer prayers, or He says no all the time, she knew differently. She knew it was only a matter of time before something would happen. And what that something was, was always a big surprise. Still, Sadie hoped the surprise was what she wanted.

There it is, she smiled, running her finger down the last page of the address book. What was Eaglefeather doing under, Z? It was a mystery to her, but at least she found the number. She'd give him a call right away.

~~~~

"Pip? Is that you?"

"Yeah, it's me."

"Why so down my boy?"

Pip didn't want to explain the situation, but he figured he owed it to her. Sadie was their closest friend, and the more people praying for Dinah and the baby, the better. It was just hard to rehash everything, so he figured he'd give her the short form. "Dinah is having emergency surgery."

"What? Right now? Is everything okay?"

"I don't know." Pip fought back the tears. He didn't know if saying it aloud was what started the emotional roller coaster, or hearing a familiar voice that made him break down. But whatever the reason, it was a long time coming.

"Is it the baby?"

"Yes!" He continued to sob. "Dinah was in labor, and then all of a sudden they kicked me out and told me they had to get the baby out fast. I haven't heard anything since."

"Why didn't you call? I mean...sorry. You must have enough on your mind."

"Sadie..." Pip sniffled, speaking quietly now, "what if they both...die...and I'm left with...with nothing?"

"Oh my dear boy. God won't let that happen! I'll start a prayer chain immediately!"

But Pip knew it could happen. It happened to others, and God didn't save them. His entire childhood had been carved that way. As much as he believed in God and the power of prayer, doubts still surfaced. "I'd appreciate that. It helps to know that people care."

"People do care, Pip! I care!"

"Thank you!"

"Now, I want you to let me know the moment you hear something. Do you understand? If I don't hear back from you, I'll call."

"Okay." Pip told her, sniffling again, embarrassed for crying.

"How long has she been in surgery?"

"It's been over an hour."

"Okay, well try not to worry. I know that sounds cliché, but just spend the time praying, and I'll do the same. Now, I need to go start the prayer chain. Love you my boy."

"I love you too, Sadie." Pip ended the call and set his phone down beside him. He rubbed his temples with his palms, and paused for a moment. He knew Sadie was right and he needed to stay positive and pray as hard as he could. It's what he had been doing all along, but the doubts were creeping in fast with every moment that went by.

God in heaven, protect my wife and child, and let everything be okay!

Chapter 2

Sadie immediately called her friend Gladys who promised to continue the prayer chain by phone. She filled her in with all the details, said a prayer together with Gladys on the phone, and then hung up. Next she went on her computer and posted a status on Facebook for her Global Missions friends. Even though she wasn't too keen on social media the way the young people were, she knew it was the fastest and best method to get the word out.

It bothered her that Pip hadn't called, until she had. For a long time, she had been praying for him and Dinah. They seemed to be lost, displaced without family or friends, or even a church family. She realized not everyone thought church to be important, and yes, one could be a Christian without going, but it helped especially when you didn't have family.

It would break her heart if those two young people disconnected from her as well. She had to do something besides pray. Usually she stayed out of things and let God do the work, but sometimes it was time to act. She'd light a fire under the boards butt to hire a second maintenance man. Sadie picked up the phone and pressed in the numbers. "Hello, Brother Devin, Sadie here. Remember when I put in a request for a second maintenance man around here?"

"Sure sure." The elderly gentleman replied.

"Well, I was wondering. Has the board made a decision yet?"

The man on the other line hummed and hawed, and that same uncomfortable feeling Sadie got last time she called, crept in. She'd tried this before, and always got the run-a-round. What was going on, anyway?

"Well, Sadie," the old man spoke softly, all of a sudden, "since I have you on the phone, I might as well tell you. The board just met yesterday, and we were going to make it official. But..."

Sadie didn't like the sound of that. She felt her forehead start to perspire and her pulse thump like she was running a marathon. "But what, Brother Devin?"

"We...um, we're shutting you down?"

"What? Why?" Sadie couldn't believe what she was hearing. They couldn't just shut her down. The place belonged to Ben and Loretta not them. There never was a danger of the place closing down before. It was willed to Ben. Sure, after the fire, they had to go into debt to rebuild, but Ben and Loretta would have told her if the lodge was in trouble financially.

"I'm sorry Sadie," Brother Devin told her. "Ben wanted to tell you himself but he and Loretta left on a two-week European cruise this morning. He didn't want us to say anything until he had a chance to talk to you...and since you asked about hiring someone else, you put me in a hard spot. I shouldn't have said anything. You're upset aren't you?"

Sadie cleared her throat. "Of course I'm upset! I can't believe this."

"Please don't be upset."

How could she not be upset? The lodge was her job, and home. She couldn't have one without the other. What was she going to do now? "You're right, Devin, you shouldn't have said anything. Now what am I supposed to do to make a living? Where am I going to live?"

"Now Sadie..." The man fumbled his words. "I...um, oh dear. This is what Ben wanted to talk to you about. I'm sorry. I'll just say it. He wanted to make sure you understood that you don't have to move. It wasn't his decision to shut the Shining Star Ministries down, it was ours. We have decided to go in another direction, that's all. The actual physical building with still be functional. You needn't worry about that. You still have a home."

Just not a job.

"Okay, well I guess I'll wait until Ben calls me in a couple weeks to explain it all. I won't put you on the hot seat any longer Devin. If the board won't fund Shining Star Ministries anymore, then that is the way it is. I just need to find another job."

"And we will write you the best reference letter possible. Just say the word."

Sadie almost gasped. Did they realize where she was living? It was in the middle of nowhere in northern Canada. She may as well be on the moon, because jobs in the region were not exactly plentiful. And that wasn't the only concern she had, she was old, far too old to be sending out résumés and reference letters and hunting down work. It wasn't fair.

She should be retiring, not looking for another job. But retirement wasn't an option. It never was. She simply didn't make enough to save for a retirement fund. Working for a non-profit organization hadn't made her rich, it actually prevented her from having the necessities of life, sometimes.

But then she stopped herself. She was not going to be bitter. Shining Star Lodge had been a blessing for so many people, including herself. She wanted to remember it that way. But what was she going to do now? Living in a shell of a lodge without guests coming and going, would be a lonely life, not to mention a poor one. She either had to find a way to make a living, or be forced to move no matter how generous Ben and Loretta were with their place. They didn't have to let her live there. They could just up and sell, but it didn't sound like that's what they intended to do.

"Sadie?" The voice on the other end called out. "Are you still there?"

"Yes, I'm still here. I'm just thinking."

"Well, you needn't worry. You still have a place to live."

"Thank you, Devin, I appreciate you saying that, but I'm afraid it gives me little comfort. I'm still worried."

"Well don't be. Ben wouldn't want that. He'll call when he gets back. Anyway. I should run. I'll let you go, Sadie. Bye for now."

And with that, the phone went dead. Was that really the end of her job, the mission, everything? After all the lives they helped turn around, after all the work she had done with the young people that were sent to her, this was how it was going to end? Oh, how she wished she hadn't called. But then, she called to ask for a job for Pip. Now she couldn't offer him anything.

And the baby...oh, she better get praying about that baby. Her own problems would have to wait for now. There were more important things going on at the moment.

~~~~

Dinah came too, groggy and out of sorts. Her vision was blurry and she felt numb. Where was she? What was going on? Where was Pip? And... *the* baby? Panic rose in her chest and she tried to sit up, but none of her limbs responded. "Help!" she tried to scream, but only small squeaks came out.

17

"Oh, Mrs. Eaglefeather," a nearby voice spoke. "You're finally awake."

She heard some mumbling, then a group of nurses quickly gathered around her.

"You needn't try to get up. Your body is still numb from the anesthetic we gave you. You had a difficult time of it."

Dinah cleared her throat and tried to speak again. "Difficult?"

"Yes! It was touch and go there for a while, but you pulled through, somehow. You sure are a fighter. You put on quite the show for all those residents, but you wouldn't remember any of that, now would you. You were out cold."

She was right. She had no memory of that, only Pip sitting at her side in the labor and delivery ward. "Where's Pip?"

"Who?"

"My husband."

The nurse furrowed her brown, and that alerted Dinah immediately. She could tell something was on her mind.

"Mr. Eaglefeather went to the nursery. But he told me you weren't...married anymore. In fact, he said he hadn't seen you for nine months. Didn't even know you were pregnant."

"What? That's ridiculous?" Dinah replied, raising her raspy voice. "Why would he say that?" Apparently her panic had alerted the entire nursing staff to come running. They tried to calm her down but she wouldn't have any of it. She deserved to know what was going on. Why would Pip say they weren't married anymore?

"Dinah! Please, calm down!"

"NO! Not until you get my husband! I want to see my husband! I want to see my baby. BRING ME MY BABY!"

Suddenly sirens went off in the hospital hallway, and immediately most of the nurses left. Dinah could hear the 'code pink' announcement broadcasted all over the ward. Tears formed in her eyes. "What does that mean? What is code pink?"

"Um...nothing dear! Don't you worry your pretty little head," the older nurse tried to calm her by closing the double doors to the hallway, blocking the noise.

"Then, tell me what's wrong?"

"Nothing's wrong! Just ignore the noise. All you have to be concerned with is your baby. You have a beautiful healthy girl. A real sweetheart. She doesn't have your coloring, but she's got gorgeous dark skin like your ex husb—"

"I told you he's not my ex, he's my husband!"

The nurse frowned. "Well, whatever you call him. He followed the baby to the nursery, but we checked his I.D first, so don't worry. He was, in fact, Mr. Eaglefeather. Tall thin fella with a silver smile?"

"Silver smile? What are you talking about?" Dinah couldn't believe this. Did they give her baby to the wrong dad?

"You know, his silver front tooth?"

"What? NO! That's not him. He's never been to the dentist in his life."

The nurse chuckled like she didn't believe her. "I'm sure we'll get this all sorted out eventually. I just started my shift, so what do I know? You've been out of it for a while, so you're probably a little fuzzy."

"Fuzzy? I think I know my own husband!"

"I'm sure you do," the nurse said, shushing her as she took Dinah's vitals, and looked at her watch.

"You need to calm down, my dear. Your baby needs a healthy mama."

Tears rolled down Dinah's cheek as she flopped her head on the pillow, frustrated and worried that they gave her baby to the wrong dad. A baby. I have a baby girl. Where was her baby? Where was Pip? All these unanswered questions made Dinah's head hurt. And she could barely keep her eyelids open. They had given her something and now she was drifting off to sleep again. No! She didn't want to, but it was too hard to fight. Maybe when she wakes, this will all be a bad dream?

~~~~

"My staff already told you officer." Dr. Uric lowered his voice. "The guy had I.D and everything. He was definitely the father. I don't know why he would have taken the newborn out of the hospital without consent, but it's not an abduction. Maybe he didn't understand that we keep newborns for at least twenty-four hours?"

The balding officer was busy taking notes and finally looked up. "So you're telling me there was no need to call us at all?"

"Well, yes and no. I mean, it's protocol when a newborn goes missing, but she's with the father for sure. Our security cameras prove that. He took her out the front doors shortly after she was brought to the nursery to get weighed and measured. But there was a shift change, and I'll have to call the night staff back in for questioning if you insist this is an abduction. They aren't going to be very happy with me."

The officer shook his head. "Fine then. We'll check the security cameras for now, but let us know when the mother is awake. We'd like to speak with her about the father."

"I'm sure that will clear everything up. The natives around here are different with their cultural beliefs." Dr. Uric tried to smile. "He probably wanted to hold her up to the moon or something. Who knows. I'm sure he'll be back. The mother is in I.C.U for Pete's sake. He wouldn't just leave her."

Chapter 3

Pip lay bloodied and bound in the half-lit linen closet.

He never even saw it coming. One minute he was waiting in the hall, praying for his wife and child, the next he was lying in a linen closet with an unbelievable headache. God? He could barely even pray. This was all too much. Why would someone knock him out? Was some mental patient on the loose and he was just in the wrong place at the wrong time? It didn't make sense.

With his feet, he began kicking the door. As far as he could tell he was still in the hospital, but he didn't know for sure. "Mmmmm." He tried to shout through a duct-taped mouth that was so tightly wrapped it hurt to breathe.

Visions of his childhood began to plague his mind. His brothers would always play tricks like this on him, especially his psychotic uncle. One time they trapped him in a cave near Deep Bay, and didn't let him out for two days. It was then, that he started his pretending games. Either he was a monkey, or a Chipewyan warrior chief. Those two were his favorites. He'd retreat in some small corner of his mind, to cope. It was a childish game that helped him through his difficult childhood. He thought he'd forgotten that part of himself, but it was all resurfacing now.

Where was grandfather when he needed him? He had nobody. It was just him and Dinah for so long. They didn't have any connections with people. They didn't have any relatives they could rely on. Nobody cared. What if nobody found him at all? But he spoke to Sadie earlier. At least she would call, that is if he still had his cell phone on him. With his hands tied behind his back, he wasn't able to check his jacket pocket where he usually kept it.

Suddenly, he heard a familiar ring. My phone! It wasn't coming from his jacket, but from the pail beside the door. The closet was dark, except for the bright light that beamed in under the door, but at least it was enough light so he could see his way over to it.

Little by little he scooted to the pail. There it is! It was ringing his favorite tune inside the pail. Thankfully it was an empty pail. Water would have destroyed it. At least something was working in his favor. Now he just had to figure out how to answer it before whoever was phoning hung up. It was probably Sadie.

Hurry up, he told himself as he tongued the duct-tape, hoping to free his mouth so he could use it to free his hands and answer the phone in time. But it was virtually impossible unless you were James Bond or Houdini.

The phone suddenly stopped ringing. It was too late. He had missed his chance to be rescued. Why was everything against him? Nothing ever worked out. Now what was he supposed to do, kick the door some more? Guess so!

Pip dropped his head, defeated. The situation mirrored how he had been feeling for the past couple years. How ironic. He didn't need to be bound hand and foot to figure out that his life was going in the wrong direction, and he didn't know how to fix it.

There was no good in it except for Dinah and the baby. And he even wondered if that had turned out. He didn't know how the surgery went, or if his wife and baby were even alive. He needed some answers! He needed to get out of there. But with no way to get his cell phone, and no way to use his hands or mouth to open the door, he was doomed.

I give up, God!

But only silence answered him back. Typical, he thought. Was God even there? Maybe He'd forgotten about him. He'd wondered that for a while. Dinah would get after him if she knew how he was feeling right now, but he couldn't help it. He felt abandoned, just like when he was a kid.

With the nightly street brawls in front of their apartment lately, and the gang violence, it was hard to see God anywhere. The crime was so bad he had to put three dead-bolts on the apartment door, just to feel safe. It was awful!

And lately, he thought they had a stalker. Some guy in a red hoody kept following them daily for a couple months. At first he thought it was his imagination, but then it became so regular that it couldn't just be a coincidence. He never told Dinah, afraid it would create worry and stress that she didn't need while pregnant. But he was sure of it now. Always the same time, and same place, in front of the obstetrics office. Maybe the guy's wife was expecting a child as well? Could be, but then why was he there every time he turned around? It freaked him out. In fact, now that he thought about it, perhaps that was the same lunatic that knocked him out?

Naaaaah! His mind was playing tricks on him. It was too farfetched even for him. No, his best bet was to stay focused and keep kicking at the door. Surely someone would hear him.

Surely!

~~~~

Strange, Sadie thought. Why wasn't Pip answering his phone? He always had it with him no matter what. In fact, his favorite past time, was playing with his phone. It was like that for all the young people these days. Everything was instant including communication. It was something she couldn't understand. Didn't they get sick of the old ball and chain? That's what she called cell phones. Still, Pip would have answered by now. Something was wrong.

As she sat in her lazy-boy and rubbed her forehead, she realized what she had to do. She had no choice but to hop on the next float plane to Saskatoon. She didn't have any customers staying at the lodge at the moment. The retreat ended a couple days ago and that was apparently the last one they'd ever have. There was no reason she had to stick around. She'd simply leave a note for Abdul.

Sadie couldn't remember the last time she'd been anywhere. Not good. It was time to get out of there and see the world. She could look for work while in the city. Maybe moving to Saskatoon would help Pip and Dinah? Maybe she could tend to the baby while they were at work?

A multitude of ideas began to race through Sadie's head. But before she let herself get carried away, she'd have to call the charter service and see if she could catch a flight in the morning. And then she had to pack. She'd be sure to load up a suitcase filled with gifts for the new babe.

Oh, how she wished Pip would answer his phone. She really needed to know if they were okay. It was driving her crazy, but she'd just have to wait.

~~~~

"Take a look at this?" the detective queried.

"Talk to me, Spencer. What do we got?" Grayson hoped it was something good, because right now, nothing was making sense. It was odd they were putting so much effort into an amber alert that wasn't really an abduction. They were told the code pink at the hospital was just a formality and the father took her. But he didn't buy it. Something smelled fishy.

"We got two aboriginal males entering the hospital at different times, dressed exactly the same. Look." The officer pressed rewind and played again. "You have male number one entering with pregnant lady here. Then, shortly after, you have male number two carrying an empty car seat. He appears to be stalking them."

"And he knows how to work the cameras. See!" Detective Grayson pointed at the video screen and shook his head. The guy was good, he'd give him that. "Boys, I think we have a bona fide abduction here. These men, the father, are two different people."

They were going to be working overtime on this one.

"You have the clip of him leaving the hospital?"

"Yup! Take a look at this." The officer fast-forwarded the video.

Grayson viewed a man exiting the hospital with a baby in a car seat. The guy didn't even rush out the door. He takes his time and even waves at the couple coming in. "Could we have this all wrong?"

"Don't know. The couple signed in as Pip and Dinah Eaglefeather, at emergency. We checked the ledger. But the nurse says they weren't married anymore and the dad didn't even know about the baby until it was about to be born. Could it be a custody thing?"

"Could be." Grayson bit his lip, thinking again. "But the guy showed his I.D before taking the baby. I don't get it. Who is this other guy, then? Doesn't make sense. He played it out over and over in his mind. "They look alike though. That can't be a coincidence. And the clothes. They're dressed exactly the same for a reason."

"Maybe the first guy just brought her in and left?" the officer said. "We have him coming in with the pregnant lady, but he never left. Seriously, we went over every inch of the video, and we can't see him exiting the building unless he got out through some restricted exit, which of course would have triggered the alarms."

"I don't know." Grayson frowned. "Something stinks, and I'm gonna find out what. I'm pretty sure it's an abduction, but there's a lot of unanswered questions, so I might be wrong. I need to talk to the mother. Maybe she knows what's going on. Who knows, boys. This all might be a big misunderstanding, like the doctor said. Cross your fingers."

Grayson sipped some coffee and went on. "Get me everything you've got on this Pipata Eaglefeather. In the meantime, I'm going back to the hospital to talk to Mom. Maybe she'll shed some light on the subject. I really hope this isn't a custody battle or some dumb polygamy thing."

"It's called polyandry."

"What?"

"Polyandry." The detective mused. "More than one husband?"

"Oh! Just what I needed to hear, Spence. Thanks for that!"

"No problem, bud." The jovial detective playfully winked, then turned and continued clicking the computer keys, grinning from ear to ear.

Grayson chuckled and walked away. The wise crack sent his mind reeling, hoping the joke was just a joke. He couldn't imagine sharing his wife with another guy. But seriously, when pit against a child abduction, he found himself rooting for polyandry, as sick as it was. To have a newborn stolen, was a parent's worst nightmare, one he was glad he'd never have to worry about. He and his wife couldn't have children. A heartbreak at first, but really, a blessing in disguise.

Regardless, Grayson was confident his team would get to the bottom of this soon enough. As long as he kept pumping them with coffee, they'd work all night.

Chapter 4

"I can't stand it!" Chloe cried to her friend Rozelyn, over coffee at her house.

"Well, does he know how you feel?"

"Of course he knows, but he doesn't care! He doesn't care!"

"Oh Chloe, I'm sure he cares. He's just busy like they all are. Me and Spence have misunderstandings like this. Mostly because he's got his mind on the job all the time. When he's home, he's not really home. His mind is always on work and he doesn't hear me. I have to nag until he clicks in. Maybe that's what you have to do with Grayson?"

Chloe was so upset she couldn't stop bawling. It was embarrassing, but she was tired of hiding it from her friend. It was the first time she opened up about the issue since it all began. She had bottled it up inside, and now she was a blubbering mess.

"I tried nagging and it doesn't work! I should've told you a long time ago, but it was private. I got my test results back from our fertility specialist, finally after four months of waiting, and he said I'll never be able to get pregnant with an elevated FSH level! And he doesn't even think IVF would help my situation.

Even though I still want to try, Grayson doesn't! He says it's a waste of time and money, and he won't even consider looking into adoption, either!" The bawling got louder, and Chloe couldn't stop.

"Oh honey, why didn't you tell me this sooner? Now it all makes sense. You've been miserable for a long time, haven't you?"

"Yes! It…it hurts sooo bad!"

"Okay! That's it!"

Chloe sniffled and hiccupped. "What?"

"You need some girl time. Let's go shopping. We'll get a mani/pedi and pig out on ice-cream and hamburgers."

"Like this? I'm a mess. Look at me." Chloe loved her friend but she bordered on the crazy side. Her idea of shopping was a whirlwind of wild adventures and she wasn't up for that today. She'd done it many times, and it wasn't happening. Not now, not when she wanted to wallow in her sorrows. She couldn't have a baby and nothing would take her mind off of that. But she knew her friend meant well. A distraction made sense but it wasn't going to work this time.

"C'mon, I'll drive." Rozelyn grinned.

"No, I can't. I'm too upset; besides, I have to work early."

"Okay, but you know the guys are pulling an all-nighter again. So can we! Just say the word. It will make you feel better. Promise!"

Chloe actually considered it for moment, then caught a glimpse of her reflection in the china cabinet. "No... absolutely not!"

"Your loss."

"I appreciate the offer." Chloe wiped her nose. "But seriously, Rozelyn, what am I going to do? I always pictured myself with kids."

"Well, why doesn't he want to adopt?"

"I don't knooooooow!" And the tears continued.

Her friend sat there with her thinking face on. Now she was in trouble. "I got it! This is what you're going to do, young lady. You and I are going to visit The Luther Home, tomorrow after work."

"The what?"

"The Luther Home. It's a home for teenage mothers. I'm a social worker. Trust me. I know these things. We don't deal with this particular home because it's privately run by a non-profit church organization, but it doesn't hurt to take a look. I'm sure they don't bite."

"And it's in Saskatoon?"

"Right here in our own back yard."

Chloe dried her tears and blew her nose. Maybe it wouldn't hurt to take a look at this place. If they handled adoption, she could at least find out what the waiting list was like and what the whole process involved. Surely, Grayson wouldn't mind her checking it out. He wouldn't be home anyway. These all-nighters had a habit of turning into two or three. "Okay, let's do it!"

"You're smiling, kiddo! Now that's more like it! I'll pick you up after work tomorrow. Now, no more crying. Promise?"

Chloe shook her head and took an uneven breath. "Promise."

~~~~

The long plane ride took its toll on Sadie. She was completely exhausted by the time she got to Saskatoon. And since Pip still wasn't answering his cell phone, she figured she'd catch a few hours of sleep and head off to the hospital in the morning. She just couldn't keep her eyes open one more minute.

Calling the hospital was a big disappointment. They wouldn't give her any information at all. They said she wasn't a relative, and they couldn't give out details like that to just anyone. It wasn't like she was Dinah's mother, or any kind of relative. The fact is, she was nobody, at least according to the hospital staff. And Dinah wasn't answering her cell phone either. Sadie sighed. She hoped that her trip to the hospital tomorrow would give her some answers. She prayed everything was okay.

The shower made her feel even sleepier. She toweled herself off and dressed herself in her favorite pajamas, and crawled into bed. Now she knew why she hadn't traveled in a while. It was hard work. The trip took all day, and wasn't exactly comfortable. A good sleep would make all the difference.

Take care of my little butterfly, Lord.

~~~~

Dinah was mobile now. She could feel her arms and legs again, and that was a relief. But the rest of her was a mess. She spent an entire day in and out of consciousness, deliberately sedated because of what was going on.

And what was going on? She still didn't know. She would spend yet another night worrying about her baby and husband. It wasn't true what they were telling her. Pip would never leave her, or leave the hospital with their baby, without telling her first. He wasn't the estranged husband they were making him out to be. She'd never heard of such nonsense. But she couldn't cry about it anymore.

It was time to sleep, yet her mind wouldn't turn off. The hospital was quieting down, but she was still fully awake. And now her milk was coming in. Her breasts hurt so bad she couldn't get comfortable. And the incision from her C-section made her scratch continuously.

All Dinah wanted to do was hold her baby for the first time, yet she wasn't even given that privilege. An unimaginable sorrow fell over her, and she wondered why this was happening. Why was Pip doing this to her? Or maybe he wasn't? But if he wasn't, then where was he? Where was her baby? All these unanswered questions consumed her. Sleep was not going to come easily.

They moved her to a different ward instead of having her stay amongst the other new mothers. It was offensive at first, but she was thankful for the quiet area they put her in. She didn't have to listen to the other babies crying, and long for her own. It would've been way too hard.

Dinah wondered what her baby looked like. The nurse said she had lovely dark skin like Pip's. Oh how she longed to see her, hold her in her arms, nurse her. It was an ache unlike anything she'd ever felt before. It was like a void that couldn't be filled.

What was she going to do? How would she survive this? What if they never find her baby? What if they never find her husband? What if he did leave her?

Dinah gave up calling Pip's cell phone. He wasn't answering, so she decided, neither would she. She turned it off and pondered. Something was still bothering her. Why would Pip wear a false tooth? He didn't have a silver cap. He hadn't been to the dentist. Why the charade? If he didn't love her anymore, why didn't he just say so? Why did he have to take her child? Their child.

Still, this was insanity? Had he finally lost his mind? He came pretty close sometimes, dealing with all his family issues from childhood, and then struggling for the last three years financially. But still, they had each other, and she thought that was enough. Was all the anticipation of the baby's birth a great big lie?

Ooooh! These mild reeling questions were not helping her headache at all. Maybe she needed a sleeping pill. As Dinah pressed the buzzer attached to her bed sheet, and waited for the nurse to come, she wondered what tomorrow would bring. She was told, the police wanted to talk to her in the morning.

That should be fun.

Chapter 5

The morning was sunny and warm, a much-needed change after the last few days of solid rain. Chloe headed out to work early as usual, hoping her day would go quickly. She could hardly wait to check out the adoption idea, even though she didn't dare mention it to Grayson when he called.

He called her from the hospital last night, but told her he couldn't tell her much about the case he was on, just that it was a waste of time going there. Apparently, he had waited all day to talk to a patient, just to be turned away because she was sedated.

 It was part of the job, the frustration part. Usually Chloe found it hard to encourage her husband in what most of the time, turned out to be an impossible task. But she tried anyway. That's the kind of person she was.

Usually these things worked themselves out, so she didn't get too worried about it. Grayson was a tough guy, and for the most part that was fine with her. Manly men were more attractive in her opinion, in fact that's what made her fall in love with him in the first place. It's just that manly men, were not good at talking about their feelings, and that's exactly what she needed with this whole fertility thing, or rather, infertility thing. She still found it hard to believe they couldn't have children.

For the longest time she thought the doctors were completely wrong. If it wasn't Grayson, she knew it was her. But still, tests were not always accurate. She had spent far too long hoping for that. But the final tests proved it. Her reproductive system was broken, and there was nothing she could do about it.

IVF might give them a chance, a 1% chance if they were lucky, but really, adoption was their best option, by far. And she thought about it continuously. How could she keep her mind focused on work? Almost every thought in her brain was about babies these days. And she had a full day of clients. They overbooked her again, but this time she wasn't going to let it bother her. Today she was going to find out her options.

Working for home-care, sometimes brought her down with the many grumpy elderly patients she saw daily. A lot of the times, their depression rubbed off on her. How many times did she hear them complaining about some ailment, or the fact that they didn't have enough money to live. Yes, she sympathized about their hardships, but sometimes it was too much for her to take. Especially the last few years, dealing with her own depressing infertility issues.

But today she wasn't going to let anything get her down. The old biddies could crab all they want, but nothing was going to destroy her excitement. Today was the start of a new path in her life. Just think of it, she could be a mother in days, or months. But working on Grayson would be the hard part. To get him to change his mind, would be challenging, but if she did all the legwork, he would have nothing to complain about. Hopefully!

Chloe looked at her watch and realized she'd be late if she didn't hurry. She jumped in her Mazda, made sure her face was okay, and started the vehicle. She was thankful for the cool summer mornings. By the end of the day, it would be hot enough, typical June weather. At least it was light out already, and that made heading to work at 6 AM, a little more bearable. But then, she had better learn how to be flexible. If she played her cards right, she'd be adjusting to feedings, and diaper changes, for her new little adopted son or daughter, soon. She grinned at herself in the mirror. I'm gonna be a mother!

~~~~

Sadie yawned as she took one last look around the hotel room to make sure she didn't forget anything. At first, she was going to stay a few nights at the hotel, but then realized Pip and Dinah didn't have anyone to help them with the new baby. She decided she was going to volunteer her services and stay as long as they needed her. If for some reason it wasn't okay, she'd just come back to the hotel. Why pay for another night when she didn't have to? It was a bit premature, especially since she didn't know exactly what was going on, but she hoped and prayed everything was fine.

At the front entrance, Sadie spotted a taxi and pulled her suitcase toward it. "Can you take me to the Royal University Hospital please?" she asked the driver.

"No problem," the Middle Eastern man with a turban replied.

The warm summer morning beamed down upon her face, as Sadie took in a breath of fresh air. It definitely wasn't the same fresh air as she was used to in northern Saskatchewan, but it would have to do. City air was hard to adjust to, but considering the circumstances, she knew she had to get used to it sooner or later. She was likely to be stuck in the city for a while, if not permanently.

~~~~

Cramping limbs, made it impossible for Pip to feel his hands and feet. The minor pins and needles he was experiencing a few hours ago, had turned into severe numbness. The duct-tape was so tight it was cutting off his circulation. And kicking the door with his useless legs, didn't attract much attention. He was starting to wonder if anyone was ever going to find him.

Pip couldn't remember much of the last few hours, except that he started hyperventilating and passed out at one point. It started as uncontrollable shaking like usual, then nausea, then sweat literally poured off his body. No wonder he was smelling something gross.

Without bathroom facilities, he soiled himself, and that didn't feel very pleasant. Even though he was very embarrassed, and the stench filled the confined space, he still hoped someone would discover him soon. If Pip had to spend another day in there, it may just be his last.

And what had happened with his wife and baby? Where did they think he was?

"Ooooh," he groaned. He couldn't stand the pain anymore. And not just the physical pain, the hurt that welled deep inside. It was killing him. The torture of not knowing what was going on, was eating him alive.

Who would do this to him...and why?

Chapter 6

Grayson tried to put the pieces together. He had already drilled the staff about the birth, going through every detail in his mind until he made himself dizzy. But it wasn't just that, he'd need another caffeine fix if he was going to be at this again all day. He was running on empty from the all-nighters.

And still the mother wasn't available. Boy, he knew she just had a baby, but surely they could provide a time for him to question her. The doctor on call wasn't exactly helpful. It was almost as if he was deliberately trying to stall his efforts. But that's how doctors were. They never really listened and always seemed to be too busy.

He guessed his poor attitude about doctors, stemmed from all the poking and prodding he and Chloe went through with their fertility issues. Rather, her fertility issues. He was fine; nothing wrong with his swimmers. But his wife was miserable, and ignoring her feelings was only going to make things worse. She wanted a baby one way or the other. Ugh! Were they going to become one of those couples that go to a foreign country to adopt a baby, only to find out later, it has severe health problems? Probably.

"Here's your coffee sir." A feminine voice interrupted his thoughts. He was glad for the distraction because he definitely hadn't intended to drift to that topic. He needed to focus on the case.

"Thanks!" Grayson said, sipping the hot drink carefully. His buddy, Spencer, and partner for almost nine years, stood gathering a team together to comb through the hospital one more time. They'd been through all surveillance cameras, but still weren't any further than yesterday. And the first sweep-through of the hospital hadn't given them any leads at all.

Where was this Eaglefeather character, anyway?

They searched his residence, but hadn't found anything unusual. The young man had simply disappeared. No credit card transactions had taken place; He hadn't gotten on any flights, or even driven his car out of the hospital parking lot. And it appeared his wife did in fact, live with him. Not sure why it was rumored that they weren't together anymore. And there was even a nursery set up in the apartment. It didn't make any sense at all. A father would want to stick around after the birth of his child, wouldn't he? Something wasn't right.

Grayson had to talk to the mother. Enough of this! They were running out of time. The odds of finding an abducted child dropped significantly with every passing hour, and he wasn't going to play this waiting game any longer. If the chief of staff wasn't going to co-operate and allow him to question the mother soon, he'd force the issue and arrive unannounced.

~~~~

Sadie tried not to get lost in the big hospital, but it was almost impossible not to. She was told to go to anti-partum, whatever that was. Fourth floor, room 408. But the sign above her said maternity ward, and she figured that's where Dinah would be. After-all, she did just have a baby. "Excuse me, nurse, I'm looking for someone. She just gave birth. I mean…I'm looking for my daughter."

Immediately Sadie cringed. She knew it was an outright lie, but she didn't know how else she'd be allowed in. It wasn't visiting hours yet, and she'd been told on the phone that unless she was immediate family, she wasn't allowed to come until 2:30 pm like everyone else. That wasn't acceptable. With both Dinah and Pip not answering their cell phones, she knew something was wrong, and she had to find out what, even if it meant she had to lie. Forgive me Jesus.

"What's your daughter's name?" the nurse behind the desk asked her.

"Dinah Eaglefeather."

Then the nurse's smile fell to a frown, which alarmed Sadie immediately. Something was wrong. My Lord, did something happen to the baby? Or Dinah? Sadie's heart started to race, and sweat beaded down her forehead. "What? What's wrong?"

"It's just..." the nurse whispered, looking around nervously, "um...she...we moved her to anti-partum for the time being. It's at the end of the hall, then turn right. 408 I believe. But...who did you say you were again?"

"I'm...her mother." She lied the second time.

"Oh...well...then you probably know already. We're trying to let her rest as long as we can before the police start with the questions. You know."

But Sadie didn't know, and that only added to her panic, even though she tried not to show it. Because of her lie, she'd have to play along as if she understood, and that was killing her. What was going on anyway?

Once Sadie arrived at the anti-partum ward, she immediately looked for room 408 and found it at the end of the hall. She couldn't just go in. There was a security guard posted at the door. What the heck?

"Sorry, only immediate family." The emotionless guard stopped her from entering

"I... I'm her mother." She lied for the third time, feeling a bit like the Apostle Peter denying he knew Jesus three times before the rooster crowed.

"I. D please."

Sadie knew she had nothing proving she was Dinah's mother, and that brought tears to her eyes. This close, but so far away. How could she make him open the door? "Look." She swallowed back tears. "You have to let me see her. I'm all she's got. Please!"

"Lady, as far as I know, you could be the kidnapper."

"What? What are you talking about?'

Just then, a nurse came out of the room with an empty breakfast tray, leaving the door cracked enough for Sadie to catch a glimpse of a tiny woman with blonde hair in a hospital bed. "*Dinah!* It's me, Sadie!"

Then, the security guard pulled the door shut. "I'm sorry ma'am but that is not allowed. You'll have to leave immediately. Try coming back at regular visiting hours."

"I can't! I have to see her, now!"

"Well, you can't!"

Sadie started to cry, then. She had enough. Not only was she worried sick about what was going on, but she was totally exhausted from the trip. She cried louder and louder in hopes that Dinah would hear. And she wasn't moving one inch until he opened the door.

The nurses from down the hall immediately started charging her way. What was she going to do now? But the door to the room slowly inched open, revealing an elfin blonde woman. "Sadie? Is that you?"

The security guard reluctantly held open the door. "Is this your mother, miss?"

"Mother?" Dinah asked, puzzled, darting her puffy blood-shot eyes, back and forth from the security guard to Sadie. "She's the only real mother I've ever known. Please, let her in!"

Sadie crashed through the door and hugged Dinah tightly. Both of them began to howl like wounded animals. "*Ooooh!* What on earth is going on?"

"I don't know, Sadie. I don't know!"

Chapter 7

"You *no* have appointment!" Chloe was told by the rude Asian man at the door of the adoption agency, as she and Rozelyn stood there. After looking forward to it all day, this was the result? It was maddening. Chloe wanted to hit the puny foreigner. "Can I get an appointment then?"

"Just wait! Boss man no like," the man spoke through the crack as he closed the door, making them wait.

"Sorry, Chloe," her friend apologized. "This is my fault. I should have done the leg work for you. Sometimes these private agencies have their own set of rules. It's crazy, but they're privately funded and there's not much we can do about it. Let's just wait and see what he says when he comes back."

"Yeah, if he even comes back." Tears welled in her eyes, and she hung her head. If being infertile wasn't enough, now this. Was she ever going to be a mother? It all looked hopeless right about now.

"Look." Rozelyn tried to calm her down. "I know this seems odd, but don't be discouraged. This agency is just one option. I thought we could tour the place and it would give you some hope. But seriously, if they aren't open to the public, there are many that are. We can drive to Regina. They have government agencies that are open to anyone. The waiting list is much longer, but still, it may be a better option than private."

"Let's just go, then." Chloe sniffled. "The guy's a jerk anyway. I don't want to deal with someone that doesn't have the decency to be polite to a future client, and I'm sure Grayson wouldn't like him either."

"Fine, you're call."

Then, as they both turned to go, the door cracked open again. "Wait! Boss no like you here now!" the Asian man spoke.

"Obviously!" Chloe spit back.

"No, here-here-here!" the man said, reaching out his arm through the crack. He held a business card out to them.

Chloe turned and reluctantly grabbed the card from his hand.

"You come back, midnight!"

"What?"

But the little man closed the door for good this time, leaving them both stunned. The business card clearly said, Appointment 12 a.m.

"As if I'm coming back at midnight. What kind of place is this, anyway?"

"I don't know, but I'm sure gonna find out." Rozelyn sighed.

"Not me, I don't want to have anything to do with it."

"Oh come on Chloe, aren't you the least big curious?"

"No!"

~~~~

By the time Grayson was allowed past the goon at the door, it was already after four. At least he was able to get a few hours of sleep in between, but it was a total waste of yet another day. Unbelievable! The hospital security staff was not co-operating very well, but at least he was finally questioning the mother. Finally!

"And Mrs. Eaglefeather," he asked, "you're positive your husband stayed in the building while you were in surgery?"

"Of course! Why would he leave?"

"I don't know. You tell me!"

"Hey now! Don't you talk to her like that! She did nothing wrong!" the voice said, defensively. It was her again. Sadie Long. Why did she have to be in the room? It was totally against protocol to let her be there while he questioned the mother, but the lady claimed she had a right to be there, and the mother insisted she wasn't saying a word without her. Ridiculous!

"Sorry, I didn't mean to be rude." He forced a smile. "It's just that my team has been working pretty hard. We want to find your baby, but time is running out. We need some positive leads. You say you've never noticed anyone following you? You didn't know the man with the baby seat?"

"I've never seen him before."

"Look." He sighed. "I've seen cases like this before and to be honest, a lot of them turned out to be domestic disputes. The nurses said you and your husband were divorced."

"No! That's not true!" The poor mother started to sob once more.

He was getting nowhere. Grayson raked his hands through his hair again. "Sorry, but I have to ask these questions. Were you having marital difficulties?"

But the woman only wailed louder.

"Oh come on!" Sadie interrupted. "Really? This is enough! Can't you see you're upsetting her? You should be out there looking for my grandbaby, not condemning this poor woman to death! You're treating her like it's her fault someone stole her child."

The investigation was going nowhere, especially with this Sadie character interrupting all the time. He was told she wasn't even related. "And who are you again?"

"You know darn well who I am!"

Grayson just stopped and crossed his arms in front of his chest. He shook his head and exhaled his pent-up hot air. He was already on their bad side, and the mother was obviously distraught. He couldn't go on, and would have to come back later when grandma and the bodyguard were off duty. That meant yet another all-nighter. Chloe would never forgive him.

"Look," he said, "I just want to find your baby. Please! I'm not the bad guy here. I have a wife at home that I haven't seen in two days because I've been working overtime, trying to find your child. My staff is working around the clock too, so cut me some slack. I do care!"

"I don't believe that, detective! You have no idea what it means to lose a child."

"I beg your pardon?" Grayson couldn't believe the old lady just said that. He couldn't figure out if he was hurt, or just plain mad. He knew all too well what losing a child meant. The experience of seeing his own baby born, had been stolen from him, and the loss felt just as real. But instead of arguing the point, he chose not to respond at all. Besides, something was coming through the ear-peace. Spencer's team had found someone suspicious on the labor and delivery ward.

Finally, a lead!

~~~~

Pip squinted, as light burst through the doorway. He moaned as he realized someone had finally found him. The brightness nearly blinded him, and he couldn't make out who exactly was rescuing him, but that didn't matter. What mattered, was he was finally getting out of the foul-smelling, hell-hole, he'd been trapped in for the last three days.

Chapter 8

The wind had picked up by midnight, and a storm was brewing, when Chloe and Rozelyn returned to The Luther Home. They stood there rapping at the door in the dark. The street light in front of the building was broken and that gave the place a dingy feeling.

Chloe didn't want to be there in the first place. If it was up to her, she'd be sleeping in her own bed right now, not doing this. But Rozelyn was persistent, and she was a wimp. "C'mon Rozelyn! Nobody's gonna answer. Let's just go. We both have to work in the morning."

"Just wait!"

"I don't want to wait!" Chloe started getting mad now. She could hear the rumble in the sky and knew there was going to be a downpour any minute. The rude Asian man probably meant noon, not midnight. Who in their right mind would schedule an appointment in the middle of the night? Someone shady, that's who! And that's probably why her friend was so curious. She was a social worker, after all.

Rozelyn knocked harder this time. "Chloe you've always been a suck! C'mon, get a backbone!"

"That's it, I'm leaving!"

"Fine, I'm sorry."

But then, a light in the second story window turned on and a little man opened it up and hung his head out. "Come-come-come!" he said, urgently.

"Does he want us to come up?" Chloe asked.

"Looks like it. C'mon!" Her friend took her by the hand, squeaked open the screen door, and went inside.

The place smelled of body odor, and cigarettes. "This doesn't feel right."

"Just follow me, Chloe." They took the winding stairway to the top and met the Asian man who motioned to follow him down the hall. It wasn't hard to figure that he was leading them to a crying baby.

"What on earth?" Rozelyn spoke up right away.

A young man was holding the screaming infant in one arm like a football, while flicking a lighter in the other hand. He lit his smoke that hung out of the side of his mouth, and swore sideways at the newborn to shut up.

Chloe froze in place. Her heart sank at how the man mistreated the baby, and she looked to Rozelyn for the next move.

"Is this your baby?" Her friend spit at the man.

"No, it's yours, for a hundred grand!"

"Uh…NOPE! That's not how it's done buddy! I'm a social worker and I'll have to seize the child. You're obviously not fit to take care of it. I'm calling 911 right now!" Rozelyn tried to work the cell phone fast.

"No you're not, lady!"

"Oh yes I am!"

But before she could punch a single number in, the Asian man karate chopped her wrist, and the phone fell to the floor. "Indian say no po-lice!"

"You heard him!" The man grinned, as he pulled out a gun from his belt and waved it around like he knew what he was doing. "Now you, take care of the kid!" He motioned to Chloe, handing the screaming infant over to her like it was a sack of potatoes.

"Chow, tie the other one up."

"Yes, boss man!"

The Asian man obeyed and then proceeded to tape up Rozelyn's mouth with duct-tape as well. Chloe just sat on the edge of the bed with the crying baby and didn't know what to do. She rocked it back and forth, but it wouldn't be quiet. "It's turning blue!"

"Well, make it stop crying!"

"I can't!"

"You better, lady, or I'll use this thing, I swear!" The Indian pointed the gun.

Chloe started crying and stuck her pinkie in the baby's mouth until it started sucking. Finally, it stopped wailing. "It's hungry. Do you have any formula?"

"Of course! You think we're idiots? Chow, get the brat another bottle."

Chow bowed and left the room.

"Now look, lady," the man spoke to Chloe. "This is how it's gonna be. Because of Chow's screw up, with him mistaking you for the client, I figure you owe me. I should've realized the stupid Asian got it wrong when he called me yesterday. But what's done is done. You're gonna play mama for a while until the real client gets here. Then you're gonna make this adoption look legit for us. You do as I say, and you won't get hurt. Do anything stupid, and your fat friend gets a bullet. Understand?"

"I understand!"

~~~~

Pip found himself dressed in a hospital gown attached to an intravenous the next morning. Vaguely, he remembered the midnight rescue, the reunion with his wife, the tears that followed. He was so thankful she was all right, but shocked at the news that his child was missing. It was unbelievable! How could a hospital let someone walk out with someone else's baby? His daughter!

Yes, he had a daughter. It was hard to fathom, especially not being able to hold her, or see what she looked like. He didn't even feel like a father, yet he was being called that by the gang of police officers who bombarded him last night with questions.

He was the one with questions. Why would someone want to knock him out, tie him up, and shove him in a closet, to steal his kid? Well, he could think of a dozen reasons why, but he didn't want his mind to go there.

No, he didn't know what was going on like they thought he did, but he was sure going to find out. For all he knew, it was a racial thing. The hospital staff probably didn't even care, because she was just another native baby. Well, he was going to make them care. She was his child, and he was going to find her.

Pip ripped his intravenous out, grabbed his clothes sitting next to him, and slowly got himself dressed. His entire body ached, but he pushed through the pain.

"What do you think you're doing, Mr. Eaglefeather?" a nurse asked as she came in.

"Leaving!"

"Oh no you're not. You're still dehydrated."

"I don't care, I'm going to find my daughter!"

The nurse put her hand on his shoulder to try and stop him, but there was no stopping him. He brushed her hand aside, and continued to dress himself. "I'm leaving and you can't stop me!"

"No, I can't, but maybe the doctor can?"

Pip was not listening. It was as if he was deaf and couldn't hear her. He didn't pause for even a moment, while the nurse pleaded with him.

"Please!" she said. "Just let me get the doctor before you go. It will only take a few minutes. Then, if you still want to leave, you're free to go."

"Oh, believe me, I'm still leaving." But Pip, being the gentle spirit he was, couldn't help but feel sorry for the young nurse who was only trying to do her job. Perhaps he could wait for the doctor. He knew Dinah had been sent home with Sadie already, and he'd be at her side to comfort her soon enough, so he decided to appease the nurse. "Fine! Tell the doctor he better hurry up before I leave. I'm not waiting forever."

"Thank you, Mr. Eaglefeather. It's my job on the line you know. I just want to pass my practicum. It's protocol to talk to the doctor before you leave—and we all just want to make sure you're okay."

"Well, I'm fine!"

The nurse forced a smile and told him she'd be right back with the doctor.

A million things reeled through Pip's mind as he sat there dressed and waiting. It irritated him that they wouldn't keep Dinah longer. She should be the one in the hospital still, not him. She had the baby; She had the C-section. Still, they needed the bed they said. They discharged her last night, shortly after he was admitted.

That thought brought a certain sadness upon him, as he stared out the window to another rainy day. It wasn't supposed to be like this, God, he whispered. But only the wind answered him back.

His daughter was his family now, a part of him that was missing. How typical. Family had always been the missing link in his life. He wanted things to be different for him and Dinah, and now look what happened. A child was supposed to be a legacy, a part of him that would be passed down from generation to generation. But how could that happen now?

As the wind whipped across the window pane once more, a chill made him shiver at the thought that his child may not even be alive. God, don't do this to me! But still no answer, only his own thoughts. His faith—the faith that had been passed down to him, was nowhere to be found—just like his daughter.

Chapter 9

Funny, Grayson hadn't heard from his wife all night. His last text told her he was going to catch a few winks at the precinct and work through the night again, and she immediately phoned him back and grumbled. That was over twelve hours ago. She must be pretty mad. Still, it wasn't like Chloe to miss work. He'd gotten a call from her boss, wondering why she hadn't clocked in this morning.

Now, searching through the house, he found that their bed hadn't been slept in either. Did she leave him? Grayson started sweating. He knew she was depressed lately because of her infertility issues, but she wouldn't leave him. Not now! Not after all they'd been through together. And he didn't completely close the door on adoption. Or wait, he had. Yes, he remembered he told her he didn't want to adopt. Could that be what got her all fired up?

"Hey, Spence," he spoke on the phone with his partner, "did Chloe go with Rozelyn somewhere?"

"Uh—yeah buddy, she left me a note."

Grayson wondered why he hadn't gotten a note. "Well, what does it say?"

"That our wives are out spending our money again, that's what. The girls always seem to do this when we have a big case. It's like they're trying to get back at us. Don't you know these things, or am I the only one that's clued into this?"

"No, I guess I don't know women like you do, pal."

"You got that right!"

Grayson furrowed his brow. "I was worried, Spence. You'd think the least she could do was call me, or leave a note?"

"That would be too simple. Women are more complex than that. You'd know that if you were a stud like me."

"Hardy har har!" Grayson's old buddy was getting on his nerves. He was too tired for his jokes, or rather, insults today. "I'll meet you back at the precinct in ten."

It bugged him that his wife was so distant lately. Perhaps it was his fault as well. He hadn't exactly been the most comforting guy, especially with his focus on the case. Still, there was something that gnawed at him. Why would her boss be expecting her to work today, if she had a day off? But then, he probably got that wrong too. She was constantly going on about how unfair her shift changes were lately.

Chloe was in the middle of a grievance complaint, if his mind served him correctly. Or was that something else? Sometimes he wished he paid more attention to his wife's problems, but it wasn't his fault he had such time restraints. And usually she just droned on and on about things anyway. It was a bad habit of Grayson's to block his wife's voice out, and just make it seem like he was listening. That had to stop, or at least he had to put some effort into listening to her more, or he'd be in the dog house forever.

But his wife's silly tantrums would have to wait. He had more important things to do right now, like find a missing baby, and he'd wasted half the day already.

~~~~

"What do you mean you closed the case?" Grayson shouted at his superior. "We haven't found the baby yet!"

Spencer sat in the seat beside him and didn't say a word.

"You heard me! It's closed! We got no more time to waste on a domestic. The father took the kid to the reserve. We got a call from some old squaw about an hour ago. She said she was the kokum, you know, that's what these people call their grandmothers."

These people? Grayson couldn't believe how prejudice his boss was.

"And sooo?"

"And so the kokum said her son didn't want the baby raised with a white woman. Apparently, the couple had broken up a long time ago, and the father lied. There's nothing we can do but let social services handle it. I forwarded it to their department, but they have a backlog right now. They said they'd get to the case as soon as possible. They'll send someone out to the reserve to check on the infant, but that's all we can do."

"You mean that's all you want to do!"

"Oh, come on Grayson, you know me better than that."

Apparently not! "And why was the father beaten and locked in the closet then?"

"Well, obviously he had help to take the child. He had to make it look like an abduction, now didn't he? Clever, really."

Grayson gulped hard. "I don't buy it! Not for one minute!" Red flags popped up all over the place. "C'mon Spence, say something. You don't buy this, do you pal?"

Spencer shrugged his shoulders and said nothing.

Grayson's mouth hung open. "After all the time we've spent on this case, you're going to pull it out from underneath me like this? Really?"

Grayson couldn't believe it. He flung the file at his boss and bolted out of the room, slamming the door behind him. His pulse raced as he reached the end of the hall, finding himself blocked with nowhere left to go. He paced back and forth, raking his hands through his hair. Breathe, Grayson, breathe!

Spencer came running after him then, and caught up to him, out of breath. "For what it's worth—I…I'm sorry, pal!"

"Don't call me pal!" Grayson glared.

"Hey c'mon, don't be like this, Gray. It wasn't my fault. I'm not the boss. I wish I was. I wouldn't have closed the case, but it's not my call. You heard him. They already passed it on to Social Services."

Grayson banged his head against the wall. "I'm so sick of the racial stink in this town. You know darn well, why they dropped this case, Spencer."

"I know."

"Well, I'm not letting them get away with it this time. Remember the Whitecap Incident? Or wait—let me refresh your memory: The native women who went missing. Nobody cared. Nobody wanted to care!"

Spencer hung his head. "I remember."

"I don't care about the color of someone's skin. I do my job, no matter what!"

"I do my job too, Gray. But they tied our hands...again!"

Grayson shook his head and tried to calm down.

"And they already reassigned me anyway."

"Well, I'm not giving up that easily."

Spencer's eyes grew wide. "Hate to break this to you pal, but boss said you're suspended."

"What? Why? For how long this time?"

"For throwing the case file, apparently. You're out for two weeks."

Grayson was fuming again. If he was going out for two weeks, he was spending it the way he wanted, and that was finishing this case, with or without Spencer's help.

~~~~

Pip had been waiting for almost an hour already, and still the doctor hadn't shown up. He was about to leave when finally Dr. Uric came in.

"Now son, you can't leave just yet," the doctor told him, as he entered the room.

"I'm not your son, and I can leave whenever I want."

"Okay fine, but let me warn you then. There will be a warrant out for your arrest."

Pip's mouth hung open. He thought the doctor was going to tell him to stay until he was hydrated, but not this. This was ridiculous. "A warrant? For what?"

"For kidnapping."

"I didn't kidnap my own baby, you idiot!" Pip knew that was the wrong thing to say the moment it escaped his mouth. He wanted to take it back immediately.

"Look here, you little jerk," Dr. Uric whispered. "Don't you push me or you'll wish you never did. I have friends you don't want to mess with. You hear me? You're going to jail for this kidnapping, or so help me God, you'll wish you were never born. You understand?"

"No, I don't understand!" Pip spit back. "If I was under arrest, then why am I not handcuffed? Why isn't there a guard at my door?"

"We don't have security for all you people."

"You people?" Pip had had enough of this insulting treatment. He was leaving with or without this ape's permission. He pulled his arm away from the crazy doctor and backed up toward the door. The student nurse at the doorway stepped aside as he came through, but Pip continued to stand his ground. "And don't think I'm not gonna look for my daughter, because I will! I'll search for her until the day I die! Do you understand that?

The doctor just stood there with his arms crossed, and shook his head.

"I didn't take her!" Pip argued. He turned, and ran as fast as he could down the hallway. He took the stairs and hop-jumped down to the bottom, then, tore out of the front doors as fast as he possibly could, never once looking back.

Tears streamed down Pip's face as he headed toward his apartment. He pulled his hood up to fight off the rain, and then brushed tears from his eyes. He was going to find his baby girl, if it was the last thing he ever did!

Chapter 10

Sadie tried to console Dinah the best she could, under the circumstances, but it wasn't helping. There was nothing that would ease the pain from the loss of a child. And this was even worse. They didn't know if the baby was alive or dead. It was the not knowing that was driving them both crazy." You have to eat something, my dear."

"What for?"

"For when they find the baby. You want to have enough milk to feed her." It was apparently the wrong thing to say. Sadie wasn't thinking. You don't say that to a grieving mother who was missing her baby so bad she couldn't even function.

Sadie had never had any children, she didn't know what it was like. She didn't know what it felt like to nurse a child, and have it totally dependent upon her. It was something she had missed out on her entire life and it grieved her to remember that fact.

She had waited too long to find the man of her dreams. Her biological clock had all but stopped working. Sadie felt guilty for having these thoughts when it wasn't about her, but still her heart ached about the whole situation, and she couldn't help but think of her own missed opportunities. Why did she wait so long? And now she was at a total loss of how to help her little butterfly.

Dinah was continuously bawling, and her pain was obvious. It was almost unbearable to take care of her. God in heaven, Sadie prayed. Help them find this little child. Don't let any harm come to it. And bring back their happiness and joy. Praying was their only hope, yet she realized the young couple was struggling in that area.

She had seen a lot in her life throughout the years, but to have a child abducted, a newborn no less, had to be an extremely stressful thing to deal with, and certainly rock anyone's faith. Still, she knew there was nothing impossible for God.

~~~~

"Leave me alone, Sadie!" Dinah cried. But she didn't know what else to say to the old woman. There was no way she could understand how she was feeling, and it wasn't her responsibility to try to get her to understand. There was no understanding this.

Leaving the hospital without her baby, was the hardest thing she had ever done. Her heart ached, literally ached, with every step she took as she left the hospital. Sure, she could've waited all night in Pip's room for him, but there was only a small chair available, and she was in no condition to sit there that long with her C-section incision. It didn't make sense to stay, so that's why she and Sadie went home. That, and the fact that they discharged her because they needed the bed.

The healthcare system wasn't exactly a five-star service. It was more like maybe one star to Dinah. In fact, it wasn't even that. She wished she could take the hospital to court for losing her baby, and for allowing her husband to be shoved in a closet and left to die.

Dinah felt herself longing to go home. And by home, she meant northern Saskatchewan, where she had spent so much of her time as a teenager. The city was full of too many people, too much crime, and too little love.

Already, she was sick of the hustle and bustle of what she called the rat race. It wasn't even human anymore. All she was looking forward to, was being a mother and holding her child, and making a difference to her baby. But now there was no baby, not at least what she could see.

She didn't even want to name the child. Sure, Sadie said it was important to give their daughter a name, but for some reason she couldn't. It hurt too much. All the what-if's danced around in her mind. What if she gave the child a name for nothing?

Tears trickled down her cheek, even after she thought she couldn't possibly cry anymore. She needed her husband, she needed her daughter, and yes, according to Sadie she needed God. But right now, she couldn't pray. She just couldn't.

~~~~

Pip finally made it home by suppertime and his heart sank when he opened the door to his wife, crumpled on the couch, sobbing.

"Did they find the baby?" Dinah sniffled, with hope in her eyes. But all Pip could do was shake his head, no, and hold her.

Sadie interrupted. "Are you okay, Pip?".

"I'm fine, but apparently I'm supposed to be under arrest."

"What?" Dinah shrieked.

Pip filled them in and told them about the crazy doctor who threatened him. He insisted it must be a mistake, and the first thing he intended to do was contact the detective that questioned him. Thankfully, he gave him his card and told him if he thought of anything at all, to give him a call.

He unfolded it and started to dial the number. "Don't worry, I'm going to do everything possible to find our little girl." He waited for the dial tone. "Hello...detective Grayson? We need to talk."

Chapter 11

Chloe named the child Lily, after her great-grandmother. She knew she really shouldn't give her a name, but she had to call her something, and Lily seemed to fit. The angelic chocolate-faced child, slept most of the time in between feedings. She had such feminine features that she knew she was going to grow up to be a very pretty girl.

The more Chloe let her mind wander, the more pain she felt. She would never have a baby of her own, she would never feel the little kicks inside of her, or the swelling of her belly, and that brought tears to her eyes. Even now, as she held the tiny newborn's hand, she realized this could quite possibly be the closest to motherhood that she'd ever come, as horrific as the circumstances were.

Lily's soft suckling lips searched for the breast, so Chloe pulled her close, pretending. She knew she'd never nurse a child, but it was nice to imagine the feeling. Still, it broke her heart, mourning over something she could never do, especially since she told herself not to, right from the beginning. Instead of focusing on what she didn't have, she realized she had to focus on what she did have. And that meant, in this moment, she was Lily's mother.

Once more she rocked the newborn and cuddled it as she sang another lullaby in the smoky filled room she had been in since yesterday.

They had placed Rozelyn in a chair where she still sat slumped over. Her hands were tied behind her back and her feet were bound as well. She was gagged and tied to the chair and hadn't been able to use the bathroom. Chloe felt sorry for her friend. She had soiled herself several times with a puddle of urine forming beneath her chair.

The Asian stood guard with a gun at the door and wouldn't leave. The big native man had left shortly after he arrived. As far as Chloe could figure, he didn't even live there. In fact, it seemed like the Asian man was the only one who ran the place. If it wasn't for him, she would have untied Roz, and escaped with the baby a long time ago. But that wasn't the case. There was nothing she could do but cuddle the newborn, feed and change her, and rock her to sleep. That, and worry about her friend. "Are you okay, Rozelyn?"

"You *no* talk to her!"

Chloe ignore the Asian man and continued speaking to her friend. "Rozelyn?" No answer. She got up, carried the child with her, and spoke directly into Rozelyn's ear this time. "Are you okay?"

"I say, you no talk to her!"

Chloe glared at the little man with the big gun. Who did he think he was, flashing that thing around? Did he think he was so big just because he had a gun? If she could only get it out of his hand. But she was worried about her friend. It looked like she was unconscious with her head hanging down unresponsive.

"I need to make sure she's okay."

"Boss say, you *no* touch her!"

The Asian shoved Chloe back down on the bed with the baby in her arms. It was hopeless. All she could do was focus on the baby, who had now woken up and started crying again. It seemed as though this newborn cried a lot. Colic maybe? She observed the restless child, and continued to rock her.

~~~

Once Grayson got to the Eaglefeather residents, it only took him a moment to realize his assumptions were correct. They dismissed the case because of his race. He'd seen it before so many times, and this was no exception. "I'm sorry, guys. I'll do everything I possibly can to help you find your baby, but with my suspension, it makes things twice as hard. I don't have access to work computers, or the database. I don't even have my badge. There's not a lot that I can do unless I go under the wire. That means, I'm basically on my own to investigate, and I usually work with a partner. Without Spencer, it will take a whole lot longer." He knew he was basically asking for help, but he didn't have a choice.

"I can help you, detective," Pip spoke up.

Grayson cringed, but knew it was the only way. "Do you have any kind of experience?"

"I once helped an RCMP officer solve a murder case, and I was just a young punk then." Pip grinned.

"It's true, detective." His wife added.

"Actually." Sadie popped up. "I can vouch for him. In fact, both of these young people are exceptional individuals. They have been through a lot and I'm sure they'll be able to help you in any way that they can."

"Well then, Pip," Grayson replied, holding out his hand for a shake, "I guess you're my new partner. Now let's get this show on the road. We got a baby to find."

~~~~

Sadie didn't like the tall dark-haired detective when she first met him in the hospital, but she sure liked him now. He really did show what type of person he was by taking on the case even with a suspension. Why was he suspended for two weeks, though?

"Detective Grayson," she decided to ask. "Are you just a troublemaker, or is your suspension directly related to this case?

"Ha—well, I can cause my share of trouble, but yes. It's related."

"I hope this doesn't cause you to get fired."

"I know what I'm doing ma'am. Don't worry. I've been suspended before. Don't get me wrong, my detective skills are up to par, I just have a boss who forgets that sometimes."

Both Dinah and Pip looked at each other with confusion on their faces. She could tell they were worried. It was hard leaving everything up to this one man.

"Shouldn't we go to the media?" Dinah asked.

"Well, we could," Grayson replied, "but I don't want to scare off the kidnapper. If he or she, or whoever took your daughter still has her in town somewhere, the best thing is for them to think we aren't looking. If the media reports the case closed, and they will, then usually criminals relax. When they relax, they make mistakes. That's what I'm betting on."

"If you say so, detective," Dinah spoke softly, trying to control her emotions.

"Look," Grayson told them, "I know you're worried. I would be too, but let me do some digging. I have a few leads I want to follow up on tonight, and then I'll pick you up bright and early tomorrow morning, Pip. Try to get some sleep, you look like you need it. Well, anyone would after everything you've been through."

Sadie could tell the detective was tired, too. Actually, she hadn't gotten much sleep in the last few days either. A good night's sleep would do them all a world of good. She just hoped the baby would be okay if they all closed their eyes for a few hours.

For some reason, she thought it was her job to worry, but no matter what she did or said, nothing was up to her. It never was. It was only up to God, and if he wanted the child to be okay, he'd protect it. Still, as many times as she tried to comfort Dinah in that regard, she didn't want to hear it. It was as if everything she'd taught her about faith had disappeared the moment her baby was taken.

Sadie didn't blame her. It was a sorrow they were all dealing with, yet, not quite the same thing as when someone dies. More like a mourning, a pain when your child, or a loved one is gone. But even still, she knew God was big enough to handle this for them. After all, he'd proved Himself time and time again, before. But for some reason, when people are in the thick of it, they forget.

Sadie needed to remind them, one baby step at a time. Rather, not a baby step exactly. She had to remember to stop using those kinds of words. Dinah would start bawling again, and she didn't want that.

Oh, why was she no good at comforting this time? In every other circumstance she used her counseling skills effectively, so what made this time different? It was personal, that's why.

It's my grandbaby!

Chapter 12

Kokum danced around the kitchen like she was born for this. She had every step perfected. Shania wished she could dance the round dance like that but she was an absolute klutz especially with the baby fat that hung around her middle.

She still missed the baby, even though it was probably for the best. She didn't want to be a mother at sixteen anyway, even though most of her friends from town were. Why did she have to be the only one that couldn't keep her baby? Well, not exactly the only one. Both girls in the Tobaccojuice family, had to hand them over to Trevor as soon as they were born too. It was the only way. Even her stupid brother Arnold said so, and he was tight with Trevor.

Still, Shania couldn't understand how Kokum could be so happy. She had lost her great-granddaughter. Didn't she understand? But then, Kokum drank too much. She always did. "I'm going to catch a ride to town with Serena."

"Mmmm…"

"Did you hear me, Kokum?"

"Mmmm?...What? Oh yah. Go! It's better than you sulking 'round here all the time. Better do somethin' 'bout that. You know what your kokum wants. And Trevor too. He told me, as soon as he cashes in with this one, he'll need another. So, get moving!"

Shania's mouth hung open. She slammed the door and started down the road to Serena's. Her dad had the truck running, and there was her friend already, waiting for her in the back of the open half-ton. At least they would be able to feel the summer breeze on their faces this time. The June sun was warm again, even after the rain.

"I hate Trevor," Serena told her. "I heard he makes a whole lot more than we think he does, and we only get a fraction of that. Can you believe it? And we do all the work. Nice boyfriend, hey?"

"I told you to dump him. I knew he was bad news all along but I got fooled just like you did. It was his eyes."

"Ha—it was a whole lot more than his eyes, and you know it!"

"Whatever." Shania tried not to grin, but she couldn't help it.

"At least I got my money, and that's all I care about."

Shania turned and squinted into the wind, as her jet-black hair danced in a swirled mess around her face. Her friend had been seeing Trevor on and off for the last three years, ever since he got out of jail.

Then, when he came to her one night, she knew what kind of guy he was. She didn't want to get pregnant, but apparently that was the plan. And Trevor had many other friends he used as well, including guys she knew personally. But it was the women who always had to experience the pain of giving their kids away.

"Easy money," Trevor told all the girls, but somehow the ten grand she shared with Kokum didn't seem to replace her little girl. Her heart still ached and it had already been two months. Almost a year for Serena, but time didn't make much of a difference. Every day without her little one felt like an eternity, and she didn't know how to stop the pain from consuming her.

"You glad you're working tonight?" Serena asked her, breaking her train of thought.

"Not really. I don't know why your stupid boyfriend needs both of us."

Serena looked at her sideways. "Didn't he tell you?"

"No!"

"He has another baby that needs to go. We gotta put on the show again."

"Oh come on, I hate that!"

"Well, suck it up if you want to get paid off-season, if you know what I mean."

Shania hated wearing the fake pregnancy forms. The girls who weren't pregnant or showing, always had to strap them on whenever some big official came to the boarding house. It was awful, and almost always brought back painful memories. But then, maybe she was the only one that had a conscience.

Both girls lay down in the truck-bed, out of the wind. The old blankets that lined it were soft enough, so she couldn't complain. They always lay down right before they reached the city limits so the police didn't stop them. "So what if they do?"

Serena was always quick to defend the jerk. "Trevor wouldn't like it. He'll beat you silly." But she wasn't afraid. He wasn't going to touch her ever again.

"So, guess what Shi?"

Shania cuddled up beside her childhood friend, eager to listen to her stories again. She always told great stories. "What?"

"Well...I don't have a story if that's what you're thinking."

"Oh boo!"

Serena pushed her bottom lip out, and gave her friend a sympathetic pout. "But I do have a surprise, though."

"Well, what is it?"

"I'm late." Serena's smile grew wide.

"What?"

"Yeah, I think I'm about six weeks maybe. Trevor is going to be stoked. I think this time I'm gonna ask for a bigger cut. You think I should?"

"Totally!" was all she could say, even though she wanted to scream. How could her friend be so stupid? The money was definitely not worth it. At least not to her. Shania would give anything to get her baby back. But now it was too late. Last she heard, someone from Ontario adopted her.

For the rest of the trip, Shania was quiet. She didn't want to let on that she was upset with her friend, and didn't want to ruin the moment. This would be Serena's third child and there was nothing she could do about it.

It was a profitable business, at least for Trevor and his Asian buddy. Though she guessed Chow didn't get much even though he did the dirty work, just like the girls. It despised her to work for Trevor, but working during off-season, as her friend put it, gave her some pocket change and kept her off the street at least. If she had her way, she'd stay in school forever and become an educated person someday. Maybe even a cop. Then she'd throw them all in jail where they belonged.

One thing was for sure, what they were doing was not only crazy, but heartbreaking. Perhaps all the other girls had turned their emotions off, but Shania just couldn't. She promised herself the moment her child was ripped away from her arms, that she'd never get sucked into getting pregnant and giving away her baby, ever again. Apparently her friend felt differently.

~~~

Chloe heard the commotion, but Chow wouldn't let her leave the room. "I have to go to the bathroom."

"You no leave."

The baby was sleeping in the bassinet beside her bed, without a peep. She lay back down and watched the little one's chest rise and fall. What was she going to do? How was she going to get out of this? She thought about escaping many times, but not without the baby. Lily was definitely coming with her.

But what about Rozelyn? They had moved her and the baby into another room down the hall, and now she wasn't able to keep an eye on her friend anymore. That really bothered her. She couldn't leave without Rozelyn.

As far as Chloe could tell, it was just Chow there all the time. There was no sign of other babies or pregnant women, or even the big aboriginal man that was there the first day. It wouldn't take that much to escape.

Chloe promised herself she would spend the day thinking of some way to sneak out with the baby. If she could only flee with the child, she could go get help and come back with the police to rescue her friend. But then, what was that new commotion she was hearing downstairs?

"You stay here with baby," Chow said, as he took out his key to lock the door behind him. "Me go check on girls."

Girls? Were there possibly others, and she just didn't realize? This was new. Chloe lay back down on the bed and moaned. She turned to her side and propped her head up with her arm, as she watched the sleeping baby once more. So precious, so little. She wondered where she came from. An Indian reserve perhaps? A product of an unplanned pregnancy? She didn't know. All she knew, was that today, she was this baby's mother, and she wasn't going to let anything happen to her.

Thoughts of Grayson, entered her mind. What would he think of this? Would he storm the building like the detective he was? Or run with the baby in his arms and never look back? Perhaps it was the only way they were ever going to be parents? Twisted, she knew, but her thoughts nonetheless. Maybe if she did what they wanted and played along, her chances of being a mother would go up significantly.

Time to play the game.

Chapter 13

When Grayson drove over to pick up Pip, he found him standing at the curb with his backpack, like a school kid waiting for the bus. It made him laugh, though he figured he'd better cut it out before the young man got in the vehicle. It wasn't funny, and he knew it.

He could see the pain and fear written all over the boy's face, and that reminded him of himself at that age, heading out on his first case. "Coffee?" Grayson smiled, handing him the hot drink, as he took a seat on the passenger side.

"Thanks!"

"So how did you two make it through the night?"

Pip slurped the hot coffee and answered, "Bout the same."

"This is your first, right?" Grayson wanted to keep him talking, find out more about the couple. Its what detectives did, yet he had to admit, the two of them sparked his curiosity. They definitely were not your average young couple. Grayson couldn't quite put his finger on it, but they were different somehow.

"First what? Case?" Pip asked, confused.

"No, first baby."

"Oh." The young man frowned, turning for a moment to hide his feelings. "Yeah, it's our first."

Grayson could feel the awkwardness. He realized that forcing the conversation was not going to work with this young fella. He'd have to leave him alone for a while, let him feel his way around. Instead of talking, they just sipped hot coffee.

The first stop was the Indian reserve where they got the phone call from. They were going to have a little chat with a woman named Moira Runningman. She was supposed to be Pip's kokum, or at least that's what she said. It was time to get a few questions answered. "So, what reserve did you come from, Pip?"

"It's not from around here."

"Where then?"

"Northern Saskatchewan." Pip informed him. "You probably haven't heard of it before. Most people haven't. It's called, Deep Bay. I was raised by my grandfather there in the bush, not on a Reserve. He didn't like reserves. He wanted to be self-sufficient, so he mostly did trapping and ran a bush plane business."

"Really?" Grayson was surprised by that. "So you're telling me you're not from around here? Like, I mean you don't have any other relatives that live around here? A kokum perhaps?"

"A what?"

"Kokum. You don't call your grandmother that?"

"I never knew my grandmother. And no, we don't call them, kokum. Not where I'm from anyway."

Grayson thought that was pretty interesting, considering somebody from the Standinghorse Indian Reserve claimed she was related. Perhaps it was a long lost relative he didn't know about? But still, the woman claimed Pip took the child back to the reserve, because she didn't want it raised by a white woman. That was obviously bogus.

"Might as well tell you, we're headed to Standinghorse Indian Reserve to check out a lead. Someone saying she's your grandmother. She called, and said you took the child out there, so she wouldn't be raised by a white woman."

"What? Seriously?"

"Yeah, my thoughts exactly."

The two of them looked at each other, and shook their heads without saying a word. Pip was distant, and gazed out the passenger window at the warm summer morning. Grayson would let him be for a while, and collect his thoughts until they got there. The trip would take a little over an hour anyway, and he needed time to process.

Perhaps the woman was a long lost relative. But why would she say he took the child to her, when he didn't? Or supposedly didn't. It was very confusing. Someone was lying, and he assumed it was probably the old woman. But why?

On the other hand, he could be totally wrong about the young man sitting next to him. He could be fooling everybody to save his own skin. Grayson didn't think so, and his gut told him the guy was honest, but still, there was always that thought in the back of his mind that Pip wasn't telling the whole truth.

There was a lot of deception going on lately, including his wife. Where on earth was she? No phone call, no text, no note, no nothing. If she and Rozelyn took a trip together, surely she would've said something. He tried to phone her one last time before he left, but still no answer. She apparently had her phone off, and that wasn't like her. He figured she must be pretty mad at him. Still, there was no way for him to know for sure. He even tried calling Rozelyn, and there was also no answer from her.

Obviously, his buddy Spencer was reassigned to a new case that was taking up his time, because he seemed too busy to answer his phone this morning. Either that, or the man was avoiding him.

Grayson guessed it probably wasn't easy being caught in the middle between his best friend, and boss, so he understood why he didn't want to answer the phone. But that made it hard, since he was the only one that apparently knew where the girls were.

It was starting to drive him crazy with worry, but he had to let it go for now, and focus on the case at hand.

Surely, his wife would show up sooner or later. Surely.

~~~

"The baby is at my cousins, I tell you." Moira Runningman insisted. Her salt and pepper, mouse-like hair, was pulled back in a bun behind her saggy neck, and double chin. She looked to be in her seventies, and Grayson could tell she was lying.

"Come on ma'am," Pip argued. "I don't know you, so why would I leave my baby with you? Are you sure you're talking about the right baby?"

"Well, let's see." The old lady scratched her head. "It was my cousin's cousin that had the baby a couple months ago. Yes, a little girl that was born on April 5th I think. She was brought to the reserve so she wouldn't have to be raised by a white woman. I'm telling you. That's what happened. It's either that, or too much drinkin' that made me think that."

Grayson realized the woman was totally inebriated and her story was unreliable. "But you called the hospital, lady, and told them you knew where my kid was," Pip said. "Why would you do that?"

"I didn't do that, did I?" The woman slurred.

"Yes, you did. In fact, I have the recorded call if you want to listen to it, Moira." He bluffed. "Now, either you did it, or you didn't do it. The recording proves you did, and we'd like to know where the child is, or we'll arrest you right here and now for kidnapping charges."

"I didn't kidnap anyone!" Moira screamed. "Leave me alone. I'm just an old woman with a bottle. I don't know nothin'. I swear!" The woman burped as she sat down on the step, and clinked her half empty whiskey bottle beside her. She wiped her sleeve across her mouth and started to cry.

"My granddaughter had the baby. Yah, she brought the baby to me—my great-granddaughter. Her baby died, you know. She's gone, and I'm a grieving kokum. Don't punish an old lady for that. I was just confused. I miss my great-granddaughter so much!"

Both Grayson and Pip eyed each other. Neither one of them had to say a word. They were both thinking the same thing. The old lady was drunk, unreliable, and this lead was a dead end. There was obviously no baby here, and if there ever was, it was her deceased great-granddaughter.

He kind of felt sorry for the old woman, but at least they had checked out the call. He could cross that one off the list, and go to the next. Trouble was, there were no more leads to follow, so he'd have to find some more.

"And what is your granddaughter's name, Moira?" But when the old woman didn't answer, Grayson realized she had fallen asleep.

Pip furrowed his brow and turned away.

"Moira? Wake up! We're not finished with you yet."

"What?...What's that?"

"Your granddaughter, what's your granddaughter's name, and where can we find her?"

The old lady shook her head, and blew bubbles from her mouth. "No no," she said, "she's my good girl, and nothing like her brother either, so don't think she's like him. Shania stays in school, and does what she's told. She's a smart one...and...um...she didn't even want to get pregnant. She's my good girl, I tell you."

The woman proceeded to shake her head like she knew what she was talking about. But obviously, she was drunk as a skunk, and they couldn't trust what she was saying. She picked up the whiskey bottle, and started chugging its contents again. Grayson knew that was their cue to leave.

In the car on the way back to the city, Grayson went over the data with Pip. "If I had the precinct's database at my disposal, I'd be able to search a few things out. We know that she's got a granddaughter named Shania, and a grandson that she doesn't like. I'm assuming they have the same last names, so that would be, Shania Runningman. The brother's name could be anything, so let's start with the girl."

Pip squirmed in his seat, opening his mouth as if he wanted to say something, then didn't. He kept showing him his phone, with a dumb look on his face. Grayson ignored the kid's immaturity for the time being, and continued to go over the details. He wanted him to understand the seriousness of detective work. You couldn't fool around with silly phone mumbo jumbo all day.

Grayson rolled his eyes and continued. "Anyway, I wish I could call in a favor with my old buddy Spencer. He'd run her name through the database for me. But unfortunately, they reassigned him to another case yesterday, and he's not answering his phone. So, I guess we gotta wait till we get back to my place, then. We can use my home computer. But I'm warning you...I haven't used it in a while, and—"

"Oh, come on! You're killin' me already!" Pip teased. "Haven't you ever heard of a smart phone? I can look up anything you want, right from here."

"Oh…um…really? How?"

"Google. Don't you know what that is?"

"Yah." Grayson worked his jaw. "I'm not that old."

Pip smirked, and typed in the girl's name, waiting for his phone to do the work. Grayson focused on the highway, and chuckled to himself. There was a lot of things that he was good at, but technology was not one of them. Computer research was Spencer's area of expertise, not his. And rubbing it in wasn't exactly funny. Smart aleck kid! Sure, his phone was archaic, but it still did the job. What was wrong with that?

"So, what do you want to know first? I got her Facebook page, Twitter account, where she goes to high school, and who her friends are."

"What? That was fast?" Grayson was quite surprised. "Man, I'll have to hire you permanently. Guess we can start with her high school."

"Goes to Bedford Road Collegiate."

"Then, that's where we're headed. We'll have a little chat with her."

Pip went serious. "What do you think she has to do with the investigation?"

"I'm thinking—Girl's baby dies. Girl needs new baby. Girl steals baby."

Pip screwed up his face. "*Maybe.*"

It was the best shot they had, and Grayson knew it, even if the kid didn't. He hoped for the young fella's sake, that this wouldn't be another dead-end. Time was running out fast, but he wasn't going to tell Pip that.

Chapter 14

"What do you mean, they were asking questions?" Trevor spoke loudly on the phone.

"Kokum said she didn't tell them anything," Shania explained. "She said she pretended to be drunk so they would leave her alone."

"Pretended? Like the old bat needs to pretend. More like, she was totally pissed and blabbed the whole thing."

"Whatever!" Trevor was being a jerk again, and that ticked her off. She knew it didn't take a lot of pretending for Kokum to pull off being drunk, but he didn't have to be so ignorant about it. Still, he was probably right. How much did Kokum tell the police? If she spilled the beans, Trevor would definitely blame her.

Of all the girls, Shania knew she was the most responsible. She always listened, always did what she was told, and never asked questions. So hopefully, Trevor wouldn't take it out on her. But just in case, she'd better suck up to him quickly. There was no way she was going down for this. "I know what you must be thinking, but seriously, she wouldn't tell. She knows she won't get paid if she does."

"You won't get paid, either!"

"Why? I didn't do anything!" Jerk! He always threatened her with that. Shania didn't really care about the money as much as Trevor thought, but still, it wasn't fair. Neither was his wrath, and that was what she was mostly afraid of. Some of the girls got hurt pretty badly the last time he accused them of talking. It turned out that he was just paranoid, like usual. "Please Trevor, listen to me! She didn't tell them anything, so you don't have to worry. Please!"

"Fine then, but you owe me big time, Shania, and you better pay up!"

She knew what that meant, and he wasn't just talking about money. She swore she'd never let him touch her again, and she meant it. That put her in a very dangerous position, one that she had to get out of quickly.

~~~~

Trevor arrived at Moira's, with his pistol tucked discretely beneath his belt. He also brought his buddy with him for medical expertise.

"What are you doing here, Trevor?"

"Oh, just came to see what my favorite girl was up to."

"Favorite girl?" Moira said, with wide eyes. "What do you want, Trevor?"

Trevor was silent, and only wore a grin as he followed the old woman into the kitchen. It was just as he remembered. She had taken him in, like one of her own that day she found him tenting on her property. He only stayed long enough for food, shelter, and the money he stole, but that didn't matter now.

If there was one thing he learned from prison, it was that you can't trust anyone, no matter how nice they seemed to be. He learned that from his uncle. Actually, he learned a lot of things from his uncle. Too bad he was dead.

"How long have you been working for me, Moira?"

"I don't know, a few years maybe?" Moira swallowed hard. Her face went beet red.

"And what did I tell you would happen if you talk to the cops?"

"I didn't! I swear!" Moira backed up into the grungy white kitchen cabinets, as Trevor inched forward and pulled out his gun. "That's not what I heard."

"Well…then…you heard wrong."

"I don't think so. Just tell me what happened, Moira, and I won't have to hurt you."

Moira started to cry like she usually did when she was drunk, like now. Trevor was used to that. He had to rough her up a few times in the past, but nothing like this. The old bat couldn't keep her mouth shut, and he was sick of it. He couldn't chance keeping her around anymore.

Trevor threw a punch at the old woman's jaw, then shoved her head against the kitchen cabinets. "It's your fault, Moira!" he shouted, thrusting the gun to her temple. "You just couldn't keep your trap shut, now could you."

"Nooo! Stop it, Trevor! I'm your family!"

"No, you're not my family. My family is dead!" Trevor was furious with the mention of family. As far as he was concerned, he was an orphan. After the death of his uncle, and the horrible death of his big brother, he lost everything. No, he didn't have family, especially not that stupid little runt.

He was going to make him pay for everything he did. And in some strange way, this was part of it. Anything that resembled family, was dead to him, including Moira, at least she would be, as soon as he pulled the trigger.

"What are you waiting for? Just do it already!" his stoic friend shouted from the doorway. "Hurry up before someone comes!"

Moira's eyes grew wide, as Trevor shouted at his friend. "DON'T RUSH ME!"

The tall, elderly man, crossed his arms in front of him, and shook his head. He stepped out of the house for a moment, and looked around nervously.

Trevor continued to shove the gun harder into Moira's temple, as he glared into her empty eyes. With a squeeze of the trigger, the old woman dropped like a crumpled doll. "Serves you right, *old bag!*"

With an old dishtowel, Trevor removed the blood-speckle from his face. He called his friend inside, and asked for his medical expertise. They wiped off his prints from the gun, and forced Moira's there instead. They positioned her in such a way, as to make whoever found her, think she killed herself in a drunken stupor.

They would believe that. The woman was good for nothing, anyway. Just an old drunk. And thankfully for his friend, he knew just how to set it up to make it look believable. "Thanks buddy!"

"No problem! Just make sure you keep your end of the bargain."

"Hey, have I ever steered you wrong?"

His friend smirked, and didn't answer. That annoyed Trevor. But for now, he let it go. It only proved one thing: He couldn't trust anyone!

Not even him!

~~~~

Bedford Road Collegiate, was an ancient high school, nestled in the heart of downtown Saskatoon. Pip hadn't gone to a traditional school, but by the looks of this one, he was thankful he hadn't. It was huge.

He and Grayson headed for the office, as they walked by the different assortment of teenagers that hung out by the front doors. It reminded him of his youth, and brought back those same feelings of insecurity that he felt growing up.

He tried to shake it from his mind.

"Excuse me," Grayson asked the receptionist. "We're looking for a student named Shania Runningman. Do you know what classroom she's in?"

"And you are?"

"Detective Spencer, and Detective Eaglefeather." He winked at Pip.

The guy had a persuasive look about him. Pip liked that, especially the part about him being a detective. Pip wished he was, but he needed to do a lot of schooling first, if he ever really wanted to train for that. He kind of liked the whole detective thing. He'd keep that in mind for future careers.

"Can I see your badges?"

Grayson bit his lip, and poured on the charm. "Well no, see, I lost mine." He winked. "And Detective Eaglefeather is a rookie."

"Then sorry sirs, I can't help you."

"Oh come on." Grayson pleaded. "We need your help."

"And I need your badge."

"Fine," he said. "Truth is, I'm suspended for two weeks and I had my badge taken away. But, this young man here had his newborn baby abducted from the hospital, and I'm trying to help him find her. You might've seen it on the news?"

The receptionist eyes grew wide. "I heard about that. So sorry! Look," she said, "we have strict rules to follow. I need to see credentials before I can give you any information about a student, or I'll lose my job."

"Please!" Pip asked nicely.

The receptionist looked around sheepishly, and then called them in close to whisper. "I shouldn't tell you even this, and you didn't hear it from me, but Shania Runningman isn't even here. She skipped school again, like usual. She's missed most of the year because of the baby."

"Right," Grayson said. "Her baby that died?"

"Died? No, not that I know of. She gave it up for adoption."

"Adoption? Are you sure?"

"Absolutely! I'm best friends with the guidance counselor here, but you didn't hear that from me. I could be fired if anyone finds out I told you this."

"Our lips are sealed," Grayson smiled. "You know what agency handled the adoption? Was it local?"

"I don't know that. Sorry."

Grayson jotted down a few things on his notepad, and closed it up. "No, you've been very helpful. Thanks for the information."

With that, Grayson and Pip left the high school, and went back to the car. Grayson started the vehicle and let it idle, so the air-conditioning could cool them off.

"So what do we do now?" Pip asked. He was sure they had another dead-end, but for some reason Grayson looked like he had something up his sleeve.

"Social Services." The detective grinned. "My buddy's wife works there. She's not in today, but I'm sure I can get some answers from some of her coworkers. They've come through for me in the past, and a few of them owe me big-time."

"Okay."

Pip was going to trust the man. Hopefully this lead would help find his daughter. "Then I guess we go to Social Services."

"Ever been there?"

"Nope!"
"Then you're in for a treat."

Chapter 15

Chloe questioned her decision to play along.

The new teenage girls that flooded the place, were suspicious. She saw some of them from her window as they came in, and they had flat bellies, then, when Chow introduced them to her, they had pregnant bellies. Hmmm.

Were they fake? If so, why?

Sure, she knew that the adoption agency was being run under the table, and that was frightening, but she couldn't understand why the girls would fake a pregnancy. What possible purpose would that serve?

Baby Lily, was fast asleep in her bassinet beside her, as she lay on the bed to rest. She just fed and changed her, and watched her little body rise and fall as she slept. Chloe couldn't believe how beautiful her warm chocolate skin, and full head of hair, was.

Her soft suckling lips searched for the breast, every time she brought the bottle to her. Chloe wondered if it was just a natural instinct, or if she breastfed with her birth mother, whoever that was.

Chloe couldn't imagine giving up such a precious little one. She must've come from some drug addict, or teenage mother, who was barely old enough to drive, leave alone take care of a baby.

Maybe she could have her? Would it be that bad? Would she be a terrible person if she wanted to buy the baby? Sure, she knew it was illegal to buy a human being, but people did it every day. Unwanted babies were probably sold for profit throughout the entire world. Why should Canada be an exception? Why should Canada be better than everyone else? Why not pay for a baby? The mother didn't want it anyway.

Even in the short time Chloe had been taking care of her, she already developed a bond. This was her child now, and nobody was going to take her away. It was just the money that set her back. Where would she get that kind of cash?

She thought about Grayson, and how she was going to tell him about this. He was a cop, and they played by a strict moral code. Convincing him to buy a child would not be easy. But she knew she had to try.

It's the how that was frustrating. How was she going to contact her husband? Chow took her phone away and smashed it. They didn't have a landline in the building, and it didn't appear that the others had cell phones, except for Chow. Not even a television, or radio, could be found in the entire place, either. They were cut off from the outside world, and there was nothing she could do about it.

Grayson was probably very worried by now.

If she could just get word to him somehow, privately; If she could just talk to him and get him to see how much in love she was with Lily, surely he would support her. Surely he wouldn't mind her spending the savings on this, instead of IVF. They both worked full-time and had more than enough to live on anyway. It wouldn't be that hard to withdraw a hundred thousand dollars.

Chloe decided she was going to talk to Trevor, as soon as he comes back. She would simply tell him not to bother with the clients who were coming, but tell him that she wanted to buy the child. Hopefully, that would be good enough to hold Lily for adoption.

Yet, her heart was torn. What was she thinking? Her best friend Rozelyn was locked away in the room down the hall. Surely, they weren't going to hurt her.

Surely, this was all just a big mistake, and they weren't as mean as they seemed.

It was probably all just a big misunderstanding. For all she knew, they could've released her friend and sent her home already. Rozelyn probably called Grayson already and told him what was happening.

But what was she trying to prove? Chloe knew that wasn't likely. She knew these people were criminals, and it wasn't a good situation to be in. What she should be concentrating on, is trying to find a way out, not playing along with their stupid game. That meant she had to face the fact that the baby was not hers, and she wasn't prepared to do that.

Chloe had burped Lily, changed her, fed her, snuggled with her, as if the child spent nine months inside her own body. No, Lily was hers now. There was no way she was giving her up, even if she had to fight for her, which she was prepared to do. Actually, she was prepared to do just about anything to keep her.

~~~~

"Can I help you with the baby?" Shania asked the woman holding the newborn, as she rubbed the itchy maternity-form under her shirt. It was bugging her like it always did.

"Um...I don't think so."

"Why not?" Shania asked. "The kid isn't yours."

Tears rushed to the woman's eyes, but she quickly brushed them away. "She is now!"

"What?" Shania whispered, and scooted up close. "What do you mean? Trevor said he had a buyer for this one. That's why we're all here."

"No—I'm going to buy her, instead."

"Look, I don't know you, or where you came from lady, except that Chow said you were hired to do some childcare. That's why you're here, isn't it?"

"No it isn't."

Tears escaped the woman's eyes again. She looked tired and distraught, and Shania knew something was definitely wrong. Part of her wanted to tell the rest of the girls, but the other part wanted to help. Her gut said to help her. "Do you know where the baby came from?"

"No, I thought someone here was the mother."

Shania frowned, "Not that I know of, but I think I have a pretty good idea where it might have come from."

Shania observed the middle-aged woman. She looked like a natural with the child, as she fed her a bottle in the kitchen. The other girls were giggling about something in the living room. And Trevor still hadn't arrived even though they were told that he was on his way. Figures!

He always made them wait around. But then, with him freaking out over Kokum talking to the police—all she wanted to do was go home. She didn't really want to see Trevor face-to-face. Who knows what he'd do to her.

But still, she came with Serena and didn't exactly have a ride home. "Do you have a car?" Shania asked. "Um...what's your name, by the way?"

"Chloe. And no, not here. But I came with a friend, and I know where her car is parked, but I just don't know where the key is. Chow has her locked up in a room at the end of the hall?"

"WHAT?" Shania leaned in close, and whispered again. "*Seriously?*"

"Mhmm!" Chloe nodded. "They made me stay and take care of the baby, and tied up my friend. I don't know how she's doing or anything, because they moved me into a different room."

"I can almost guarantee, she's not doing well. You don't know what kind of people you're dealing with. You don't want to mess with them, and you certainly don't want to buy a kid from them. First of all, if you think they're gonna let you go, you got another thing coming. And that baby has a buyer. If you try to fight them, you'll wish you never did."

Shania couldn't stop her own tears from falling now. She remembered the pain of giving birth to her own child, holding it, nursing it, only to have it ripped from her arms. It was the most incredible heart wrenching loss she had ever experienced.

"They took my friend's baby." She sobbed, not wanting to reveal her own story. "She tried to get it back; She tried everything, but Trevor wouldn't let her. There was nothing she could do. He's done that with all the girls, and he'll do that with you, too."

"Then we have to get out of here. Can you help me find my friend?"

"I think so, but we have to be quick. Trevor's supposed to be on his way."

Shania felt a connection with this woman. She wanted to tell her about her own baby, but she couldn't. She wanted to help her, but felt torn between her, and her friend Serena. She couldn't leave Serena, could she? Maybe they can all leave together?

Maybe it was time to rat on Trevor for good?

Chapter 16

By the time they got to the Social Services office, it was late in the afternoon, and almost closing time. Luckily, they still had a half hour left to get some questions answered. Grayson knew they spent too long having lunch, but he was glad he spent the time to get to know the kid.

Pip was exceptional. The things that this young man had been through, were very traumatic, and just the simple fact that he was still sane, told Grayson a lot about him. Usually people who've been through that kind of trauma, grew up with mental problems. He saw them go through the system; He put many of them in prison, and usually crimes were committed by wounded people just like him.

Really, it was amazing, and according to the young man, it was because he found God. Grayson didn't really know what to think about that. He figured having faith in something, couldn't hurt.

He also told Pip about his wife's struggles with fertility. Grayson didn't know why he felt compelled to tell the young man about that, but he figured it was because he needed another guy to talk to. After Spencer abandoned him, he needed somebody to talk to that understood women things. Pip seemed to have that in common with him, mainly baby stuff, as weird as it was for guys to discuss.

"Welp...Let's go find your little one," Grayson said, as he opened the door to the Social Services building. Pip grinned for real this time, and followed him inside.

"Grayson!" One of the female voices from down the hall, caught his attention immediately. He and Pip decided to head in that direction.

"Avari, darling? What's up?"

He'd known Avari for as long as he could remember. She, Chloe, and Rozelyn had gone to school together.

"Did you get any leads on her?"

"Well, kind of. That's why we're here," Grayson told her, wondering how she knew he was on the case. He guessed tongues were wagging like usual.

"Great! Come to my office and sit down, then. I've been worried sick."

Grayson furrowed his brow, as he eyed Pip. He could see confusion written all over his face, as well. Why was Avari worried sick about a child abduction that she wasn't personally involved with? Or maybe she was?

Did Pip know this woman?

As they both took a seat in Avari's office, Pip went completely silent. Grayson decided to listen to what his friend had to say first, before asking questions about Shania Runningman.

"So, what leads?"

"Were checking out a young girl that might have something to do with the abduction."

Avari's eyes grew wide, and her mouth hung open. "So they're calling it an abduction now? Since when?"

Then, Avari started to cry, and looked away. She grabbed a Kleenex, and wiped her eyes, and blew her nose. "I just don't get it. Why would someone want to abduct her?"

"That's what we're trying to find out."

Pip looked dumbfounded, but still said nothing.

Grayson wondered why Avari seemed overly distraught. But then, she was a woman. They tended to be more emotional. Perhaps it was that?

"We've been trying to help with the search all day. I personally called every single hospital in the city, but I haven't found out a thing. So, if you know something, please, spit it out."

Now Grayson was completely confused. Why such an interest? He knew that the hospital had passed the case on to Social Services, but they weren't usually so vested. He assumed the file would go to the bottom of the slush pile, since they thought the child was with its grandmother.

"Man, I'm impressed, Avari. You guys don't usually work so fast."

"I beg your pardon?"

Uh-oh, Grayson knew he put his foot in his mouth. She was obviously ticked off by that remark. He'd have to do some backpedaling, quickly."

"I mean, it's…it's great that you care so much."

"Why wouldn't we?"

Grayson sighed. She was still ticked off. He decided to take a different approach, and introduce Pip. "Um, no reason." Grayson felt his underarms drip with sweat. "Say, let me introduce my new partner. He decided to help in the search as well. Actually, he's been a lot of help to me since Spencer dumped me.

"Dumped you? Pfft…can you blame him?"

Grayson's mouth hung open. He couldn't believe his ears. This was the oddest conversation he'd had in a long time. But then, Avari was an odd woman. She was one of those hyper organized people, and very opinionated most of the time. Usually everyone just let her talk, because if they didn't, she'd tell them where to go without batting an eye.

Still, something seemed off.

"I don't blame Spencer." Grayson loosened his collar, and tried to breathe. "Let me rephrase that. Spencer can do whatever he wants. It wasn't his fault."

"Of course it wasn't his fault!"

"Okay—" Grayson spoke cautiously, wondering why she was being so intense. "I tried his phone all day, but he doesn't answer."

"Well, he can't exactly answer his phone when he's sedated."

Sedated? Like medicated? What on earth was going on? Grayson didn't understand anything this woman was saying. Was she on another planet or something? His thumping pulse went into overdrive.

"Did you hear me, Grayson? I said they have him sedated. You can't expect him to answer his cell phone like that. Good grief, the man's going through enough as it is, without you picking on him."

"Picking on him?" Grayson snapped back. "And what do you mean, sedated?"

Pip shrugged his shoulders when he looked over at him.

"Because of the...abduction."

Grayson blurted out a laugh, suddenly. "*Pfft—What?*"

"Okay—I've had about enough of your games, mister. I think you'd better leave!" Avari ordered, standing up suddenly. She pointed to the door like he was a delinquent schoolboy, sent to the principal's office.

"What—Why?"

"Because, you're a totally insensitive jerk, and you're making a mockery out of this whole case. I happen to care about my friend, even if you don't. That's what people do Grayson—They care! I can't believe you didn't know he was sedated. Good grief, what planet are you on? That's what happens when you have a nervous breakdown—They sedate you!"

"Nervous breakdown? Why?"

Pip interrupted, then. "I think we're talking about two different things here, people." We're trying to find my baby girl. She was abducted from the hospital a few days ago. This has nothing to do with you, lady, or this Spencer guy, or anyone else for that matter. It's personal, and it's painful...for ME! I'm the one who should be worried sick, not you!"

Avari's face went red. Her mouth hung open, and she gasped as she drew her hands to her burning face. "Oh—*No!*" She stumbled over her words. "I...I didn't realize. I'm sooo sorry. This is about the Eaglefeather baby, isn't it?"

Pip shook his head.

Avari sat back down, and fanned her red face. "I got that case the other day. It's at the bottom of my pile. I haven't even read through it. You mean to tell me, you think this is a newborn abduction, after all? I thought the grandmother has it?"

"Well, she doesn't!" Pip snapped back.

Grayson couldn't say a word, but his mind kept reeling about Spencer. What was going on with him, then? Why did he have a nervous breakdown? What abduction was she talking about, if not the baby's? The ringing in his ears, and the thumping of his racing heartbeat, made it impossible to focus on what the other two were talking about."

"Grayson? Are you okay?

"Hmmm?"

Avari gave Pip a concerning look, and Pip shrugged his shoulders in response. "Earth to Grayson. Is anybody home?"

Grayson tried to focus, and gave his head a shake. He was tired, he was confused, and now he was worried as well. He had a very bad feeling about this whole mess. Rubbing his sweaty brow, he took a deep breath. "I'm here. I'm just...just puzzled."

"Well, I'm sorry. I thought you were talking about Rozelyn. My mistake."

"Rozelyn?"

"Yes. You probably don't know, then. They found her car at the bottom of the river this morning. She wasn't in it, but still. Spencer broke down, and was rushed to St. Paul's hospital. He's on the mental health ward."

Immediately, Grayson bolted from his seat. He stumbled over his chair, and shook his dizzy head. *"No—Noooo!"* He backed out of the office. "Um...she...I—" He could barely put two words together, and took off running.

Pip instinctively charged after him.

~~~~

The old man was a good detective, but he was definitely not an athlete. Pip found him doubled over in the parking lot, trying to catch his breath. "What got you all fired up?"

"Nothing, kid! Leave me alone!"

"What—Why?" Something was wrong. Pip knew it. "Give me the keys. You're in no condition to drive."

"I'm fine!"

"No, you're not! Why are you so ticked off?"

"I'm not ticked off—Here!" Grayson threw him the keys, and headed toward the passenger door. "Get in, then! I'll fill you in along the way."

Pip drove the car away, and headed west on 22nd Street. He followed Grayson's directions to St. Paul's hospital, and realize he was going to see his sedated friend.

"Look, I get that you're upset because of your friend, but I need to know if you're still helping me find my daughter. If not, I'll understand, but I can't waste an evening at the hospital. You understand?"

"I understand completely, Pal."

"Pal? What's that supposed to mean?"

"That means, you're a selfish little punk! Okay? I've been working on finding your daughter for days, off the clock even. But the moment the focus is taken off of you, you go ballistic."

"I'm not the one that's ballistic, you are!"

"I AM NOT!"

But Pip didn't want to argue. He worked his throat, and tried to calm down before he said something he would regret. He didn't understand what was going on, and there was obviously something bothering Grayson.

Pip decided he would take a bus home to check on Dinah, after he finished driving the jerk to the hospital. Then he'd figure out what to do next. He was not wasting another minute on Grayson's wild goose chases, or volunteering to be his target for insults. As far as he was concerned, the man was the worst detective ever. No wonder he was suspended. All these so-called leads, were just a bunch of dead-ends. His baby was first priority, and Pip needed to find her soon, even if he had to do it himself.

Chapter 17

Grayson called everyone that he possibly could, and nobody knew where his wife was. It created such a headache, that he couldn't stand it anymore. He was losing control, and that wasn't like him. Now his hands wouldn't stop shaking.

Great! What was the kid doing back?

Suddenly, Pip was standing there, watching through the glass. What did he want? Grayson reluctantly unrolled the window. "Jeepers kid, you scared the heck out of me. I thought you said you were taking the bus?"

"Well, apparently I missed it."

"So…catch another."

"No."

"What do you mean, no?"

Pip sighed heavily as he came back around the driver's side. He opened the door and plunked down. "Look. I'm sorry, okay? Whatever I did, I didn't mean to. But you—well, I know when something's wrong…and something's wrong!"

Grayson just sat there glaring, trying to hide behind his anger.

"From what I've seen of you, you're a good man. I appreciate everything you've done for me, and now I'm gonna return the favor, even though I'm worried sick about—well, you know. So first, you're gonna tell me what's bothering you. And second, I'm gonna pray for you…because that's what you need. Got it?"

"Got it."

Grayson's hands palsied violently, as Pip sat there observing. He supposed he was waiting for an explanation. Breathe! Finally, with fits of sobbing, Grayson broke the silence. "It's…it's my wife…she's…she's missing! She was with Rozelyn!"

"What? The Rozelyn you guys were talking about? Your partners wife?"

"Yes!" Grayson realized Pip was finally connecting the dots.

"And do you know this for a fact?"

"Yes! She went shopping with Rozelyn, and I thought she was mad at me because I haven't been able to call. I was so busy with the case, that I—"

"Oh—sorry."

~~~~

Pip felt guilty that the detective neglected his wife to help him. The poor man had focused all his energy on finding the baby, and nothing on himself and his personal life. Pip understood the tendency. He had grown up his whole life feeling responsible for everyone else's happiness. He put all his energy into other people, instead of himself, and that was exhausting.

"You think your friend has some answers for you?"

Grayson fidgeted. "I don't know, maybe. Probably not."

"And he's sedated, right?"

"Right."

Pip breathed deeply, and tried to find the right words to comfort the man. "Okay, so this is what we're gonna do: Were gonna go see your partner. We're only staying for a few minutes if he's not awake. If he is awake, then take all the time you need. After that, you can go your way, and I'll go mine. Or, I can help you find your wife. Maybe we can find our missing girls, together?"

Grayson listened, with wide tear-filled eyes.

"But before we do that," Pip continued, "I'm gonna pray for you."

"Okay." Grayson wiped his nose with his sleeve. "Thanks kid."

"No problem."

~~~~

Sadie gently brushed Dinah's hair as if she was a little girl. It brought back memories of when Dinah first arrived at Shining Star Lodge. It was a healing lodge designed for rehabilitation. Dinah was lost in so many ways, and it took a great deal of time, energy, and prayer, to help her find her way.

Now this. God, help my little butterfly through yet another turmoil.

Sadie also said a prayer for Pip. When she first met him, he was such a broken boy. She couldn't believe the hardship he had faced his entire life, but she was proud of him for becoming the man he is today.

Still, she hoped that God would do something to move them back to Deep Bay. It was his home, and a place where he could bring up his own children, and change the dysfunctions that poisoned his past.

But it wasn't easy to change dysfunctions that were passed down from generation to generation. The ugly things left horrible scars that usually maimed for life. But with hard work, and strong faith, Sadie knew it was possible. God was a capable healer, she'd seen it many times. He could turn anything around.

Sadie hoped that was the case about her job. Was it God's will or not, for her to continue living in Deep Bay? If so, what was she going to do for income, now that her job had been pulled out from underneath her?

All these questions, and no answers, made Sadie tired. She thought of all sorts of ideas for employment, both in Saskatoon, and in Deep Bay. It was just hard focusing on which place she should live. So much depended on whether or not they find the baby.

So far, Pip and the detective had found nothing. Dinah was beside herself after talking to Pip an hour ago. He told her he was going to work all night to find the baby. But personally, Sadie hoped he would just take care of himself for a change. She hoped he'd at least come home for a few hours of sleep.

But the boy was stubborn, and she didn't blame him for wanting to keep going. She would too, if someone stole her baby. She couldn't imagine the pain and heartbreak it would cause. It felt bad enough to be the grandmother of a missing child.

Yes, Sadie knew she wasn't really Dinah's mother, and the baby wasn't really her grandchild, but still, it felt like it. And the pain was just as real.

God in heaven, please find my grandchild - Alive!

~~~~~

Pip watched from a distance, as his friend stood over his partner's bed. He observed the conscious man, wiping his tear-filled eyes, as he spoke to his friend. Then, the two of them pointed in his direction and motioned him to join them.

Pip wrung his hands. He didn't do well in situations like these, but headed for the bed anyway. Grayson introduced him to Spencer, and Pip shook his hand. It was a firm handshake, and he could tell he was a good man. Grandfather always taught him that you can tell a man by his handshake.

"I told Spencer how the case was going."

"We're gonna find your baby, young man," Spencer told him, as he started to emotionally break down again.

Pip nodded, and said a silent prayer for the poor man, but he was interrupted by a knock at the door. It was someone with a badge.

"Well, hello boys." The man grinned. "You two sure can get yourselves into trouble."

"Pip—my boss Rourke."

"Pleased to meet you Rourke." Pip shook the man's hand, but it was wet like a fish, and not firm at all. He figured so, from what Grayson had already told him about the guy.

"We have a lead." Rourke continued. "I came all the way down here just for you Spencer, so you better pay attention. And Grayson, you're back on the job, so listen up. Got prints off the steering wheel of your wife's car that belong to an Arnold Runningman. Found him in our database. He's been in and out of prison."

"Did you say, Runningman?"

Grayson and Pip eyed each other, knowing exactly what the other was thinking.

"Yeah, 19-year-old punk kid. Lives on the Standinghorse Indian Reserve." Rourke gave him a piece of paper with directions scribbled on it. "Take a drive, bring him in for questioning. You know the drill."

"Gladly!" Grayson beamed. "But not without my badge." He held out his hand smugly, rubbing it in.

"Fine! Here's your stupid badge. Now get to work!"

Grayson and Pip took off so fast, they didn't even have time to say goodbye. Pip knew how important the information was. It was finally something, not just for him, but for both of them.

A lead.

Chapter 18

Chloe took a bed sheet and ripped it into a long strip. She crossed it in front of her belly, and behind her back, and over her shoulders, then back in front to tie it. A Moby Wrap. Something she looked up on the Internet many times, perfecting it each month while hoping for a positive pregnancy test. Sadly, the tests were always negative, and she decided not to keep putting herself through that anymore. But at least she became a pro at tying a Moby Wrap.

Gently, she took the newborn and pulled the wrap over the baby's body, setting her securely in place. Sure, the material was supposed to be stretchy, but the bed sheet worked just as well. Now, Chloe had her hands free. She could sneak down the hall with Shania, break into Rozelyn's room, and get her downstairs and out the door before Chow noticed.

"Shania?" she whispered, cracking the door and peeking her head out. Where was the girl? She was supposed to meet her five minutes ago. Should she go on her own, or wait?

On tippy-toe, Chloe patted the sleeping baby, easing the whole door open this time. She looked both ways and made sure the coast was clear. Slowly and cautiously, she creaked down the hall, stepping on the noisy floorboards as she went along.

Chloe was prepared to do whatever it took to rescue Rozelyn, and get to her car. At this time of evening, Chow was in the kitchen cleaning up. She could hear him clanking dishes. And the other girls were quiet as mice, for some reason. Shania still hadn't shown up, but she couldn't wait any longer for the girl. She must've gotten cold feet.

Hopefully, Chloe stuffed enough diapers and bottles into the wrap, and the baby would be okay while she and Rozelyn escaped. She just gave Lily a bottle a half hour ago, and changed her bum a couple times. She should be good to go. Now that the newborn was sleeping, it was the perfect time to break out.

Finally, Chloe reached the end of the hall. It was now or never. She'd have to pick the lock herself, if Shania didn't show up. Maybe she could use her own Bobby Pin? She didn't really know how to pick a lock, but she was going to learn, fast. With a shaky hand, she pulled the pin from her hair, and jumped suddenly, when she saw the girl. "Finally! I thought you weren't coming back."

"Well, I had a hard time getting away from the girls."

"You didn't tell anyone, did you?"

"Well—just one." Shania cringed. "I couldn't help it. She's my best friend. I told her to keep it quiet, though. We can trust her."

"I hope you're right."

"I'm right," Shania told her, moving her aside as she picked the lock with a nail. It appeared to be much easier to use than the Bobby Pin.

It only took a minute before Chloe heard the lock, click. The door eased open. On the floor near the bed lay her friend, covered in blood and gagged. She ran up to her immediately and felt for a pulse. Thankfully, she had one.

Chloe slapped her friend lightly across the face, trying to wake her. Within seconds, Rozelyn opened her eyes wide, like a wild woman, and started to moan. "It's me. Shhhh, we're getting you out of here."

The both of them lifted her to a sitting position on the bed, and pulled off the duct-tape. Underneath, was a black and blue face that looked to be in pretty bad condition.

"Can you walk?"

Rozelyn nodded her head.

"Then let's go." Chloe took one arm, and Shania took the other. They made it back into the hallway, and then to the edge of the stairwell. Hopefully, Chow was still in the kitchen, clanking his pots and pans.

Then, without warning, a voice startled them both. "There you are, you brat."

~~~~

It was Serena—she had broken her promise.

"Please!" Shania whispered. "You said you wouldn't stop us."

"And I won't. Just hand over the fifty bucks Chow gave you this morning, and I'll give you a head start before I tell Chow."

"What?"

"You heard me." Serena grinned with her hand out. "Pay up!"

"No!"

"Shania, just give it to her," Chloe whispered, rocking the baby, who was now starting to make noise. "I'll pay you back later."

"Yeah—She'll pay you back later!" Serena mocked.

Shania gave her friend an evil eye, and glanced at Chloe. She had no choice but to give up the money. It was a dirty move from Serena. But then, she probably stabbed her in the back before, and she didn't even realize. That would explain a lot. But Shania had no time for rehashing old wounds, or new ones. She dove into her pocket, and threw the money at her ex friend, swearing a string of colorful swear-words, just to make a point.

The baby started making loud fussing noises, and Shania knew it was now or never. They had to get out of the door before Chow heard the commotion. "Let's go Chloe!"

"You won't get far," Serena said, poking at her. "Trevor's only five minutes away, and he'll catch up to you, easily."

Shania ignored Serena's barb and pushed through the front door with Chloe, the baby, and the injured woman. If they went through the alley, they would less likely be seen by Trevor, if, in fact, he was really only five minutes away.

"Give me the car keys, and I'll go get the car?"

"Oh no!" Chloe moaned. "I forgot to get the keys!"

"You're kidding me, right?"

"I'm sorry!"

"They took them—first day." Rozelyn lisped through a fat lip.

"Great!" Now they were up the creek. Without transportation, they would be caught for sure. If Chow didn't get them, Trevor would. Tears formed in Shania's eyes. "What are we supposed to do now? We can't get far like this."

"We can find someone who'll help us."

"This is downtown Saskatoon, lady, and it's getting dark. There ain't nothin' down here but hookers, pimps, and dope heads. Trust me, we'll have to walk pretty far to find someone that will actually help."

"Then we'll walk," Chloe said, with her nose in the air. "C'mon—Let's go!"

The woman was determined, she'd give her that. But reality was, it was only a matter of time before Trevor and his buddies pounded the crap out of them.

And that would be the end of that.

Grayson turned on the light, and revealed the bloody murder site. It was a horrific scene of blood splatter against white kitchen cupboards." Oh boy!" He stopped the kid from coming any further. "Maybe you'd better step outside?"

It was too late. Pip already saw it. Grayson didn't expect the kid to react the way he did. He watched the young man crumple to his knees, and hold his choking throat. "Pip? What's the matter? Breathe!"

But the kid couldn't catch his breath.

Grayson had seen this before. It was a full-blown panic attack, just like his friend Spencer's, posttraumatic stress disorder, he'd gotten from his stint in the military a long time ago. Spencer hadn't had an attack in years, but Grayson remembered it well. He figured it was part of the reason his partner was in the hospital right now.

"Pip! Look at me!" he shouted, trying to get his attention. "Look at me! I breathe - you breathe! Got it?"

Pip shook his red face, still gasping for air. Grayson held him by the scruff of the neck, and narrowed his eyes on him. He directed him to inhale, and then exhale. Over and over. "I breathe—You breathe!"

Slowly, Pip mirrored Grayson until he regained control. His breathing began to steady, but he repeated the same instructions just to be sure. "I breathe—You breathe! I breathe—You breathe!"

Finally, Pip raised his hand for Grayson to stop. "I'm fine," he choked. "*Really!*"

"You don't look fine. Your face is still red."

"I just couldn't catch my breath."

"I think it's a whole lot more than that." Grayson told him, point blank. "You have PTSD. Does this happen a lot?"

"No! I got it under control."

Grayson eyed the kid, and didn't say anymore. He must've gone through quite an ordeal to have that kind of an attack, but then the picture in front of them wasn't exactly pretty. Most people couldn't stomach it. Detective work had desensitized Grayson already. But then, there were pros and cons to that too. "I'll have to call homicide I guess."

Pip stood up, leaned against the wall, and shook his head. "This is awful. Who would do something like this to a little old lady?"

"I don't know—but we're gonna find out. I have a sneakin' suspicion this has something to do with both our cases. I just don't know what, yet."

"I think I'm going to take you home for a few hours of sleep, though. I don't like what happened to you here. In my opinion, you should probably take it easy after something like that. Ever been to Afghanistan?"

"Nope. Just Deep Bay."

Chapter 19

The night air was warm and sticky, as Chloe and Shania supported Rozelyn. They ran through the downtown alley with baby in tow. Lily was sleeping again with the swaying motion, but Chloe's back was killing her from running too long.

"Maybe we can steal a car?" Shania suggested as they stopped for a moment.

"Do you know how to hotwire one?"

"My brother showed me, but I totally suck at it."

"Then I guess we won't be doing that, because I don't know how to either." Chloe had to give this young girl some credit. She had proven herself trustworthy, bringing them this far, and she had nothing to gain. Or did she? Chloe didn't really know. All she knew was, they had to get somewhere safe, fast. "We need a place to hide."

Shania was silent as she sat there catching her breath. Chloe noticed a couple bums rummaging through a nearby dumpster. She looked at her dark surroundings, and realized they were sitting ducks. Still, at least they had the protection of the dumpster to hide behind. Better yet, they could crawl inside. "Let's get in."

"Seriously? It's dirty!"

"Better that, then dead. C'mon!" Chloe found something to stand on, and then boosted the girl inside. Then, between the two of them, they helped Rozelyn flop inside. She wondered how she would get in herself, at first, but then realized she had to take the baby out of the wrap, and hand her over to Shania.

Within minutes, Chloe had the wrap off, and handed Lily's warm sleeping body over the other side. Then, she boosted herself up with effort, reminding herself that she had to lose a few pounds, and certainly, she wasn't as young as she used to be. Thirty-seven is far too old to be doing this kind of stuff.

But then, she'd always told herself the opposite. She felt young, she was young, except for the premature gray hair since college. But she'd always told herself it was never too late to conceive a baby. Fat chance, now!

As Chloe moved around the half-empty dumpster, she kicked the garbage to one side, clearing an area for the three of them to spend the night. It wasn't half bad. She expected more of a stink, but it wasn't the worst smell in the world. Rozelyn didn't seem to care, she collapsed into the mess right away.

After checking Rozelyn's vitals, she realized her friend had passed out again. Hopefully she'd be alright until morning. There wasn't much she could do about it anyway. There was no way they were getting far on foot.

Once Chloe was sure her friend was breathing, she reached for the baby again. Shania seemed more than happy to give her back, a little too happy. They both slumped down, and looked at the stars as they shone brightly in the night sky. Only a light breeze blew the overhead wires around, on the pole beside them. Chloe observed the teenage girl, and wondered what her secrets were. "Tell me the truth - is this your baby?"

"No! I don't have a baby!"

"Just checking. I could tell it bothered you when you held Lily."

"Lily? Shania's mouth hung open. "Since when is her name, *Lily?*"

Chloe knew she had some explaining to do, but she wasn't embarrassed. Lily was her baby now, and nobody was going to change that. "I named her. Like I said before, she's mine now." Thankfully Rozelyn couldn't hear. She wasn't ready to explain that to her.

"Lady, you're nuts! They're not gonna let you keep her."

"Well, I'm sure whoever gave her up, didn't want her, or couldn't take care of her."

"And what makes you so sure?" Shania suddenly wept.

Chloe realized she struck a nerve. The girl started banging her head against the dumpster, trying to muffle her sobs.

"I'm sorry," Chloe said. "I didn't mean to upset you. Obviously this baby came from somewhere, and I don't know if you know where she came from or not, but I assumed she was from an unwanted pregnancy."

"Well, you assumed wrong."

"I'm still going to adopt her."

"Good luck with that."

~~~~

Sadie heard Pip come in the door, followed by the detective. It looked like they had a pretty difficult day. Pip filled her in with a few details when he called earlier, but that didn't explain the uneasiness she was sensing.

"What happened?" she asked. "You look like you've seen a ghost."

Grayson plopped down and groaned. "Either you say something buddy, or I will."

Sadie's eyes grew wide, as she did a double-take at Pip.

"Fine," he mumbled. "The detective said I had a panic attack, I guess."

"You guess? I saw it first hand, and I've seen a lot of things. You had a pretty bad panic attack, and I don't know if it's a good idea to continue working with me."

Sadie sighed, and figured she'd better fill the detective in. He had already been through several traumatic events in his life, but nobody understood the extent of it. She counseled him for years, under a doctor's advisement. He was able, for the most part, to avoid the triggers that caused his attacks. In fact, he hadn't had an attack since before he and Dinah married, and she hoped the worst was behind him. "Can I ask what triggered it?"

"It was a murder scene," the detective told her.

"Well, that would do it. You see detective, Pip witnessed more than one murder in his life. He was just a child the first time, and then he was unfortunate to witness more during his teenage years. He's fully aware of his PTSD. It's been a long time since his last episode, so we thought the worst was over."

"I can speak for myself!" Pip fumed. "Don't talk to me like I'm not even here. I know my stupid head doesn't work properly. It's not my fault that I had an attack; It's not my fault I walked into a murder scene. Why didn't you stop me, Grayson?"

"I tried!"

"Look." Sadie interrupted, "I'm a trained counselor, and I'm sorry we're talking about you son, but you've been through this before. It's good to talk. You know that."

Pip got up and started pacing the living room. He put his hands on his head, and started punching his temples, crying.

"Pip! Stop it!" Dinah shouted, suddenly entering the room. Great! They woke her up. Sadie had hoped the girl had finally fallen asleep, but apparently no such luck.

"Ooooh!" Pip moaned, as he ran into his wife's arms. "I'm so sorry I let you down! I'm a stupid head! I let you down! I let you down!"

"No no no! Shhhh!"

"Come! Sit down you two." Sadie patted the couch beside her. "This is all too much for you. What happened is nobody's fault. You understand? God lets things happen for a reason, and he doesn't just walk away afterward."

Dinah brushed Pip's tears from his face, and held him in a strong embrace. Sadie could see the obvious pain, and the panic attack was just a small part of that. The two young people were mourning the loss of their child, yet at the same time, hopeful they would see her again. It was a position Sadie would never fully understand, even though she was very much a part of this. "God knows your pain, and he wants to comfort you. You need to let him."

Pip sniffled, and wiped his runny nose with his sleeve. "Well, I prayed a couple times today. That's a start."

"Yes, that's a start, my boy." Sadie smiled. She could see his mood changing already.

"I even prayed for the detective. Turns out his wife is missing, too."

"What? —No! I'm so sorry!" Sadie did a double-take. "What happened?"

The detective fidgeted in his seat. "We don't really know, yet. She and a friend went shopping, and they found her abandoned car in the river."

Sadie couldn't believe it. It was horrific news. Both men were going through very similar situations. Either God was playing a cruel joke on them, or He threw them together for a reason. From her experience, there was probably a very good reason.

"We're working on both cases together," Pip said. "Or, at least we were. He didn't want my help at first, or even my prayers, but I did it anyway, didn't I Grayson?"

The detective nodded and fidgeted in his seat. He didn't look very comfortable, and Sadie hoped to change that. An evangelist at heart, she couldn't pass up the opportunity to help the man. "Are you a believer, detective?"

"Are...are you asking me?" he stuttered.

"Yes—You!"

"Well, I said my share of prayers, if that's what you mean. Met my wife at a funeral, so I guess that's like church. I...I don't think either one of us are religious, like you people. We don't practice anything, but—got nothin' against God."

"Good!" Sadie smirked. She'd met his kind before. The sitting on the fence kind; The kind that is neither for, nor against God. In her experience, that was the best kind of person to work with. If you're not against God, you're for God, and that was a good place to start.

"You know," she said, "I used to be like you. There was a time in my life that I didn't think I needed God. He was just something that I never thought about until I went through the loss of my mother. It was devastating. I found myself blaming God. Now, how could God be blamed, if I didn't recognize Him for playing an active role, in the first place? That baffled me. Why would I think that?"

The detective shrugged and leaned in to listen.

"Turns out He played a bigger role in my life than I thought, so I started digging into the Bible, and the more I dug, the more I found out. It goes without saying, that I realized I had to acknowledge Jesus Christ as my savior, the Holy Spirit as my helper, and admit that God was, in fact, real.

"And so I did. I basically told Him I believed in Him and wanted Him to be part of my life, as basic as that sounds. Now sure, there was nothing that could bring my mother back, but God helped me through the pain of losing her.

"I started praying, and the more I did, the more comfort I felt. I became so good at praying, that others started asking me to pray for them. I remember the very first prayer group I was involved in, we prayed for a friend and her husband, who were told they could never have kids. Six months later, they were pregnant. And now they have three beautiful children. God is still in the business of making miracles, so I know he can find my little grandbaby, and I know he can find your wife too. Just ask Him."

The detective rubbed his forehead. He looked as if he wanted to bolt out of there as fast as he could. Sadie chuckled to herself. She tended to overdo it sometimes. Perhaps this was one of those times. Still, in her boldness, God usually worked wonders. She hoped this was one of those times.

"Grayson has a problem with fertility, too," Pip blurted out.

The detective did a double-take, stood immediately, and cleared his throat. "Thanks a lot, kid. I think it's time to go."

"I said too much. Sorry!"

"No skin off my back, kid." Grayson shrugged.

The man's face was red as a beet. There was no fooling Sadie. She knew better. He was definitely upset. She could read people's faces quite easily, and decided she would add this particular item to her already growing prayer list.

Sadie couldn't let the man leave before one last plug. "Promise me you'll think about what I said detective."

"Oh—Sure!"

Did he just roll his eyes? Sadie mused, but understood that it was completely understandable, especially with her tendency to over-preach. But then, God had used her preachiness before, and this was no exception.

"Be ready at 9 AM kid," the detective told Pip, before he left.

"Then I can still go?"

"Against my better judgment—yes."

Sadie saw the gleam in Pip's eyes, and then again in the detective's. Yes, bringing them together was definitely something God brought about. Not only that, but He also brought them hope.

And that was not nothing!

~~~

Grayson tossed and turned all night long. How could he sleep after that? The woman was obviously a nut. How could Pip reveal such personal information? He told him about his fertility struggles in confidence.

It wasn't him anyway? 'A problem in the baby making department'—Jeepers, Grayson groaned. He didn't have a problem, his wife did. How embarrassing—and in front of a bunch of women, even. Now they must think he's got erectile dysfunction or something.

Grayson wanted to scream, but all that came out was a bunch of sobbing. He missed his wife, and her snoring, and all of her silly habits. He missed their fighting over adoption, their infertility discussions, all of it.

He'd give anything to have her back right now.

It was all too raw and painful. The kid wasn't the only one having a hard time, though he'd never admit it. He was no better than the kid, trying to hide, and pretend there was nothing wrong.

Reality sunk in as he lay there. His wife was missing! Will he ever see her again? Grayson knew these thoughts would only keep him up longer, but he couldn't help it. He'd go crazy if he stopped thinking about her, and he'd go crazy if he didn't.

In the back of his mind, he wondered if there was any merit to what the old woman said. What if all he had to do was ask for God's help? Was it really that simple? Grayson didn't think so. If it was, then everyone would get their way, and that wasn't realistic.

Grayson knew how ugly it was out there? Bad things happened every day. Child molesters, murderers, rapists, they harm the innocent continuously. He'd seen it over and over. Yet, God's supposed to care? Ha! Where was He, for those people? How could He allow such things?

But, here he was, doing the same thing the old lady did. How could he blame a God he didn't acknowledge? Maybe it was habit? Maybe it was all those Sunday School classes his mother dragged him to, when he was a little kid? Something made him think that God was responsible?

Sure, he was familiar with the Bible, kind of. He just didn't want to tell the old lady he knew more than she thought he did. But, it was something he grew out of. As far as Grayson was concerned, God was just for little kids and fairytales. Still, the whole God thing kept coming up, even as an adult.

Grayson wondered if he was looking at it all wrong. If God had so much power, that he was responsible for things that go wrong, maybe he was also responsible for things that go right? It was a long shot, but maybe it was worth looking into.

If he was going to blame God anyway, he might as well ask Him for help. God, he prayed for the first time, since he was seven years old in Mrs. Friesen's Sunday School class. If you're listening, help me find my wife, and let her be okay. And while you're at it, help us find the kid's baby girl, too."

With that, Grayson felt a sense of calm. He curled up into a ball, inhaled his wife's pillow, and closed his eyes for the first time in days. Sleep, oh blessed sleep!

Chapter 20

Those idiots! How could they let them escape? The clients were due to arrive any time, and now Trevor had no baby. Quite frankly, he was sick of the whole thing. Firstly, the clients were taking too long. If they wanted the kid, they had to pay a holding fee, or he'd sell to someone else. They knew that, yet they were still dragging their feet.

Stupid Chow! He was supposed to be watching the girls. They all deserved the beating they got last night, every single one of them. Even Serena. He didn't care if she was pregnant again. It didn't mean he couldn't wail on her, same as everyone else? She was just money to him, anyway. Still, she should be thankful he went as easy as he did on her...for the kid's sake...for his investment.

The dawn peaked through the old downtown buildings, and Trevor was glad he got an early start. He'd catch up to them in no time, especially if they were still on foot. They were slow, and he was fast, so he figured he had a little time to waste. He squatted under his favorite graffiti sign, and lit a match under a spoon. When it turned to liquid, he sucked it up through the syringe and poked himself in the arm.

The high, was a reward for putting up with the stupid broads. They were destroying his reputation, his business? Didn't they care? After all he had done for them, this was the thanks they gave him? Unbelievable?

And now, because of the old biddy, the police were investigating. It was only a matter of time before they caught on to what he was doing. He'd have to cut his losses and move on before they find him. There was no way he was going back to prison!

He was better off heading home, living off the money he'd made so far. And Grandfather's cabin would be the perfect place to hide, at least until things died down.

First, Trevor needed to find the brat. It wasn't just the money he was after. Sure, taking her made business sense, but it was never really about the money for this one. It was his birthright—payback, for everything the runt took from him.

~~~~

Rozelyn was still unconscious. Chloe wished she was able to sleep so soundly, but no such luck. She hadn't gotten much rest all night. The baby woke several times for feedings, and now she had no more formula left. She didn't know what she was going to do. The baby was wailing impatiently for food.

Shania woke to the screaming. "Oh, my ears."

"We need to find some help. I'm out of formula."

"It's too early. The businesses aren't open yet."

"Well, we have to do something, because Lily is starving." The infant thrashed her little arms and legs, red faced and screaming. Chloe knew they had to do something to keep her quiet, or risk being found by the wrong people.

"Give her to me," Shania suddenly grabbed the wailing infant, and lifted her shirt. To Chloe's amazement, the newborn latched on to her exposed breast.

"I still have milk."

"I see that." Chloe wasn't surprised. She had her suspicions all along.

"She's yours, isn't she?"

"NO! I told you she's not!" the girl cried.

Chloe observed Shania, as she breastfed the newborn like her own child. Obviously, the girl had done this before. "I don't understand!"

"I had a kid, lady! Satisfied?"

Chloe cleared her throat. "Okay." Didn't the girl tell her earlier that she didn't have a baby? Was she the newborn's mother, or wasn't she? If she was, this was a game changer. Would the girl still allow her to adopt the child if she was the mother?

"Did you have, this, kid?" Chloe asked again, this time more sternly. Maybe the teenager was just embarrassed, and didn't want to talk about it.

"NO! I keep trying to tell you. Now be quiet, or the baby won't suck right. She's used to a bottle, not me. Remember?" Shania wiped her tears with her forearm, and brushed them away from her face.

Chloe sat there, numb. She didn't know what to think. Was the girl telling the truth, or making up stories? Obviously, she had a baby, or she wouldn't have breast milk. Fifteen minutes went by, as she mulled over the new information. The baby nursed the whole time, and fell asleep when she was done.

"So, I thought you were pregnant?"

"It's a fake bump." The girl reached behind her back with one hand, and ripped open the Velcro that kept the pregnancy form in place. "See?" She tossed it onto a heap of garbage beside her.

"I thought something strange was going on. You guys had identical bumps."

The girl shifted the sleeping baby over her shoulder, and burped her. As Chloe watched its head bobble, she realized how tiny and frail the newborn really was. It was time for them to get to safety, so this nonsense could come to an end.

"We usually have to wear the fake bump whenever Trevor expects clients. It adds to the image you know."

"And what's the image?"

"A legit adoption agency."

Chloe frowned, and realized just how much danger they were really in. Getting away from there, was the absolute best thing they could have done. Now they had to find someone that would help, before Trevor found them. "Is she almost done?"

"I guess. I don't really know. I didn't nurse for long, when I was in the hospital."

"What happened? —I mean, if you wanna tell me."

"I had to give my baby to Kokum. They sold her, and I never saw her again." Shania choked up. "I...I was supposed to follow the doctor's orders, and make my milk dry up, but I couldn't. I hid it from everybody. I thought maybe—I thought somehow I would get my baby back, and I wanted to have enough milk to feed her when I did."

Shania's eyes flooded with tears, as the poor girl explained herself. It made Chloe's heart ache, listening to her story. Watching her with the newborn, was even more painful.

"And what did the doctors say, when you had to explain where your baby went?"

"I just told everyone at school that I gave her up for adoption, even though Trevor gave me heck for saying that. I guess I was supposed to say she died, but I forgot."

"Oh, you poor thing!"

Shania cringed and went on. "Anyway, I was forced to sign a death certificate, so there was no way to link her back to me. For legal reasons, Trevor told me there needed to be something official saying my baby died."

"A doctor needs to sign off on something like that."

"He did, he came right to the reserve and everything."

"Hmmm," was all Chloe could muster. The whole thing stunk. What doctor in his right mind, would sign off on a death certificate, without taking the body in for an autopsy? And wouldn't there be an inquest?

But even with all the questions, Chloe knew she wasn't going to get any real answers, at least answers that made sense, anyway. There was obviously something strange going on, but she wasn't going to get to the bottom of it now.

Chloe was just relieved that the baby wasn't Shania's. Maybe there was still a chance for her and Grayson to adopt the newborn? Maybe Grayson could even help find Shania's baby? He was good at that.

But even in her attempt to justify what was going on, Chloe felt like throwing up. How could she adopt a child that likely was stolen from its mother—just like Shania's situation? It was insane, but she pushed it from her mind, anyway. It is the way it is.

~~~~

Trevor paused as he stood at the end of the quiet alley, listening. They were in there all right! All he had to do was sneak up on them. Too easy!

He pulled the gun from his belt, and cocked the trigger. It was at times like this, that he really enjoyed his job. He was glad he had the brains to start up his own business. It helped, that he met the right people in jail. They taught him the ropes.

Grandfather wouldn't be pleased. But who cares about him, he was dead anyway. Still, Trevor wasn't going to let his mind drift back to his childhood. The only thing good about it, was sneaking off with his uncle, so they could get high together. They had more fun than either one of his stupid brothers. They were the idiots, not him.

Thankfully, his uncle taught him everything before he died. And his death was the most painful childhood memory of all. He had been forced to take counseling while in prison, which revealed a lot. The loss of his uncle, turned his entire world upside down. It drove him to mess up in the first place. If it wasn't for him, he wouldn't have wasted all that time in jail. And now the runt was going to pay!

Suddenly, Trevor kicked a small can by accident. Clumsy feet. Hopefully the girls didn't hear. "Hold it right there!" he shouted, rushing to the dumpster.

Immediately, they held their hands above their heads. The fat one lay there like she was dead. He didn't worry about her. "Hand over the kid!"

"No!"

"Then I'll shoot you dead, lady."

"Wait—wait!" Shania tried to stop him. "Don't shoot her Trevor. Please! I'm begging you! We'll give you the baby!"

"You better!"

But the old broad turned away, and wouldn't let her have it. If it was a fight she wanted, he'd give her one. First he grabbed Shania's hair, and yanked her over the top of the dumpster. He punched her ugly face like a boxer, and kicked her silly. "Now, stay there you stupid witch!"

Shania lay there full of blood, curled up in a fetal position on the ground. She moaned, and sobbed, and whimpered. Trevor went to the dumpster a second time, and pointed the gun inside. This time, he aimed at her fat friend. "I'm gonna say it one more time, lady. Hand over the kid!"

"No!" The woman clung to the kid. Did she really think she could win?

"Then, you give me no choice." Trevor cocked the gun, and let the fat friend have it.

Hysterical screaming, echoed in the alley.

Without warning, someone attacked him from behind, sending him careening forward. She hit him in the head with something—something! And it hurt, bad! Everything was fading. He touched his scalp, observing his bloody fingers. She really hit him. Stunned, Trevor teetered, crumpling against his will.

Chapter 21

Morning came early, as Grayson headed out the door with coffee in hand. He wanted to get a fresh start, and he couldn't think of a better way to do it. Still, no call from his wife, though. No word from the precinct. Calling Chloe's cell repeatedly hadn't been productive. Where was she? He didn't know if she was alive or dead, but he was hopeful.

After thumbing through the Bible this morning, he found a comforting passage from Psalm 46:10 - Be still and know that I am God. That wasn't as easy as it sounded. He couldn't be still, but he could admit that God was in charge, and that was at least something.

Grayson was glad he wasn't in charge. There was only so much he could do, and the rest was out of his hands. Still, he always tried to do his best. Having Pip's case to keep him busy, was helpful. He usually never worked two at once, but this time, it was necessary.

Thankfully, his boss wanted him on the job. It was actually a conflict of interest working on a case that involved family, but he knew many other detectives were helping as well. That put his mind at ease.

Grayson assumed the reason he was assigned to his wife's case, was so he didn't go crazy with worry. At least his boss was sensitive to that. But what he didn't know, was that he was still working the newborn abduction case. That was going to remain a secret.

For some reason, Grayson had a gut feeling that the two cases were connected somehow. The same name kept popping up: Runningman. A coincidence? Grayson didn't think so. With his experience, there was no such thing. Yes, something was definitely up, and he was going to find out what.

Grayson hadn't heard from anyone at the precinct yet, so he decided he would stop there as soon as he picked up Pip. The kid was becoming a valuable player. Actually, Grayson liked him. He was smart, computer savvy, and had hidden experience that he knew nothing about.

Something traumatic happened at Deep Bay. He remembered the case from long ago. It was a diamond smuggling ring, with connections to a bank robbery, where a women's son got shot. At the time, it was quite the intriguing case, even though he wasn't assigned to it. If Pip was mixed up in that, Grayson could see how traumatized he'd be. He already told him about some of it, but obviously not everything.

Hopefully, the kid wasn't going to have any more panic attacks. If he did, Grayson decided he was going to send him packing for good. There was no way he was capable of handling a mental health issue like that. No, Grayson didn't need that. He was stressed enough as it was. Still, he was willing to give the kid a chance. That's more than anyone else would give him.

~~~~

Early morning had always been Pip's least favorite time of day. He was definitely not a morning person. Still, he'd do anything to find his daughter, even head out at the crack of dawn, with a police officer he barely knew. But, Grayson wasn't a stranger anymore. He was someone he could trust— *a friend.* It really bothered him that Grayson's wife, and his partners wife, had both disappeared at the same time as his daughter. *What was up with that?*

Could either one of those women be capable of kidnapping his child? Pip didn't think so, yet he didn't know the women either. If Grayson was any indication, his wife was probably an outstanding citizen. But still, he could be wrong.

"Ready, buddy?" Grayson smiled at the door.

"Yeah." Pip could tell he was the opposite of him. Morning cheeriness was written all over his face.

The sun was fresh and new, with a hint of warm breeze. Normally on a day like today, he'd head out trapping if he was back home. Oh how he missed those days. Oh how he missed home.

Even after years of living on his own, and moving away from Deep Bay, he still longed for its simplicity. Life was way too busy. The hustle and bustle of the fast-paced rat-race, was severely choking him, little by little.

Before the baby was born, Pip was looking for a new job. That was put on hold since the abduction. And now, breathing in the warm June air, he felt the pangs of homesickness again, and longed to move his family there someday. Maybe he could find some kind of work—do some manual labor to pay the bills? Maybe even work for Sadie? She suggested that a while ago, but nothing since she arrived. Would he ever be able to get back to his roots?

~~~~

"How you holding up?" Grayson's co-workers asked him, when they arrived at the precinct. It was awkward. Their sympathetic eyes, made him feel sick.

"Oh, hanging in there—Rourke in?"

"Nope!"

Typical! He had no respect for his boss. Grayson was used to him being AWOL most of the time, and that was the majority of the week. He couldn't believe how they could pay him that kind of salary, with such little productivity. It was unbelievable, yet predictable. He shifted his jaw and pretended not to be annoyed. "Anyone get a lead?"

"Nothing since the homicide," one of the detectives spoke. "We put out an APB on Arnold Runningman, but so far nothing. No prints on the old lady's gun, either, just her own. They're calling it a suicide. Does that help?"

"No!" It didn't make sense. Why would the old lady kill herself after their visit with her? Sure, she was a drunk, but she didn't look suicidal to him. Then, most people don't, he figured.

Grayson scratched his head, and went through the paperwork, as Pip sat in his swivel chair, spinning. "Can you stop that?"

"Sorry."

It wasn't like Pip was really bothering him, but it was the whole situation. It didn't seem right. Something was missing, and the whole thing stunk. They were back to square one on both cases. Sighing, Grayson set the paperwork down and scratched his head. "Look kid," he swallowed, "I didn't mean to growl at you. I'm just sick of everything. Nothing makes sense."

"I got it."

The poor guy was obviously hurt. He forgot about Pip. It couldn't be easy, knowing your child was out there somewhere, kidnapped, or possibly even dead. If the evidence wasn't going to link these two cases together, Grayson was. The common denominator was, *Runningman.* He wasn't going to wait for his deadbeat boss to give him orders. He was connecting the dots himself.

"Pip, I'm sorry. Let's start the day over."

"Fine."

Grayson beamed a smile at the kid, and hoped that was enough. Let's go over the facts. Now, Arnold Runningman is connected to my wife's disappearance. The old lady—now deceased—Runningman, is connected to your case. If we can't find Arnold Runningman, then let's go after the granddaughter. We know her name is Shania Runningman, so let's go find her.

"Now you're talking." Pip grinned.

Grayson teased, and slapped him on the shoulder on the way out. "Let's go back to school, my boy. It'll be like you never left."

"Not funny!"

Chapter 22

"Hi, remember us?" Grayson poured on the charm, as he and Pip entered the front doors of Bedford Road Collegiate, for the second time. The same secretary as before, sat behind the Plexiglas.

"Hope you have a badge this time."

Grayson winked, and held up his badge attached to a chain around his neck, and smiled. "I came prepared this time, See?"

"Well, I hope so." The secretary leaned into a whisper, and smiled. "I really don't want to lose my job, mister handsome detective."

Okay, that was too much. Grayson bordered on flirtatious behavior sometimes, and he didn't even know why. He chalked it up to job relations, or at least that's what he told himself. Memories of his wife's scoldings, came to mind. She always made a point of getting after him whenever he got too friendly with the ladies. It was a bad habit, and he meant nothing by it, but he had to stop it. She was right? Of course, she was always right, and that's what was killing him. He actually missed that. *He missed her.*

Grayson cleared his throat. "Remember you told us about Shania Runningman?"

"Yes, but she isn't at school again today. Not surprising!"

Grayson figured that, but it wasn't why he came. All he wanted was information about her—the kind only friends knew. "That's fine. What I'm really after are names. Could you possibly give me a list of her friends?"

"Well, actually, a big group of her friends are absent too." It's beginning to be quite a problem. But hey, if they don't care about their education, then neither do we."

"Jeepers! I was hoping to talk to some of them."

"*Jeepers?*"

"His favorite word." Pip laughed, standing there with a smug look on his face. "I tell him it makes him sound old."

"Okay okay. Can we get back to business?" Grayson eyed the kid. "Is there anyone I could talk to about her?"

"Um—yah. You could talk to Gloria. She's the guidance counselor. She's not at liberty to divulge any personal information, though. But maybe she can help. I'll give her a call."

"Fine. Thanks." Grayson tried to keep it professional. He couldn't say he wasn't disappointed that the girl's friends weren't there. But at least the guidance counselor was available.

Suddenly, the bell rang, signaling the change of classes, and the hallway flooded with pimple-faced teenagers. They nearly knocked them over. The two of them stood there like fish out of water. Man, was he glad he wasn't that age anymore!

Gloria Martins met them in the busy hallway and introduced herself. "Sorry about the chaos. Come with me gentleman. We have a lot of students since the doors of immigration opened. It's been crowded all year. Come into my office."

Grayson nodded and Pip followed, as they both took a seat.

"Now, how can I help you gentleman?"

"We're trying to find Shania Runningman."

The round pug-looking woman looked confused. "Well, you were told she wasn't at school today, were you not? She hasn't been at school all week."

"Yes, but we thought maybe you'd know where we could find her—like maybe favorite hangouts, friend's places, work, you know."

The woman bit her lip and paused for a moment. "Is she in some kind of trouble, detectives? Because Shania's a sweet girl, and usually isn't a troublemaker. She doesn't have a very good home life, but generally she's a pretty good kid. In fact, I have a lot of hope for her. If she puts her mind to it, she could have a good future. We've discussed scholarships, but I'm afraid this year's a bust, with her having the baby. She's failing too many classes simply because she just hasn't been here."

"So, she did have a baby?"

"Of course. She put her up for adoption right away, but I'm afraid you'll have to discuss that with Social Services."

"Yes, we will. But her grandmother told us the baby died. Do you know anything about that?"

The lady shrugged her shoulders and gave them a funny look. "I can't think of any reason why she would say that. Shania certainly didn't mention it. That could explain the absenteeism."

"Did she have a part-time job or anything?"

Gloria stopped then, and went to her file. "Why yes, I think she did. Let me just check to be sure. I don't remember every detail about the students here. My mind isn't like it used to be. Um, yes," she said, flipping to the next page. "Here we go. She works at The Luther Home, on Second Avenue. It's downtown."

"Right." Grayson jotted it down in his notepad. "Anything else you can think of— like friends, siblings?"

"Well, there's Arnold, her older brother. We expelled him at the beginning of the year. He assaulted another boy, and well...he's generally like that. Like I said, the family life isn't what it should be. They both live with their grandmother after the parents took off. Sad, really."

"The grandmother was shot and killed yesterday."

"Oh nooo!"

"They say it might be a suicide, but I'm thinking murder. It's still under investigation."

"Do they think Shania did it?" Gloria asked. "Because I can tell you, that sweet girl couldn't possibly be capable of that...but her brother Arnold, he would be the one. I'd track him down—not her."

Grayson closed his notepad and looked up. "Well, you've been very helpful ma'am. We'll be in touch with you if we need anything else." The three of them rose, as the woman got up and guided them to the door.

"Oh, no problem gentleman. I always like to co-operate with the police."

As he and Pip left the office, and headed for the front door, Grayson decided to skip the goodbyes to the secretary, and leave without turning around. He was proud of himself. Chloe would be proud of him, also.

Chloe—could her disappearance possibly have something to do with this Arnold Runningman? He felt sick thinking about it. What did a stupid punk like him want with his wife? Grayson didn't even have to answer that. He already knew.

~~~~

Grayson went quiet for some reason, as they drove to the Social Services building one more time. Pip mulled over the information that Gloria told them.

The Runningman family didn't sound very pleasant. Surely Social Services had more on them.

They were no closer to finding his daughter, or Grayson's wife, but at least they had some leads to follow. He was told they were going to have a quick chat with Avari again, and then head to Second Avenue.

"Isn't The Luther Home an adoption agency?" Grayson asked Avari when they arrived.

"Yes, it is. They're listed here as the agency that handled the Runningman adoption. It says Shania Runningman had a baby girl a couple months ago, and the infant was adopted at only a few days old. Now, that's not your typical adoption, others take much longer. But the home is private. They run by a different set of rules."

"And so," Grayson asked, "what's a young girl who gives her baby up for adoption, doing working for the same agency that gave her kid away? Isn't that a conflict of interest? It's pretty unethical if you ask me."

"Granted, it is strange."

Grayson fidgeted, and gave Pip a weird nod, most likely meaning they were about to go. He was used to his funny gestures, and motions, and odd idioms and words from the 60's and 70's. That was his personality, he guessed.

All three of them rose and headed to the doorway. Pip was trying to play detective and put it all together, but it didn't make sense. There were so many twists and turns in both cases, that it made it hard to keep things straight. They did in fact, seem connected by the same people. Or maybe it was just a coincidence?

"Where to?" Pip asked before thinking. He regretted the question immediately. He knew the answer, and should have said it before Grayson had a chance to give him a hard time. But it was too late.

"Oh—c'mon, kid. Fill in the blanks," Grayson teased. "I thought I was doing a better job teaching you, than that. Where do you think we're going?

"The Luther Home?" Pip cringed.

"Bingo!"

~~~~

By the time they approached The Luther Home, it was midmorning, and the humid June air was kicking up some dark thunderclouds. The place looked dingy, like no one took care of it. The old white siding was dirty, broken, and uneven in places. It was a two-story building with four windows on top, and four windows on the bottom. Grayson and Pip stood at the door and knocked.

"Are you sure we're at the right place?" Pip asked.

"I'm pretty sure of it. It's the only 1531 on Second Avenue. Look." Grayson pointed. "The numbers are right there."

"Wow! This place is a dive. I'd never adopt a baby here?"

"Me neither Pip, but some people are pretty desperate, I guess."

They knocked again, and stood there waiting, while the breeze picked up. Quite frankly, the place was so rundown, Grayson thought it might be abandoned for a moment, until he heard somebody slide open the upstairs window. An oriental man popped his head out. "Go way, go way!"

"Police!" Grayson held up his badge, for cause-and-effect. "Open the door!"

The oriental started shouting, from what sounded to be curse words in his own language. Grayson didn't know who he was directing his words to, but he didn't like it. Either he opened the door, or he'd break it down."

"Warrant! Warrant!" the oriental man yelled.

Ridiculous! Grayson couldn't believe the man. He was not going through the process of getting a warrant for a few simple questions. But he knew if he knocked down the door, he'd never hear the end of it from Rourke.

"Let me try," Pip said.

Grayson didn't know how much better the kid would be, but he figured it was worth a shot. He sure didn't get very far.

"My friend was just kidding," Pip called up to the oriental. "We're not cops. Do we look like cops? Seriously, we have money for the boss, so come down here and open up."

"You lying!"

"No!" Pip insisted. "Honest!"

"YOU LYING!"

Great! This wasn't working, either. Grayson realized he'd have to bust the door down, and explain it later. He would suck up to Rourke, somehow. But just as he was about to force his way through the door, a teenage girl slowly creaked it open.

"Hello?" Pip said, going in first. Grayson didn't like that. He should have waited for him to make the first move. The kid was unarmed, and almost anything could happen. He reminded himself that he'd have to give him heck later, and explain the danger he put them both in. For now, he'd let it go. At least they got in. The pregnant girl didn't look very dangerous anyway, with that bruise, and fat lip.

Grayson shoved the kid aside, and stepped in front, blocking it so the girl couldn't close in on Pip.

"I'm detective Grayson," he said, "and I'd like to ask you a few questions."

"Okay," the native girl whispered. She stared at Pip with wide eyes.

"Is this The Luther Home?"

The girl shook her head, telling them it was. She still couldn't take her eyes off the kid. She was mesmerized by him. Very odd. He wasn't that good looking. "Excuse me." Grayson tried to get her attention. "Do you know this guy?"

Pip turned and looked at Grayson oddly, obviously wondering what the heck he was doing. But Grayson went on without explaining himself, waiting for the girl to answer.

"Um—" she said, "He looks like my boyfriend."

"Pfft—What?" Pip choked, screwing up his face. He defended himself to Grayson, immediately. "I— I'm not! I've never seen her before in my life."

Grayson chuckled, finding the whole thing funny. A case of mistaken identity? Or, the kid had some explaining to do. In any case, they had more pressing matters. He cleared his throat, pulled himself together, and washed the smirk off his face.

Pip just glared.

"We need to speak to the oriental upstairs," Grayson said. "Can you get him?"

The young girl agreed, and left for a few minutes, leaving them standing there. Grayson observed the surroundings, it looked and smelled just like the exterior of the place. If this was an adoption agency, he was a monkey's uncle.

"I know what you're thinking, Grayson," Pip whispered.

"Now, how do you know what I'm thinking?" he grinned, trying to tease.

"I can tell. It's written all over your face. I do not know that girl. I've never seen her before in my life. I swear!"

"I believe you!"

"You don't sound like you believe me." Pip frowned, and folded his arms.

Grayson fought the smirk that was forming, and told himself to focus on the investigation. It really was hilarious, but it wasn't the time or the place for it.

Suddenly, a short oriental man scurried down the steps toward them. He looked angry, and Grayson knew it wasn't a good way to start a conversation. He held up his hand. "Whoa whoa whoa! Just calm down! All we want, is to ask you a few questions."

Grayson knew he handled that badly. Telling an upset person to calm down, was the opposite of what he was trained to do. He wasn't thinking straight. But still, he needed to push on with the investigation, no matter how much he screwed up.

"You go way!" the little man argued. "You *no* stay here! Boss man come back!"

Oh, so there was a boss, after all. At least they were getting somewhere. "Could we have the name of your boss, and how to get a hold of him, please?"

"Here here!" The oriental man gave him a business card, and tried to push him and the kid backward. "Now—go go go!"

Normally Grayson wouldn't let that happen. If he was thinking clearly, he would have drawn his weapon after being shoved like that. But he was off his game. He took the business card, and decided to get the heck out of there. "C'mon! Let's go!"

The oriental man shut the door before they were all the way out. *What a guy.* Something was definitely wrong, and Grayson was going to find out what.

Just before they got to the car, Pip spotted someone across the street. It was a native guy, leaning against an old graffiti sign. The man's face was bloody, and he looked like a bum. He curled a lip at Pip, and spit a gob of something on the street. *Strange.*

Grayson didn't recognize him, but obviously Pip did, and that bothered him. If the kid had enemies, that may explain the kidnapping. Still, the expression on Pip's face didn't seem like he'd just seen his enemy, it looked like fear—*like he'd seen a ghost.*

Chapter 23

Shania's head throbbed, but she was used to it. Trevor beat her up before, but this time he went too far. She'd never seen him actually shoot a gun. He had a few of them, but mostly just boasted about them like an idiot. Now he really did it. The woman was either dead, or almost.

Chloe was in shock ever since they stole the car. She stared out the window, off into space like she was stoned. The baby slept soundly, and Shania drove, even though she didn't have a license. Without Chloe's help deciding what to do, she figured the best place for them was back on the reserve. Maybe they should've gone to the police, and they still might, but for now, she needed to talk to her grandmother.

As they pulled into the reserve, Shania noticed yellow police tape draped around the entrance of her house. She gulped and felt sick to her stomach. Kokum! *If he hurt her—he was dead.* Quickly, she stopped short and pulled the shifter into park. Within seconds, she ripped out of the vehicle, and ran inside. A pool of blood spread out throughout the kitchen floor, wafting a horrible stench. Immediately, she burst into sobs. *Trevooooooooor!!!*

The bile in Shania's throat rose to the surface, and she ran to the bathroom to throw up. Her body trembled as she heaved and sobbed. *How could he do this?* He was an animal! She sat there on the bathroom floor for a moment, *numb.* Outside, thunder rumbled. A storm was coming from the west. It fit the rage she was feeling. *Let it pour!*

Suddenly, the floorboards in the living room creaked. "Who's there?" Shania shot up, and wiped her mouth dry. She crept into the hallway, and peered into the living room. A dark figure stood in front of the window pane, shadowed by flashes of lightning, making her jump.

"It's just me, Shi," the voice spoke calmly.

"Arnold?"

It was her brother. As much as she disliked him, he was a welcome sight. *At least he wasn't Trevor!*

"What happened?"

"Kokum's dead!" Arnold told her, point blank.

"I figured."

Arnold twisted his face. "She shot herself in the head, stupid old woman!"

"Kokum wouldn't do that."

"How do you know? She was a drunk," he told her. "The police said her prints were all over the gun—typical suicide."

"You're lying!" Shania dried her tears. She looked him straight in the eyes, trying to read him. Usually that's all it took. What she saw was the same dark eyes as always. She couldn't trust him—never could. Did he have something to do with it?

"I thought you hated the police? Why would you talk to them?" she asked. Shania knew her brother would never give the police the time of day, leave alone cooperate with a murder investigation. And that's what she figured this was—a murder!

"I'm not lying, Shania?"

"Yes, you are! I know what you've been up to!"

"*Well*...I know what you've been up to too, *little sis!*" her brother retorted. Suddenly, he pulled her backward into a chokehold, and held her there.

"Stop—it!"

"Not until you smarten up! I know who's in the car, and she better have the kid, otherwise you're dead. Trevor's on his way right now, and he's leaving to go up north. He's taking me with him, Shi, so don't screw it up on me!"

Shania's eyes widened, and she took a deep breath. If that was the truth, then she and Chloe were in grave danger. Why did she have to come here? She should've gone to the police. Now it was too late, and Trevor was coming to kill her for sure. *Just like Kokum.*

Arnold wouldn't let Shania go, and dragged her to the kitchen. He fumbled through the drawer with one hand, reaching for a butcher knife. When he found the largest one, he dragged her to the living room, and threw her down on the dirty green carpet, kneeing her in the back. He pulled her wrists together, tying an old skipping rope around them. With the knife, he sliced through the rope to cut off the ends.

He lifted her to the nearest chair and duct-taped her in. With one of Kokum's old scarves, he tied her ankles. Then, like an afterthought, he stuffed another one in her mouth for a gag. The butcher knife to the throat was his final attempt at scaring her. "Now, shut up and sit there you stupid witch! You don't even know how badly you screwed things up for me. Trevor might not let me go with him, now. But he'll change his mind when he sees what I did to you. He'll change his mind when he sees that I have the kid?"

Shania just sat there with wide eyes, stunned.

~~~~

Chloe couldn't move. She didn't even remember getting into the car. And now it was beginning to storm. The once bright sunshiny day, had now turned dark, lighting up the sky. Thunder rumbled like her growling stomach. Her mind was reeling through the chaos of what happened only a few hours ago. Was Rozelyn dead? She couldn't believe he shot her. Her heart thumped against the tiny sleeping baby snuggled against her chest.

What the heck was she doing?

Was this all about the baby? How selfish of her! She jeopardized her life, and others, just for the chance to be a mother. How could she ignore her friend's needs, for a stranger's baby? *How could she not?* For as long as she could remember, Rozelyn had been her best friend—the friend who had it all. She raised two kids of her own, and sent them out of the nest, early. She and Spencer traveled every chance they got. And Chloe was always so envious. *Well, not anymore.*

At least her friend had a chance to be a mother. Chloe always made a point of reminding Rozelyn that she was doubly blessed. Now those blessings were all for nothing if she really was dead. Whose fault was that? *She only had herself to blame!* Overwhelming shame, gripped the pit of her stomach. What would Grayson say? What would she tell Spencer?

Lightning flickered in the sky, with a bolt hitting a nearby field, and the thunder cracked loudly this time, causing her to jump. Now the baby was awake. She'd have to find Shania. The only thing that calmed the child was the breast. Chloe needed to get out of the vehicle, but hail started pelting the hood. The downpour was so heavy, she couldn't see the house in front of her. Guess she'd better stay put and try to comfort the baby herself.

Where was Shania, anyway?

When the hail quit, Chloe observed the shabby house with yellow police tape strung around it. It was about 500 feet in front of the vehicle. The door was left open and hanging off its hinges. Did she dare go in? Where on earth did the girl take them? What happened to going to the police station? Was she that out of it that she didn't notice they headed out of the city? How stupid? Now what were they going to do?

The rain was still coming down, but not as hard. It was time to take a run for the house. But before Chloe could, a figure appeared beside the driver's door, and opened it. "You okay, lady?" It was a native man with black hair poking out of a red hoodie. He beamed a silver front tooth at her as he smiled. Should she trust him?

"Lady?" the man asked again.

"Oh—I'm okay, but I'm looking for Shania."

"In the house—C'mon, before you get soaked."

Chloe nodded. It wasn't exactly the best place for a newborn. She'd have to trust the guy, or the baby would catch cold. Besides, if Shania went inside, it was obviously safe to go in.

"What's your name?" The man held out a hand to help her out.

"Chloe."

"Pleased to meet you, Chloe! *I'm Arnold.*"

Chapter 24

All the way back to the precinct, Pip was quiet as a mouse. Grayson had no idea what was wrong. Obviously, the situation at the adoption agency didn't exactly go as planned, but surely that wasn't it. Could it be the guy he saw across the street? "Who was that guy?"

"Nobody!"

"Well, it doesn't sound like he was nobody. You're all choked up."

Pip didn't answer and just turned away. He glared out the window in the rain. It was the oddest thing. One minute he was playing detective, and the next minute, he was closed mouthed. "Look, if you don't tell me what's going on, I can't help you. Either you spit it out, or I take you home. You can find your own daughter, and I'll find my own wife."

"Fine then—*Take me home!*"

Grayson couldn't believe it. What had gotten into the guy? He sighed, wondering whether or not he should follow through with his threat. But it appeared they were already at the precinct, and pulling into the puddle-filled parking lot. "Okay then—I just have to run some names through the computer, and I'll drop you off. You can go your way, and I'll go mine. That is… unless you have something to share."

"Nope!"

Stubborn kid. That was that, then. Grayson would be better off, anyway. He could move a lot fast without a punk kid tagging along. He didn't need his antisocial behavior. And certainly, if he didn't trust him enough to tell him what was wrong, then why bother trying to help him?

Grayson decided to use the underground parking lot because of the sudden downpour. They pulled into the stall. "Look kid." He shifted into park, and sat there. "Why don't you come inside? We can see what we can dig out of the data base. It's pretty unique. You'll love it. Maybe by then you'll loosen up."

Pip nodded, working his jaw.

"Okay then, let's get going." Grayson was glad the kid came around. He'd give him another chance. And surely, what was bothering him couldn't be all that bad. For all he knew, he got a text from his wife. She was probably scolding him or something. That would explain the poor mood.

Modern technology was getting out of hand. *Texting mostly.* Sure the young people laughed at him for not knowing how to text, or for not using his cell phone every minute, but at least he didn't have someone hounding him everywhere he went. He had a basic cell phone for emergencies only, and that was that.

Grayson could admit he was technologically challenged. He hated it. But now, without help, he didn't know how he was going to do the research. Usually his partner handled all the computer work, and that was embarrassing since Spencer was ten years older than him. He always teased him and told him to take a class. Thankfully, Grayson was able to get away without one. Even now, he if he played his cards right, Pip would work the database for him.

He needed that stubborn, antisocial, kid.

~~~~

"According to this, The Luther Home isn't even listed under adoption agencies," Pip told Grayson.

"So—What's up with that?"

"Don't know."

"See if you can pull up, babies born on reservations in the last two years."

Pip tapped away at the keys as Grayson sipped his coffee. The kid was still pretty closed mouthed, but he was loosening up enough to talk, now. That was at least a little progress.

"I have something—Looks like a lot of the babies were born on the Standinghorse Indian Reserve. Twenty babies in the last two years."

"Interesting." Grayson pulled his chair closer to the screen. "Can you find out the status of each child for me?

"Sure." Pip clicked away like a Pro, bringing up information in seconds. "Three live births—the rest deceased."

"What did you say?"

"*Deceased!* That's what it says."

"Whoa! What's going on here? Either they have bad water out there, or something strange is going on. How can that many babies die in one place? Does it say how they died?"

"Nope."

Grayson scratched his head. Could The Luther Home have something to do with this? It smelled pretty fishy to him. Twenty babies gone—abductions perhaps? Could there be a connection to Pip's daughter? "Pull up the death certificates. I want to see the doctor's signature."

Once again, within seconds, Pip had it up on the screen. "Look at this? The same doctor signed every certificate."

"Well, what do you know," Grayson guffawed. "Good old Dr. Uric."

"I know that name. That's the jerk doctor who bawled me out in the hospital."

"*The one and only.* I didn't like him either."
Grayson was eager to find the other names. "What
about Arnold Runningman? I want to know
everything we got on him and his sister, Shania. Let's
see if we can connect the dots between your case and
mine. And while you're at it, run the name on this
business card." He flipped it over. "Trevor
Standingontheroad, I think."

"*O—kay.*" Pip said, nervously.

"While you're doing that, I'm going for more
coffee." Grayson patted the kid on the back. He did
good work, but Grayson could tell there was
something still bothering him. Surely, he'd spit out
whatever it was, eventually. Maybe it was none of
his business? The kid was kind of shy like that.

~~~~

Pip brought up the first name—*Arnold
Runningman.* He was in and out of Juvie his entire
life, which was only nineteen years. Wow, Pip
couldn't believe it. He was raised by his grandmother
for the past eight years—previous to that, in and out
of foster care since the age of five. This guy was
pretty messed up.

He could relate. Pip was raised by his grandfather
after his parent's died, but Grandfather was a good
caregiver. He was lucky. It could have been way
different. He missed the old man.

Shania Runningman had a clean record. He
searched the archives a few times but nothing came
up under her name. It was odd, but Pip knew how
that could be. One kid turns out great, and the other
one, bad. Just like his own family.

"Got anything?" Grayson came back with hot
coffee.

Pip took the brew, and filled the detective in. It wasn't rocket science. One had a record, and one didn't. He couldn't figure out how there was a connection between them, and both their cases.

"And what about the guy on the business card? Did you bring him up?"

Pip wasn't sure what to say. He couldn't tell the detective. He didn't know how. The moment Trevor's picture popped up, it confirmed what he already knew. He had seen him across the street, and it was still turning his stomach. Now he knew. This was definitely the kidnapper! But to tell Grayson, wasn't exactly going to be easy.

His chest was growing heavy, and Pip knew if he didn't get out of there soon, he'd have another panic attack. *Run!* Within seconds, he bolted out of his seat, and shot off toward the bathroom.

"Hey man? What's up?" Grayson asked.

Breathe! Pip told himself. But he couldn't catch his breath. He couldn't respond. All he could do was run, crashing into the bathroom stall. He locked himself in, hyperventilating. Already he could feel the spinning sensation take hold. He sat down, dropped his head between his legs, and tried to suck in air. *Breathe, you idiot! Breathe!* But the more he told himself to breathe, the more he couldn't. He gasped and choked, and then realized Grayson was listening. He was right outside the door.

"You all right, kid?"

But Pip couldn't answer; He couldn't speak. The air wasn't getting into his lungs. Was he going to die? Panic overtook every muscle, paralyzing him completely. He raised his head again, and gripped his throat to try to make it work. But the air wouldn't come. Then, with one kick, the detective had the door open. It banged his knees. Grayson yanked the door the other way, and nearly broke it off. He was shaking him now—*then a hard slap.*

"I breathe—you breathe!" Grayson instructed him.

All Pip could do was gasp.

"*No!* Follow me kid. I breathe—you breathe! I breathe—you breathe!

Finally, Pip managed to copy him, breathing to the rhythm. The spinning stopped and he felt his heartbeat slowdown. The lightheadedness disappeared as well. The air was returning to his lungs again, and he realized he wasn't dying today!

"You got this kid!"

Embarrassment washed over Pip's face as nausea set in. This time, he turned and puked in the toilet, and Grayson stepped outside the stall. *Why did this have to happen now?* The whole thing made him look like a fool. *Stupidhead!*

"You done?"

"Yah."

Grayson led him by the arm and walked him back to his desk. He figured this had to be one of the most embarrassing moments of his life. Why did he always look like a weakling around the detective? He burped, and wiped the sweat off his brow. At least the guy had patience with him, and he actually cared enough to help him. Two panic attacks in the last forty-eight hours was not a good thing. *Stupidhead indeed!*

"I think I'm gonna take you home, buddy," Grayson told him suddenly. "You're no good to me like this."

"No—*Please!* I'm fine!"

Grayson looked sideways at him and shook his head. "What set you off like that?"

"I don't know," he lied.

"Well...*don't do it again!*"

Pip nodded and tried and cracked a smile. Grayson sure was good at calming people down. Pip guessed that was why he was the detective, not him. In fact, he didn't think he'd ever be one now. *Not with that stunt!*

Suddenly, a commotion in the back pulled Grayson's attention off him, and onto the female officer running toward them. "Grayson!" She waved a paper in the air. "You better hear this!"

"What's up?'

"We have a female—mid forties, enroute to RUH as we speak. Gunshot wound, multiple fractures. Found her in a dumpster near Fifth Avenue."

"So?"

"Grayson...*She's Rozelyn!*"

"And my wife?"

"Nothing—*Just Roz.*"

Pip watched as the man's hope melted. A feeling he knew all too well. At least now they were going to get some answers. He wondered if it was a good thing, though. Sometimes knowing, was far worse than not knowing.

Chapter 25

"Shut the kid up, already!" Arnold yelled at Chloe. He never did have any patience. Why would she expect him to be any different now?

"I'm trying!"

"Well, try harder!" her brother shouted again!

From the moment Arnold brought Chloe into the house, the woman lost it. Just the sight of blood alone, made her puke.

"She's hungry! *I told you that!*"

"Then give her your boob and shut her up!"

"I can't!" Chloe eyed Shania and then Arnold. It was inevitable, and Shania knew it. She nodded, mentally giving her the okay to let out her secret.

"Shania's been nursing her."

Arnold's eyes grew wide, and he laughed. Figures! He thought everything was a joke, including the baby she gave birth to. His reaction, and the way he belittled her, made her want to punch him in the face. *Jerk!*

"Unbelievable!" he said. "It's been two whole months since we sold your brat, and still you're pretending like she's coming back. *Well, she's not!* Wait till Trevor hears about this one—*Ha!* He'll laugh so hard he'll crap his pants."

Shania furrowed her brow, and cursed through the scarf gagging her mouth. The muffled noises sounded more like wounded animals, more than anything else.

"Can you untie her?" Chloe spoke softly. "She can't nurse the baby if she's like that, and it's the only way to stop the baby from crying."

"Fine!" Arnold turned to her, scowling. "But I'm locking you both in the bedroom then. I don't trust either one of you.

~~~

Chloe watched Shania as she nursed the baby, again. She couldn't quite put her finger on it, but there was something amazing about the whole process. She wished she could experience what that felt like someday, but there wasn't much hope of that. She may not get to experience giving birth, but adoption was the next best thing. If she was lucky she'd get to keep Lily, but she didn't know how that was going to happen now.

They had fled from one danger to the next, and being locked in yet another room, didn't help matters much. Surely there was some way they could escape.

She wished she was a stronger person instead of weak and helpless. The shock of witnessing her friend get shot, didn't help Chloe's nerves either. Yes, she could handle a lot of difficult circumstances at work, but this was not work. This was not a typical day taking care of home-care patients. *Definitely not!* It was something entirely different, not just for her, but for Shania, too.

As mature as the teenager was, she realized she was just a kid. Chloe wondered what kind of a family she must've come from, to fall into a life like this. It was sad, really. She had already had a child of her own, and didn't look anything more than sixteen.

Apparently she lived here. *How awful!* And with a brother like that, no wonder she fell in with the wrong crowd. *Poor thing!*

Looking around the room, it appeared there was no window, which was odd because that was a safety feature all homes were supposed to have. But she figured, homes on reserves must not have to follow the same rules.

If they were going to escape, they'd have to break out. And behind the locked door, was a guy who seemed to be cruel and obnoxious. She was sure he was capable of almost anything.

The blood in the kitchen worried her. What happened there? Did she even want to know? Just the thought of seeing that mess again made her stomach turn. However, she'd have to go through the kitchen if she wanted to get out of the house. There was only one door in and out, and that was the one. Another health code violation.

But first, she'd have to figure out a way to unlock the door. "You don't happen to know any tricks to get out of this room, do you?" she asked Shania, as she burped the baby.

"Not really. This was Kokum's room...my grandmother. If my brother locked us in, then it wasn't by the door lock. It's broken. He must've put a padlock on it. That would be the only way the door would lock. Besides, I already checked, and when I yank on the door, it sounds like he chained it."

"Great! I thought maybe we could pick it like we did the other door."

"I doubt it."

Chloe could still hear thunder outside. She hoped the power didn't go off in the storm. They needed it to search the room for a way out. Maybe the closet would give her some ideas? "You ever been inside this?"

"No—but hey, don't you want the baby back?"

Chloe observed the teenager as she held Lily uncomfortably. It was obvious she didn't want to get too attached. She wondered if she shouldn't let her. But fear crept in, and she worried she might take the child, and keep her for her own.

"Um—yeah, I'll take her now," she grabbed the infant, cooing the baby and talking to her softly "You can go back into mama's sling where you're safe and sound." Chloe fussed with the baby carrier and folded it on either side of the child's tiny body, and then pulled up the bottom piece of material over-top her bum. "There you go. Now let's check out that closet."

"What's behind the clothes?"

The teenager shrugged, and looked disinterested. She brushed her tears away, and acted strange. It wasn't Chloe's fault the girl had issues. There was nothing she could do about it anyway. Rozelyn was the social worker, not her. Rozelyn—why did she have to think of her now? It was hard enough to keep going, without remembering her friend. Did she die of her injuries?

Chloe shed her own tears now, and tried to hide them. She sniffled and pushed past her emotions.

"It looks like the walls aren't even finished back here," Chloe said, regaining composure. She rummaged through the clothes, trying to get behind them. She went down on hands and knees and crawled through the mess.

Suddenly a dizzy spell came over her, and she sat back on her heels and took a breath. "Maybe I should've let you hold the baby, after all," she called to the girl. "Lily's heavy, and it's pretty hot and squishy in here. Do you think maybe you could come and help me? Shania?"

But the girl wasn't answering. She was probably still pouting on the bed. Chloe decided to take another deep breath and dive back in for a second attempt. "It's too dark in here!" Chloe complained, annoyed that she was now caught between the shoes, and a big pile of dirty clothes that almost made her gag. *Gross!*

"Good grief!" A voice from above, shot into the dark closet. "Here—let me help!"

Finally! Shania flung open the double door to the closet and attempted to remove all the clothes that were hanging there. She slid bundles of them off the metal pole, and dropped them on the bedroom floor. Gradually, more light beamed in, along with fresh air. "Thank you!"

"You're welcome! Now move over and let me see what you're doing."

"Fine!" Chloe crouched on her heels, and instinctively grabbed her head as it started spinning again. "Sorry—just let me catch my breath."

"You okay, lady?"

"Yeah!" Chloe nodded her head, swallowing hard with guilt. The girl had more compassion than she had, obviously. And after she refused to comfort the teenager earlier. Shame flooded over her. How could she be so selfish? She made a mental note of that fact, promising herself she'd work on that particular personality flaw, immediately. "Are you okay?"

"Um—yah."

Chloe crawled toward Shania and paused. "You know, I was thinking. If we kicked the drywall in, we probably could bust through to the other side. What's behind it?"

"My room—*My closet.*"

"*Perfect! We could kick* a hole through the closet and crawl through. But, it would be pretty noisy. We'll have to do it quietly or your brother will hear."

"Right." Shania observed the wall. "Well, I think we could do it. I heard Arnold go out, so it's perfect timing."

"Really? Are you sure he's outside?"

"Yup!"

"Then let's do it!"

~~~~

Trevor's blood was boiling when he got out of the vehicle. Everything was all screwed up now, and he didn't know who was to blame. Probably all of them. *Good for nothing nitwits!* Now he had to get out of there in a hurry. The police were on to him, especially since he saw them across the street from The Luther Home. Seeing the ugly runt wasn't exactly what he bargained for. Gave him a good scare, anyway. He won't see his daughter, *ever*, and that's a promise!

It was a miracle that both the stupid broads came back with the kid. Bunch of dumb women, running around with their tails between their legs. *Man, were they ever stupid!* But at least their stupidity bought him more time. He had the kid again, and that meant payday.

Still, the potential buyers hadn't come yet, and that bothered him. He gave them plenty of chances to come up with the money, and now it was time to move on. He had to find another buyer quickly, before he headed up north. And that didn't leave him a lot of time. Hopefully, Arnold had some suggestions. He owed him big time for having such a stupid sister.

"I don't know anybody?" Arnold wined.

"Look, you're my main man. Do some snooping around town if you have to. Just find me a buyer, and find one fast!"

"But I thought we were leaving. You are taking me with you I hope?"

Trevor smirked, hoping to light a fire under the kids butt. He would play with him a bit, and make him sweat. Maybe he'd find him a buyer faster. But really, Trevor never planned on taking him along in the first place. The only reason he needed him was because he resembled the runt. "Nope, I think I'll go by myself."

"*Whaaat?*"

"You heard me! But...*If you find a buyer today,* I might reconsider."

"*Done!* Let me make a few calls, and you'll see. I'm a man of my word."

Trevor admired the guy's enthusiasm. He was catching on quickly. At least something was going right. As for the girls, he could hardly wait to wring their little necks. They'll wish they never crossed him.

"C'mon inside Trev," the kid slapped his back, enthusiastically. "I have the women locked up in the bedroom."

"*You dog!*"

Chapter 26

There was nothing more either one of them could do at the hospital, that was for sure. Rozelyn was in a coma, and barely hanging on to life. At least she was alive, and that was more than he could say for his wife. *He could only hope!* "C'mon Pip, let's go see the crime scene. There might be something useful for us there."

Pip nodded his head and followed the detective without question.

Grayson knew, if they had any chance of finding his wife alive, they'd have to get their hands dirty. And that meant playing the twenty-question game with the CSI's. They usually hated that, because apparently, they weren't finished with the scene yet.

Quite frankly, he didn't have time to wait for them to get all their ducks in a row. He needed answers, now, even if it meant doing his own CSI work—though he was sure they wouldn't be very happy with that.

It started to rain again, this time more steadily. The thunderheads had passed, and now a continual monsoon-like rain lingered. It was typical June weather in Saskatchewan, but that made the job even harder. Grayson hoped the CSI group had gathered enough information before everything went soggy, or there wasn't going to be much helpful information for them.

On the ride over, the patter of rain hitting the windshield, echoed through the vehicle. It was hypnotic, with the back and forth motion of the windshield wipers. That brought Grayson's thoughts back to his wife. If he had only been a better husband, maybe his wife wouldn't be missing. If he hadn't argued about adoption, maybe she wouldn't have stomped off and gone shopping with Rozelyn.

How many times had he told himself he should listen to her more intently? And did he? *No!* It was his fault she was missing, and now some lunatic had kidnapped her, *or worse.* Grayson knew what worse meant, he'd seen it every day on the job, and that made him feel sick to his stomach.

His wife was out there by herself, forced to do who-knows-what, for her captors. She might be the one with a bullet in her head, and maybe not as lucky as her friend Rozelyn—hanging onto life by a thread. *God, help my wife wherever she is!*

As he and Pip pulled into the alley leading to the crime scene, they could see the yellow police tape skirting the area. Grayson sat there staring into space, while Pip spoke. "Are we getting out?"

"Yeah." He didn't want to get out really, especially in the rain, but he knew he had to take a look. If there were any clues that could help them in this investigation, he had to know.

The two of them grabbed a couple umbrellas tucked under the seat and opened them up as they headed outside. The pelting rain calmed Grayson's speeding pulse as they walked to the dumpster.

"This it?" Grayson shouted to a CSI agent through the downpour.

"Yup! We combed it through, already. Don't know what you think you can find."

Grayson ignored him, and peeked inside, anyway. *Nothing but garbage.* Surely he didn't have to go through that. "C'mon Pip, let's go ask them what they found. I don't want to rummage through a mess like that, and I don't think you want to either."

"Definitely not!"

The two of them headed for the CSI vehicle, and took a look at the sealed bags of crime scene treasures. One in particular caught his eye. "Is that what I think it is?"

The CSI agent shrugged his shoulders. "A baby bottle? You came all the way out here in the rain for a baby bottle?"

Grayson smirked at the kid. Pip's eyes grew wide. "Maybe. Can you check to see if my wife's fingerprints are on it? And while you're at it, check to see if the prints match a Shania Runningman, or an Arnold Runningman. Oh, and check prints for Trevor Standingontheroad while you're at it."

"Got it boss!"

The two of them hurried back to the vehicle to get out of the rain. They folded their umbrellas and threw them on the floor, shivering wet as they drove away.

"You think this seriously has something to do with my daughter?"

Grayson nodded his head. "Don't get your hopes up or anything, but this is just too big of a coincidence if you ask me. I told you before that I think the two cases are linked somehow."

"But that would mean—*your wife*—Do you think she took my daughter?"

"No, *I didn't say that.* But my gut just tells me that Roz and Chloe were at the wrong place at the wrong time. They could've stumbled upon the kidnappers somehow. Let's just see what the evidence shows us first, before we jump to conclusions."

The whole thing smelled fishy to Grayson. He certainly hoped his wife wasn't capable of kidnapping a baby. Even as desperate as she was to have a child, he knew she was not a criminal. He knew she could never do such a thing. But still, what did one case have to do with the other? It was driving him insane. "I think we better take another trip to The Luther Home. It seems suspicious doesn't it? And both Arnold and Shania Runningman have connections to the place for some reason. They tie into my case, and it's about time we find out how."

Pip shrugged his shoulders oddly, as if he didn't agree.

"What, you don't think so?" It certainly looked like the kid didn't agree with him. He had a funny look on his face, that made Grayson second guess himself.

"If you have something to say, spit it out, kid! You think we're barking up the wrong tree?"

"No...*I don't!*"

"Well, it sure looks like you do."

"No, you're right. Let's go." The kid looked as white as a ghost, and started breathing heavily.

"You're not gonna have another attack, are you?"

Pip shook his head.

"I hope not." Grayson frowned, focusing on his driving now. He hadn't been a detective for as long as he had, to ignore his gut. And right now, his gut was telling him a lot of things. One of them was that the two cases were definitely connected, and the other, was that the kid was hiding something.

~~~~

Dinah hadn't heard from Pip all day. She hoped he and the detective had gotten further in the investigation today than they had yesterday, but for some reason she didn't think so. She had given up hoping for a miracle, and that was the most depressing thing of all.

"You've got to have faith, sweetheart," Sadie kept telling her. But too much time had passed. Was it really healthy to remain optimistic? The emotional roller coaster she had been on, was exhausting.

"I *do* have faith! What I don't have, is hope. If there was something to go on, maybe it would be easier, but we haven't heard a thing. Why not? I'll tell you why not. Because someone took my child and is a million miles away by now."

Dinah started to bawl, just like she'd done every day since her baby disappeared. It was becoming a regular pattern already. Her depression was becoming more severe, but she didn't care. All she wanted to do was give up and die.

"Oh, my little butterfly. Don't say such things. You need to get your mind off of this. Why don't you try writing again? That usually helps."

"Well, not this time. Nothing helps, and I'm going crazy just sitting around waiting!"

Sadie immediately folded her hands and started praying silently to herself.

"And stop that! There's only so much praying a person can take. We need to do something. I need to do something!"

Sadie sighed, and looked up. "And what do you suppose we do? You're recovering from a C-section. You can barely move, leave alone help the detective with the investigation. And you have to use the breast pump every two hours. What kind of help would that be?"

"I don't know, but I gotta do something, or I'm gonna go nuts! Please, Sadie! Help me do something, anything!"

Sadie scratched her head and sighed again. "Fine! This is against my better judgment, but if it makes you feel better, I'll take you wherever you want to go.

"Great! I'll call a cab. We're going back to the hospital. I want to question the staff again—now that I'm not so out of it."

Sadie cringed. "*Oh dear!*"

Dinah smiled for the first time in a long time. Finally, she felt the depression lift, and hope rise from the ashes. She felt empowered as if she could soar on wings like eagles; run and not grow weary; walk and not faint. Yes, she was at least doing something.

And that made all the difference in the world.

~~~~

Sadie thought she must be crazy letting the girl help.

She found the wheelchair in the front lobby of the hospital and ordered Dinah to sit in it, whether she wanted to or not. Besides, the only way the girl was helping, was if she agreed to be pushed around by Sadie. *That was that!*

Behind the chair, hung an oversized bag containing Dinah's breast pump, and paraphernalia she needed for their little excursion. It was ridiculous really, but probably necessary, considering the girls depression lately. If this made her feel better, then it was definitely the right thing to do.

"So where did they say this doctor is?"

"C wing. It's supposed to be at the end of this hall."

Sadie looked around, and stopped for a moment to get her bearings. "Over there," she pointed. "I guess it helps when you read the signs, doesn't it?"

They both laughed out loud, and Sadie liked that. At least the girl's cheerful self was making a comeback. Oh how she had missed that. Her little butterfly had been far too sad since all this happened. Happiness was long overdue.

"Excuse me," Dinah spoke to the doctor at the nursing station. "The nurse on the phone told me to come see you. Do you remember me?"

"Oh, well yes." The doctor gave her a cheerful smile. "Mrs. Eaglefeather, isn't it? You're hear about the baby?"

" Yes! I want to go over the details with you?"

"Details? You mean the recent news?"

"News?" Dinah asked, excitedly. "What news?"

The doctor whispered, and looked around cautiously. His actions were suspicious, as if he had some gossip he didn't want anyone else to hear. "Let's talk in private," he said, motioning them to the side of the hallway, as he continued to whisper. "I have some information you might find interesting."

"What is it? Did they find my baby?" Dinah glowed.

"Well," he whispered, "I shouldn't tell you this, but I heard they found your baby on an Indian reserve, nearby."

"*Whaaat?*"

"It's true!"

"How do you know this?" Sadie asked, wanting to hear the details. But surely if it was true, Pip and the detective would have told them this. But maybe it was recent news, like he said? Maybe the case had just been solved, and they hadn't been informed yet?

"I have friends who do medicals for the Standinghorse Indian Reserve, and that's how I found out. Would you like me to take you there?"

"Take us there?" Sadie swallowed hard, turning to the girl.

"Absolutely! *Yes!*"

Sadie wanted to tell Dinah to calm down and not get her hopes up, but she couldn't squash what little hope she had. No, she wasn't going to take that away. In fact, she hoped this was their missing child, as well.

"Let me call my husband so he can meet us," Dinah told the doctor.

"Oh—definitely not!" The doctor placed his hand on Dinah's cell phone. He grinned sheepishly and took it from her, setting off alarm bells immediately. Something wasn't right, but Sadie would give him the benefit of the doubt. He obviously knew more than they did.

"It's all hush-hush you know," the doctor continued to whisper. "Let me take you out there and we'll confirm it's your child, first. After all, I wasn't supposed to say anything. It's their surprise."

Sadie assumed, *their*, referred to Pip and the detective. How sneaky! That's probably why they hadn't heard from them all day. Pip had his phone off and didn't want to ruin the surprise. *Little bugger!*

As the doctor wheeled Dinah down the hallway toward the parkade, Sadie followed behind them. They arrived at the nursing station, so the doctor could tell his staff he was done for the day.

"Have a good night, Nurse Beckett."

"You too, Dr. Uric."

And off they went to find the doctor's car.

Chapter 27

Within minutes, Shania and Chloe had booted a hole through what used to be the closet joining her room to her grandmother's. It wasn't even that noisy. The drywall lay in crumbled pieces on the hardwood floor, with white powder everywhere.

Arnold was still outside when they tiptoed through the bloody kitchen and peeked outside. Stupid Trevor was here. Now they were in for it. "Quick!" Shania jumped. "They're coming in! We have to hide!"

The two of them looked around quickly for a hiding place, but couldn't find anything. There wasn't even a decent closet big enough for both of them, except maybe the bathroom, and that would probably be the first place they'd look. They scurried around like mice, going in every direction, until suddenly, Shania felt the back of her shirt being pulled.

"*Get back here you witch!*" Arnold yelled, grabbing her. She dangled there like a puppet.

Trevor went for the baby, immediately. "Oh no you don't, lady! You have something of mine." He took her by the scruff of the neck as well, and plunked her down on a kitchen chair. Then he took his belt off, and pulled her hands behind her back, buckling them to the chair. The baby was still tucked into her sling, unharmed. "Now…One move and your dead, lady!"

Shania struggled with her brother, but he pinned her down on the floor, punching her, then kicking her in the side repeatedly. The pain was unbearable with each thrust of his boot. She felt the room spin and then she vomited blood. She tried to get up, but now both Arnold and Trevor were letting her have it, right to the stomach with their boots. "Stop!" But they wouldn't listen to her, or Chloe either, who was screaming from the chair, with the now crying infant.

"That will teach you, you stupid broad!" Her brother had finally stopped, and stood there winded.

Shania wouldn't give up. She spit blood at Trevor, only to receive another blow. He spoke with every boot, telling her just how much he despised her. "I—hate—you!" He kicked harder, wiping the blood-spit from his face. "*I—gave— you—everything!*"

"NO YOU DIDN'T!"

"Yes—I—did!"

"Like what?"

Trevor stopped short, and leaned down to shout. "I knocked you up! Remember the kid?"

"HOW COULD I FORGET?" Shania bawled and moaned, remembering. This animal had fathered her child. He also took her away. She cried so hard she couldn't see anymore.

And then a wallop to the head.

"You stupid witch!" Trevor booted again. He was out of breath, but continued anyway. "I never should have trusted you! Never! I never should have trusted any of you!"

"Trev!" Arnold pulled him aside, trying to make him stop. "She's my sister, man! *Stop!*"

But Trevor wouldn't hear of it. He screamed as loud as he could, raging once more. "That's exactly why I'm doing this! Because she's your sister! Family doesn't mean anything to me! *Nothing! —Nothing! —Nothing!*" He continued assaulting her until she couldn't move, couldn't speak, or barely breathe. Shania's punctured lungs wouldn't allow her the dignity to say what she needed to say, but her thoughts lingered resolute.

Screw you!

~~~~

They couldn't keep her in the chair for long. The baby needed tending to, and she was the only one that could, now that they killed the girl. The assault had taken its toll on Chloe, bringing her nausea back, as she viewed the bloody mess on the floor. *Monster!*

The two aboriginal males dragged Shania's badly beaten dead body to the nearest bedroom and threw her in like trash. *How sad.* Chloe could feel the bile rising in her throat, but she didn't dare puke. Not with them on the rampage.

She overheard them both talking as they came back into the kitchen, looking through the cupboards for something to eat like nothing happened. "She had it coming," Trevor spoke.

"Um—yah," was all Arnold could say. He looked terrified.

Trevor pulled out a box of Cheerios from the cupboard, and proceeded to pour himself and Arnold a bowl full. He grabbed an old jug of milk from the fridge and smelt it, pouring it on top. The two of them chomped the cereal like pigs, completely ignoring her sitting on the chair. Jerks!

"Better get me a buyer for the kid by the end of the day, pal!" Trevor spit through his Cheerios.

"I told you I would!"

"Better not be any more surprises, or I'll really lose it."

Really lose it? Chloe wanted to slap the man. What did he call what just happened? Nothing?

"Don't worry."

"WELL I DO!" Trevor suddenly slammed his fist on the kitchen table, rattling the dishes. "You're a loser, Arnold. Just like your sister! I never should have trusted you two. You better come through for me, or it's your neck on the line this time!"

"I—I will!"

"You better!"

Arnold swallowed hard and continued to shovel spoonfuls of Cheerios into his mouth. He slouched, hanging his head like he was already defeated. Suddenly, Chloe realized she could solve both their problems. Even though she'd have to deal with criminals, she'd ignore her conscience long enough to pull it off. Yes, she'd tell them what she planned to do, as soon as they were done eating.

She was the new buyer!

~~~~

Trevor burped, and looked out the window. *Raining again.* It was a non-stop deluge. Man, he had to get out of this hole. He'd been doing this adoption scam too long, and now he was paying for it, literally! He got sucked into thinking he could trust the people on this reserve, but guess not. He couldn't trust anybody, especially family. He got lost in it for a while, thinking he could make his millions here, but that was a joke. Not with these people. Not with anyone.

Trevor remembered a time when he was a teenager, growing up with his uncle. Man, he missed him. He would have told him to leave, a long time ago. But no, he had to hang around for the money, and the women. It was sweet while it lasted, but now it was time to move on. His uncle would always remind him that nothing was ever permanent. You had to keep moving if you wanted to survive.

He'd gather some of the old woman's supplies to survive in the bush for a while, lay low, until things settled down. Then, after a while, he'd start the old business up again, under a new name. He knew how to do it. A prodigy of his uncle, meant he was an expert at counterfeiting anything.

Trevor grabbed an empty box and started stuffing it with blankets, rubber boots, jackets, and anything he could find to survive the elements in the north. Even though it rained up there, too, it was much harsher. A rain like this could turn to snow, even in the middle of June. He'd seen it happen.

Arnold was working fast, filling boxes with food. Trevor chuckled to himself, just looking at the fool. He actually thinks he's coming along. What a retard. Didn't he know? *I work alone.* Especially laying low. Look at him all sheepish and shaky like a coward. He reminded him of only one other person like that— *The runt!*

Which reminded him. He'd have to do something with the brat, or cut his losses and leave her behind. But he knew what that meant, and as much fun as killing was, he didn't exactly want to kill his investment. The other two were expendable, but not the baby. She was his paycheck for all the runt had put him through.

Across the room, Trevor watched as the woman bounced the kid in the swaddle thing. He supposed she'd need her hands, eventually. Maybe he could tie her feet instead of her hands? He squatted beside the shrieking child, and the woman. "Come on, lady! Shut her up!" He already had a headache from the stupid thing.

"I'm trying!"

"Well, here then." He bent forward. "I'll free your hands—but no funny business." Within seconds, he had the belt unbuckled that held her to the chair.

Then he quickly fastened her legs so she couldn't get away. "There! Now, make the kid shut up!"

Immediately, the woman started patting the baby's back, and the child started cooing. "There. Better?" What was she talking to him for? Didn't she know she'd better close her trap or he'd close it for her? Did she want to make him mad again?

"Could I ask you something?" the women said.

"No!"

But she kept on, and wasn't intimidated by him at all. "If I found a buyer for the baby, would you let me go?"

"Maybe—But I want a hundred grand first."

"Well then, we understand each other quite well. I just happen to have the money in my bank account. Would you prefer a money transfer—*like today?*"

"Lady..." He grinned. "If you can wire me a hundred grand, today, I'll even give you my car to get back to town. On one condition though—and you know what that is."

"I know. I won't say a word about what happened, or about the adoption agency, or how I got the baby. I won't turn you in."

"You do, lady, and I'll hunt you and the kid down, and kill you both with my bare hands." He really hoped she was serious, because it didn't look like knuckle-head in the kitchen was going to come through for him anytime soon.

"I understand. But, I trust you have adoption papers? It has to be...*legal*. You know."

"I know."

He took out the forged adoption papers from his pocket for the lady to see. But she couldn't touch. Not until she wired the money into his account, and he got confirmation of the transaction.

"If you let me use your cell, I can wire the money right now."

Trevor grinned, and gave her his smart phone. "No funny business. Got it?"

"Got it!"

Chapter 28

Pip and Grayson stood at the door of The Luther Home, again. This time they were able to talk to the Asian man quite easily. He seemed very compliant, not like the last time. His broken English told them the owner had taken off to the Standinghorse Indian Reserve in a hurry.

He apparently skipped off without paying the man, and that was obviously annoying the Asian. Grayson could see how upset he was, by how much he talked with his hands. He waved them in the air like a wild man. "Me *no* like boss man. And *no* like Runningman, either!"

Runningman equals Arnold, equals Shania, equals the connection to both their cases. *Bingo!* It was a connection, albeit a pretty weak one. Still, it was something. Grayson just didn't know what. "And you know for sure, that he went out there?"

"Me sure—sure!"

Grayson and Pip, immediately ran back to the car in the rain, so they could head to the reserve.

"I have to call my wife first," Pip told him, shaking his wet black hair as he pulled out his phone. "Great! I need to charge it. Can I use your phone?"

Grayson pulled out his phone as well, and frowned. "Sorry bud, mine's dead too."

"Ugh! Well, let's stop by the apartment, then. I haven't checked in all day. Dinah must be worried sick."

Grayson nodded, and shifted into reverse. He really hoped this wouldn't take long. They didn't have all day. In fact, they probably didn't have much time at all. "Hurry it up then."

Within minutes, they were at the apartment. Grayson did a little speeding to get there, but it was one of the perks of the job. You never get a speeding ticket, *ever!*

"'Went to the hospital for some follow up,'" Pip read the note, puzzled. "'Don't worry. Be back soon?'" Pip scratched his head. "Why didn't she call me first? You think I should worry?"

"No, I'm sure she's fine. And besides, both our phones were dead, remember? Just leave a note and tell her something generic, so she doesn't worry. Like, don't hold supper because you're gonna be working late. Works like a charm."

Pip bit his lip and started writing the note.

Grayson regretted making that wisecrack. Yes, it had worked like a charm, but now, under the circumstances, he felt guilty that he used the generic excuse on his wife in the first place. If he would've respected her feelings more, maybe she wouldn't be missing.

But nope! He wasn't going to let his mind go there right now. He was going to focus on the case, because the case meant getting her back. And getting her back was the objective, not feeling sorry for himself. Surely, this connection would pan out, and they would find his wife and baby unharmed.

Hopefully!

~~~

"Ever wish you lived in a sunny climate?" Grayson asked, grumbling about the rain again.

"Nope!"

"Why not?"

"Born and raised in the bush, my friend." Pip told him. "You don't know what rain is until you've seen it hitting the shores of Reindeer Lake. There's nothing like it. Makes you want to spend your entire life up there."

"You miss it a lot, hey?"

"Every day!"

"Why don't you go back?"

"I've been trying for years. Just aren't any jobs up there," Pip shifted his jaw, hoping the detective didn't notice how the conversation had brought on his melancholy mood. Stormy weather always made him homesick, even without the twenty questions.

They were driving for almost an hour now, feeling mud slip under the tires after turning onto a dirt road. The pelting rain didn't help, as more dark clouds hung in the distance. They would lose light soon, and that made Pip nervous. If his intuition was correct, this guy the Asian was talking about, was him. And the last time he saw him was back home, a long time ago.

It was bittersweet, but Pip didn't want to think about that now. It might not even be him, and all his anxiety would be for nothing. If it was him, he'd deal with it somehow. Somehow!

"Watch it!" he yelled suddenly, as a deer jumped out, causing the vehicle to veer right. "Look at them all." He noted a few dozen animals in the ditch, just hanging around in the rain. "That was close!" But it wasn't the end of it. Pip heard the familiar *thump thump thump* of a flat tire, and moaned. "Oh nooo!"

"Great! We have a flat—and no spare!"

"What? No spare?"

"No spare! I forgot to bring it for a maintenance check last week. Jeepers anyway!"

"Now what?" Pip groaned. They sat on the side of a muddy back-road in the pouring rain. He didn't have a good feeling about this, especially being so close to the reserve.

"Welp…we can sit tight and wait for backup, or, head out on foot."

Pip sighed, and realized what Grayson was gearing up to do. When he reached for the umbrellas, he confirmed it. "Oh no we're not—We're not going out in this."

"Oh yes we are, bush man! Thought you loved this stuff."

"From the inside."

"Well—suck it up!"

Great! Me and my big mouth!

~~~

They were lost, and Sadie knew it. The fool doctor had taken them the wrong way. Not that she'd ever been out to The Standinghorse Indian Reserve before, but she could read, and the map definitely said they were supposed to turn. "It's supposed to be south!" She pointed as they sat on the side of the rural grid in the blinding rain.

"*Wonderful!*" The doctor moaned. "I'd call for directions from here, but there's no cell service, apparently. The man threw his phone down in the empty passenger seat.

Sadie was glad she chose to sit in the back with Dinah. The man was creepy. And now they were lost in a rain storm. Now what?

"Look…" She pointed on the map. "I think if we turn here, we should get back on track."

The doctor looked over his shoulder and grabbed the map from Sadie. "Well, guess we better turn around, then. Sorry gals."

Sadie gave him a smile, and heard Dinah let out a faint gasp. She looked embarrassed, grabbing her chest. It was obviously time to use the breast pump, and they were stuck in the car. Great! The poor girl. Perhaps she could do it in the car, discreetly. It did have battery backup. "Just pump, dear!"

"I can't!"

"Oh—go ahead!" the doctor piped up, eavesdropping. "I'm a doctor, remember? Don't need to be shy around me."

Dinah sheepishly bit her lip, and darted her eyes from the doctor to Sadie, then pulled her state of the art, electronic breast pump out. Women in the old days expressed milk the good old-fashioned way. Nothing wrong with that, but a little more time consuming. Apparently time wasn't an issue now, since the old doc got them lost. He was attempting a U-turn in the middle of the road, ever so slowly.

"There now," the doctor said, "looks like we're headed in the right direction, again. I only hope this won't set off the schedule."

"What schedule?" Sadie asked.

"Oh...um...I mean...I hope they're still there?"

Dinah's eyes grew wide, and the familiar sound of the breast pump went off in a rhythmic pattern. Sadie shifted her jaw. "Didn't you phone them to let them know we're coming?"

The doctor swallowed hard as his face turned red. "Um...well...no. I wanted it to be a complete surprise for everyone."

"And so, nobody knows we're coming? If we break down, or get lost again, nobody will come find us." Sadie spit out, annoyed. "And they could be gone before we even get there."

"I didn't say that, lady. I just meant that they have their own plans, and I only hope that I can catch them before they leave."

There was something the man wasn't telling them, and that made Sadie nervous. Could they really trust him? Maybe this was a mistake? Did he, or didn't he say the baby was out at the reserve? If so, then why would he be worried that they were going to leave?

"I thought you said my husband was out there?" Dinah asked, nervously.

"What? —No!" the doctor told them. "I didn't say anything of the sort."

Sadie's heart sank. This was a mistake. Who was he talking about when he said, "This was their surprise?" Who was the *'their'* he was referring to, if not Pip and the detective?

Dinah wore confusion all over her face, as well. Not only that, but she was starting to cry again. Obviously, she wasn't the only one thinking something was wrong.

What was going on, anyway?

Chapter 29

"There!" the woman glowed. "The money has successfully been transferred to you. Here's the confirmation number."

"Let's see!" Trevor took his cell phone back and slid his finger across the screen, thankful for the archaic WIFI Arnold had in his house. It was the only way to connect. The cell tower coverage was so sparse it made him sick.

"See?" the stupid woman gloated.

"It better be there."

"So—she's mine then?"

"Take the kid and beat it lady, before I change my mind. Here's the paperwork. Remember, you never saw me. This meeting didn't happen. You open your trap, and I'll personally cut your tongue out and gut you like a fish—same with the brat."

"Got it!" she said quickly. "Now, can you kindly untie me and hand over your car keys? You promised me I could have your vehicle."

Trevor growled and unbuckled her ankles, then handed her the car keys. What did he care? It was stolen anyway. He'd like to see her explain that one when she gets back to town. And anyway, he could always take the old Tobaccojuice truck next door, to get up north. Serena's dad wouldn't care one way or the other. He was always drunker than a skunk, anyway.

The woman grabbed the papers and stuffed them into the baby sling, and set off toward the door. Then, suddenly, Arnold stood in her way. "What? You're just gonna let her go?"

"She paid for the kid. That's all I care about, retard."

"*Retard?* What? —I…"

"You heard me." Trevor was becoming very annoyed at Arnold's mouth. What was he thinking? It had nothing to do with him. It wasn't even his business. He didn't have a right to tell him what he can or cannot do, especially now when he failed to find a viable alternative to the mess he and his sister put him in.

"I say we kill them both." Arnold demanded.

"Well, I say no!"

"But she can identify us!" the kid yelled this time, infuriating Trevor to no end. How dare he defy him in front of one of his clients. Totally unprofessional!

"She can identify, *you!* Me—she has an agreement with. Am I right?" He turned to the woman for confirmation. She nodded a quick, *yes.*

"Well—then I'm gonna be the one who turns *you* in!" Arnold swore.

"No you're not!"

"YES I WILL!" he shouted, continuing to block the woman. But Trevor pushed them out of the way, and forced the idiot's squirmy body into a chokehold. The lady darted out the door as fast as she could. Trevor paused to hear her turn the engine over, and roll out of there.

Good! No witnesses.

"Please Trevor!" the kid choked. "*Don't!*"

But Trevor didn't hesitate. He snapped the kid's neck like a twig, and watched his lifeless body drop to the floor in his grandmother's blood.

Ashes to ashes dust to dust!

~~~

Chloe could barely breathe. Her heart was pounding so fast, she thought she would have a heart attack. Rain blurred her vision as the wipers worked overtime. *Drive you fool, drive!* It was unbelievably stupid, but she pulled it off. The baby was hers. All she had to do was get home.

Did she really get away with it?

It was dark and stormy, difficult to drive in, but the weather wasn't exactly first and foremost in her mind. Still, she had to focus, but found herself unable to see much of anything, except the taillights of a parked car. Was that—*Was that a police car?*

Sure enough, as Chloe crept up to it, she recognized the vehicle. It had a flat tire and was covered in mud—*A squad car.* It was only recognizable to someone who knew them like the back of her hand. She'd memorized the look of it over the years. Grayson practically lived in his. *Grayson.* Why did she have to think of him now? Was he looking for her? What would he say about this?

She shook her head. Why was she thinking about him now? She had to stop it. There was no time for a conscience, only time for action. What was she supposed to do? She had to do this! She had to! *There was no other choice.*

As Chloe idled beside the cruiser, she tried to see if there was anyone in it. Her heart pounded as she checked it out. The messy, mud speckled windows, made it impossible. She was wet, she was scared, and shaking profusely, but the baby was tucked warmly into her sling.

There was no other choice. She had to get out of the vehicle. Chloe opened the driver's door and stepped out into the dark night. The rain pelted her head as she shielded the child, but not well enough. Once again, the baby started crying. "Now now, Lily. Mama's here!"

Ping ping ping, went the seat belt alarm, as she looked inside the vehicle. It had been abandoned.

Why? Chloe couldn't see anything that identified the squad car, and she didn't want to stand in the rain any longer. The baby would not settle down. She didn't have time for this anyway. What if they changed their minds and came after her and the baby? No, she had to get going.

If someone else came along and found her with the child, what would she say? How could she explain her whereabouts? How could she explain Lily? At least at home, she could clean up, buy some baby stuff, and present the child as her own. Even to Grayson, she could say she'd been out of province to adopt the child. Would that work?

Oh, everything made her nervous. Even the pelting rain on the hood of the vehicles made her jump. She had to get out of there—*think!* As Chloe turned back to her car, she suddenly felt a bout of nausea. It was too much. This was all way too much. Her head spun as she lost her balance and puked beside the wet muddy tire. *Ohhh!*

Chloe was sick with worry, with shock, and wondered how she was going to get out of this mess. She slid back into the driver's seat and wiped her sleeve across her mouth to clean up. Instinctively, she looked in the rear-view mirror, and caught a glimpse of herself. Who was that savage women?

Certainly not her!

~~~~

Grayson could hear a vehicle speed away as they snuck up to the back of the house. He and Pip ditched the umbrellas, and peered into the side window, just in time to see the murder. He hoped the kid wouldn't freak out, because he knew the protocol—Draw your weapon and wait for backup. But, there was no way to call for backup. Yes, he should have called from the squad car before he left. That was his first mistake. The second, was letting Pip come along. He wasn't ready for this.

There was a murderer in there, and he just broke someone's neck. Grayson kept checking on the kid, and so far, no panic attack. He looked fine—too fine. "Are you okay?" Grayson whispered. Pip nodded, but didn't say anything. He just went back to the window. He seemed fine. In fact, the only emotion that Grayson could see was anger. He figured anger was better than panic.

"Get down! We can't go in without backup!"

"*I'm going in!*"

"Oh no you're not! You don't have a weapon, I do!"

"I don't need a weapon. I just need my bare hands!"

"*Oh—ho!* Right!" Grayson gasped. "What's gotten into you? One minute you're panicking, and the next minute you want to be a hero!"

"*Well*—I'm not gonna just sit here!"

Grayson looked into the kid's eyes and saw frustration. He didn't understand why, but he knew how it could affect a person. Seeing someone murdered in cold blood wasn't exactly the kind of thing you could dismiss easily, leave alone keep your cool about. He had to make a move, either that, or watch the kid botch it up and endanger them both.

"Okay—we're going in. But I take the lead. You follow me, do what I say, and maybe you won't die today."

"I just want him *dead!*"

Brutal! The kid was full of rage for some reason. Grayson furrowed his brow and didn't respond. He put his index finger to his lips to shush the inexperience kid, and readied himself to knock down the door on three. *One, two, three...*

Chapter 30

Pip's pulse was racing, and he was so light headed, he literally felt like he was floating. He wasn't panicking, but maybe he should be. This new-found courage, if that's what you call it, was dangerous. It was something he hadn't experienced before. He knew it wasn't right, but he couldn't stop his mind from reeling.

God help me!

He couldn't think straight; He couldn't calm down. He was so full of rage it drove him to think unspeakable things. And it was that, that made him charge past Grayson, ignoring the detective's warning to stay behind him.

After all, it was *his* fight!

~~~

Pip deliberately charged past the detective like an elephant. Was he insane? What was the matter with the him? The weapon flipped out of Grayson's hand, and dropped to the floor a few feet away, because of it. "Hold it right there!" Grayson shouted anyway, even without the gun.

The kid was out of control, and there was nothing he could do to stop him now. He was punching the side of the guy's head, repeatedly. *Ridiculous!* He screwed everything up.

"*Get off!*" the man shouted, twisting and turning while Pip clung to his back.

"NO!"

"*Then I'll cut you, runt!*" The man whipped out a knife.

That was not good. The situation was completely out of control, and all Grayson could do was stay out of the way. He had to find the gun, fast. Where did it go?

Pip kept punching the man in his temple until finally, the man overpowered the kid. He held him by knifepoint, using the blade as a means to keep him in a chokehold. "Forget about the gun, cop, or, I'll slice his neck wide open!"

Grayson froze immediately, and rose from the floor. He didn't find the gun in time, nor did he have any power over this botched situation. He was furious, and glared at Pip to make him aware of that.

"Our boy screwed up, didn't he?" The man grinned, forcing the knife harder. "Yeah, I can see that. He's normally a screw up, aren't you runt? Tell him, tell him what kind of a screw up you are!"

Pip's face burned red, and tears began to leak.

"Yup—Nothing but a cry baby!" The man laughed. "You never change, Pipata."

And then Grayson's eyes grew wide. *He knows him!*

"Oh—what? You didn't know?" The man sneered at Grayson. "Yes, we're brothers. Aren't we little bro?" The aboriginal cocked his head sideways, as he continued to hold Pip at knifepoint.

Grayson went over the details in his mind. Why didn't he help Pip when he attacked his brother in the first place? How stupid! He could have avoided this situation. Anyone else would have went to Pip's aid immediately. But then, he wasn't anyone else. He was a trained professional, who knew better than to get himself caught up in a dog fight. He was taught to assume the perp had a weapon in every circumstance. *And he did!* Still, the guilt consumed him.

Seeing Pip's wild rage, made him realize just how much trouble the two of them were in. If this was, in fact, his brother, then there was a deep-rooted anger here, and a personal vendetta neither one of them were not going to escape very easily.

"So, what do you want, buddy?" Grayson asked, with his hands raised.

"I want my brother to *pay!*"

That wasn't the answer Grayson had hoped for, apparently Pip either, judging by the dirty look on his face. "Pay for *what?*"

The kid moaned as the knife dug deeper.

"For destroying my family!"

"I didn't...*destroy*...anything! *You did!*"

The brother's face became red with anger, and he lowered the knife to adjust his hold. Grayson knew that was his opportunity, so he bolted toward the two of them. He went for the back of the guys knees making him lose his balance. The knife dropped to the floor, and the tackle began.

Pip punched his brother in the head. Grayson yanked the guys arms behind his back and forced the brute to the ground. "You're under arrest, pal!" He slapped the cuffs on, glad he brought them with him. "You have the right to remain silent. Anything you say or do can be used against you in a court of law."

"I'm gonna kill you, *runt!*" The man spit.

"Sit down and shut up!" Grayson ordered the prisoner. He sat him down on a chair and found something to tie him in. "Now, you're not going anywhere!"

Pip paced the floor in front of them, going back and forth nervously, raking his fingers through his hair. "Tell me where she is, *Trevor!*"

Suddenly, Pip's brother threw his head back, and roared. "*Ha ha ha!* I still have the upper hand, even handcuffed. No matter what you do Pipata, you'll always be the lowest man on the totem pole."

"TELL ME WHERE SHE IS!!!"

Grayson decided to stay out of it. Obviously, this was between Pip and his brother, and it didn't take a brain surgeon to figure out the rest.

"You'll never find her."

"*Trevor, please! She's—she's my little girl!*"

"Not anymore!"

Pip punched his brother in the chair repeatedly, and Grayson didn't stop him. This was his fight, and he respected the kid enough to let him have it. Instead, Grayson just sat there and watched the assault. Sometimes these things were necessary.

"DID YOU KILL HER?"

"No." The guy spit blood. "That would be too easy."

"THEN WHERE IS SHE?"

"You'll never find her. I sold her for a hundred grand, and she's long gone!"

Pip screamed, "NOOOOO!" Then lit into him again, punch after punch.

Grayson knew it was time to step in now, or the kid would kill the only one connecting him to his wife. Sure, he deserved everything he was getting, but he needed some answers as well. "*Pip!*" Grayson stopped him mid-swing. "*That's enough!* I need to question him."

Pip stopped, reluctantly, and stormed to the couch to decompress. He buried his head in his hands and moaned. Grayson kept an eye on him, just in case. He didn't need any panic attacks.

"Know anything about this woman?" Grayson showed him a picture of his wife. "We have an amber alert out on her." He thought he'd explain it that way, since alerting the perp to the fact that she was his wife, probably wouldn't go over very well.

The man's eyes went wide, and then he shook his head. "Ha ha ha! You guys are pathetic! I ain't telling you, squat!" He grinned sideways through his bloody teeth, laughing as he spit a gob of red. He knew her all right—he was just playing with him. Not good! *You won't be laughing when I get through with you buddy.*

Feeling his neck burn, Grayson fought off the urge to punch the guy out. And the Indian cleverly eyed him, waiting for him to break. But he didn't. He'd been trained to deal with jerks like him. Instead, Grayson roughly frisked the man, feeling around for a cell phone. He patted his back pocket. There it is! *Sucker!* But it only had one bar of battery life left in it. *Great!* He'd need to call for backup right away, and with any luck, they'd have his ugly mug in jail before midnight.

Grayson went into the bathroom, and closed the door to make the call in private. It went straight to voicemail, so he left a message for his boss. *Man, he hoped he checked it regularly.* It wasn't exactly something that could wait.

As he used the bathroom facilities and flushed the toilet, he realized he'd better call 911 just in case. But while he punched in the number, the phone suddenly died. *Great!* Maybe the guy had a charger?

"Hey, ugly face!" He called from the bathroom. "Got a charger for your phone?"

"*Ha ha ha!*" the jerk roared. "You guys are giving me a good laugh today. Why would I give you a charger to call for backup? You think I'm an idiot or somethin'?"

"Um—yeah! Actually, I do!" Grayson chuckled, raking a kitchen chair over. He took a seat backwards in front of the Indian. "You see, you and me are gonna get something straight. First, you're gonna tell me who you sold the kid to, and secondly, you're gonna tell me where the woman in the photo is. *Got it?*"

"Oh—Man, this is hilarious!" The guy roared with laughter again. Grayson didn't know what he thought was so funny. It wasn't a joke. If he didn't watch it, his mouth was going to meet his boot.

"You'd better wipe that grin off your face, buddy," Grayson went on.

"Or what?"

But before he could answer, Grayson turned his head to a flicker of light outside. It wasn't lightning. It looked like headlights coming into the yard, and it was too soon for backup. "Expecting someone?"

"Yeah, backup for *me?*"

Not likely, but Grayson decided to search for the gun just in case.

Chapter 31

It was his wife!

Pip couldn't believe that both she and Sadie came all this way for nothing. And the stupid doctor who lectured him, had driven them out there. Why? It didn't make sense. "I don't understand. Tell me again why you're here?"

"The doctor said our baby was here," Dinah sobbed.

Pip gave the doctor an evil eye and then looked at Grayson for assurance. Surely this was a mistake. He couldn't have taken them all the way out there on a rumor.

Grayson confronted the doctor immediately. "Who told you the baby was out here?"

"I—um—Oh dear." The doctor frowned. "Perhaps I was wrong. I thought I was helping."

"*Well, you're not!*" Grayson blurted out.

Bringing the girls into this mess was the last thing they needed, Pip thought to himself. And in front of his deadbeat brother of all things. Not only was this dangerous, but totally off the wall. Usually doctors don't get so involved with their patients. Something else was going on. "Take them home!"

"But...I want to stay with you," Dinah said.

"NO!" Pip eyeballed Trevor, as he sat in the chair where they put him. "It's not safe. We have...*police business* to take care of."

"Pfft, you're a total joke, runt?" Trevor laughed again. "And this is getting funnier by the minute."

Then Dinah spun immediately. "*I know you!*"

"Hello chubby cheeks," Trevor grinned. "Come give your brother-in-law a kiss."

Dinah's mouth hung open, as she put the pieces together. Her face turned red and Pip knew she was seething. He tried to stop her from charging past him, but he couldn't hold her back.

"*You creep!*" She slapped Trevor's face. "WHERE IS MY BABY?!"

"Ha ha ha!" Trevor laughed. "You think I'd tell you?"

Then Dinah slapped him over and over, screaming. She crumpled, as Pip caught her fall.

"So this is what's going on!" Sadie fumed, looking at the doctor. "I thought you said..."

"I said a lot of things, lady," the doctor smirked, drawing his weapon. "Now, all of you—*move over there!* He pointed with the gun. "Except for you, cop. You can untie my business partner here, and when you're finished, you can tie up your friends."

~~~~

Dr. Uric. Now it was all coming together. His name was on their blacklist, and the leading physician questioned in the Eaglefeather abduction, not to mention his name was on the Runningman baby's death certificate. And now this. What a coincidence. Now all he had to do was find the connection to his wife. *And then he'd find her!*

As Grayson's mind raced, he followed instructions exactly. He tried to hurry, so the doctor didn't kick him again. He untied Trevor, and grabbed the duct-tape they handed him. Reluctantly, he went about taping up his friends. He hurried with shaky hands, trying not to be intimidated by the gun.

"Now it's your turn, cop," the doctor told Grayson. Trevor tore the duct-tape with his teeth and pushed him down in another chair, wrapping his ankles, wrists, and mouth. He couldn't move, or barely breathe, because the tape was so tight.

"Now hand me the gun, Uric," Trevor reached out his hand to the doctor.

"No, it's mine!"

This was interesting. Grayson listened intently.

"I did all the dirty work, you scum bag!" the doctor went on, narrowing his aim at Trevor. "After all those babies I got for you, this is how you treat me? You still haven't paid me my full share yet, *and you promised!*

"So! I told you I'd wire it tomorrow."

"It's always tomorrow with you," Dr. Uric's voice shook. "*I need it now!*"

"Well, you don't get it now!" Trevor inched forward, causing the doctor to back-step.

"But I tied up the loose ends for you, just like you said."

"I didn't tell you to bring them *here,* you idiot!" Trevor continued to inch forward.

"I'm not an idiot!" Dr. Uric growled. "I'm the one with the PHD, remember? Without me, you wouldn't have this so-called business."

Trevor crossed his arms and smiled, letting the doctor finish.

"I let you take the upper hand too long. Well not anymore. If you're pulling out, then give me my share! NOW!"

Trevor shook his head.

"What's does that mean?" the doctor fumed, waving the gun. "No? Don't tell me you don't have it. And don't tell me, tomorrow, cause tomorrow you'll be gone. Give me my share, now! I know you have it, you obviously just sold the girl."

"Yes! I did. And you're not getting any part of it."

"Why you—"

Then Trevor charged Dr. Uric, and the gun went off into the ceiling. The two of them struggled for the weapon, until the stronger and much younger one, overpowered the weaker. It was obvious who that was.

"Now get your hands where I can see them," Trevor said, out of breath.

Dr. Uric immediately raised his hands in the air, and pleaded his case. "Please! Trevor! You can't do this! *I beg you!*"

But there was no mercy where Trevor was concerned. He pulled the trigger without batting an eye. The body crumpled to the ground in a heap, and Grayson turned his head away. So did everyone else.

All he could hear were whimpers from the two women. "When I get back—you're next!" the man said to the group, as he bolted from the room.

Good! That would give Grayson more time to escape. The metal edge of the chair would make a good knife to cut through the duct-tape. If he hurried, he'd be free before the scum bag returned.

~~~

Sadie continued to pray.

She'd done nothing but pray for the last hour, but still couldn't break herself free, even though Grayson seemed to be making progress. How could this happen? *God! Please help us!*

The two young people looked completely defeated. They both hung their heads and hadn't moved in over a half hour. If she could only talk to them, she'd be able to comfort them somewhat. But no, their mouths were duct-taped, same as hers.

Dinah had such red, tear filled eyes, she could barely keep them open. Her front was wet with engorged milk as well. *Poor thing!* When will this end? What could possibly come of this grim situation?

Sadie felt her own heart pounding. How could she be such a fool and fall for the doctor's deception? What if he had taken them somewhere and killed them, and dumped their bodies on the side of the road? No one would ever know. Thankfully, God was taking care of them. *He always did!*

It was dark outside now, with occasional flashes of lightening in the sky. The stormy summer night was a fitting reflection of their own experience - *Dismal.* The continual moisture had practically ruined the roads leading in and out of the reserve.

If they ever manage to get free, she hoped they could drive the doctor's car out of there. That is, if they could get through the muddy roads. What they really needed, was to call the police. Sadie didn't know if that had been done yet, or not. It seemed Pip's brother had taken all the phones. He went around collecting them when they first got tied up.

Sadie glanced over at Grayson and it looked like he had finally freed his hands. He nodded his head at her and wringed his wrists in front of him. The duct-tape was shredded and his hands were now free to remove the binding on his mouth.

Within minutes, the detective had freed himself, and immediately crouched behind the sofa, looking for something. *What was he doing?* Then, surprising her, Grayson popped his head up with a revolver in his hand.

"*Mmm, mmm!*" Dinah tried to speak, eyes wide with horror. Turn around!

Suddenly, Trevor jumped from behind him like a crazy person, and tackled Grayson to the ground. They rolled on the floor in front of them—in the blood and all.

"Get—off—me!" Grayson fought.

The two of them struggled for the gun which Grayson held firmly, trying to keep it from the big man. Then they rolled back and forth, back and forth.

God help us!

Sadie's heart pounded in her chest. *Come on detective, get up!*

But it was too late. The Indian had won. "Get up pig!" he shouted, out of breath.

"*Please!* Just walk away!"

"I don't want to walk away! I want to see my brother's friends squirm and beg like my family did before they died. *Right, Pip?*"

Grayson stood there with arms raised to the ceiling, sporting a bloody nose and contusions on his face. He was completely out of breath and Sadie knew that was the end. There was no way they were getting out of this one.

"Sit down cop!"

"*Trevor!* Just walk away! There's no need to hurt anyone!"

"*I said shut up!*"

"You don't want to do this!"

"Oh—yes I do!"

Then, suddenly, a shot rang out, piercing the detective in the leg. He crumpled to the ground and moaned. Then another one, hitting him in the arm. And then as he aimed again, Pip moaned loudly with wild eyes. "Mmm! Mmm!"

Trevor turned to his brother and said, "What? You think you can stop me? I don't think so. I want you to see him squirm. And when I'm finished with him, I'll move onto the women, and you're not gonna like that. Last thing you'll see is your wife pleading for her life, just like—"

Trevor stopped short. He took a deep breath, and looked as if he was wiping away tears. This was her shot! Sadie suddenly started moaning, "Mmm! Mmm!" Motioning the man to come remove the duct-tape from her mouth.

He turned his head, annoyed, but came over to her anyway. "WHAT?"

"Mmm! Mmm!"

"Fine! I'll let you have your last words." Within seconds, the duct-tape was removed from Sadie's mouth, and it stung.

"Don't do it!" she blurted out.

"You can't stop me, lady!"

"*Please!* Listen to me for a minute! You don't have to do this! There is another way!"

Trevor stood there smugly and eyeballed the woman, laughing under his breath. "Yeah? And what's this *other way?* Hmm?"

"God!"

"Ha ha ha! You're a nut, lady!"

"Well, then I'm a nut! But I'm not going to meet my maker without at least offering you an alternative to this awful mess you created."

Trevor stood with his arms crossed, and rolled his eyes.

"God can forgive you for all of this! Nobody has to die. You can walk away from this a free man."

"How's that?"

"By repenting!"

Trevor roared with laughter this time.

"It's not funny," she went on. "All you have to do, is be sorry for the pain you caused. Ask God to take it away. I bet it feels terrible."

"You don't know, *squat!*"

"I know enough to know that it aches every day. *Doesn't it?* When you hurt the ones you love, you pay for it forever. It's something that sticks with you no matter where you go, and what you do. I know that you'll never be free unless you ask God to take the pain away. You might be able to run now, but you'll never escape the legacy of what you've done here. *Not without God, that is!*"

"Shut up, lady! SHUT UP!"

Now he was mad. Sadie said too much, but she didn't care. She was sick of a lifetime of heartache, simply because people didn't have the common sense to nurture and love their families. Must this kind of legacy continue? So many people had been hurt over the years, because of what happened in Deep Bay, and the lives that were lost there.

When would it stop? When would people realize that they could truly be free from the sins of their fathers, by reaching out to the father who created them? Her heart was sick, but she could see it went in one ear and out the other. Did she really think she could change him?

Trevor paced the floor in front of her, and she realized she had one last chance to see if she could stop him from making the biggest mistake of his life. "Untie me, son!" She smiled softly, catching his wild eyes.

He stopped in place and cocked his head, squinting at her as if to say something. Then, a long pause as he narrowed his aim—and shot her point blank.

"*Mmmmm!*" the muffled voices cried.

Life was fading, quickly. Wickedness devoured the last bit of hope Sadie had, until there was nothing left at all. *Nothing!*

Chapter 32

Pip was livid!

How could his own flesh and blood do something so heinous? Every muscle in Pip's body ached at the sight in front of him. Blood was everywhere, and all he could do was sit and do nothing to help his friends.

"She's next, wimp!" Trevor grinned, aiming the gun at his wife.

Everything seemed to move in slow motion. Was this even real? Would he shoot the only person in this world that mattered to him? Of course he would. He was Trevor. The guy who called him names and made fun of him his entire life.

"Mmmmm! Pip tried to speak, begging with his eyes. If he would only give him a voice, he'd surely be able to stop him. "Mmmmm!" He tried again.

"Oh, what? Little baby boy can't speak?"

"Mmmmm!"

"Well, I guess I can take the tape off your mouth. I'd like to hear you scream when I mess with your woman, and then put a bullet in her head."

Pip's eyes grew wide. There was no way he was touching his wife, not in a million years. How was he going to save her? He looked to Grayson, who had now passed out on the floor. Sadie was motionless too. What was he going to do? *God?*

The man was a maniac, and he was embarrassed to be related to such a monster. He could see Dinah was visibly distraught, with tears streaming down and makeup running black rivers down her face. Oh how his heart ached for everything she'd been through. And now this.

Trevor reached in and pulled the grey duct-tape from Pip's mouth. It burned his skin from the ripping, and made him move his jaw back and forth. At least he was able to say something now, not that it would do any good. "Trevor—Whatever I did, I'm sorry! But please—don't hurt my wife!"

"Ha! I can't believe it. Even after all of this, you still play the innocent little mouse. I can't believe it!" Trevor fumed, barking off a string of swear words at him.

"WHAT DID I DO?!"

"It's what you didn't do, brother. You should have stopped them from killing Uncle Leon. He was my best friend. He was the only one that cared about me. It wasn't his fault he got tangled into that crap at Deep Bay. He was an innocent bystander."

"He wasn't an innocent bystander! He made my life a living hell. He made Dinah's life a living hell. Do you even know what he did to her?"

"Mmmmm! Dinah cried behind the duct-tape, and nodded her head.

"Shut up, witch!" Trevor turned to her for a moment. "I know what she did, Pipata. I know what kind of a person she is. I know that she's just a whore!"

"SHE IS NOT! She's my wife—*my family!* You're my family!"

"Family? Ha! What does that even mean? We're supposed to be brothers, yet you never came to visit me in jail, not even once. You preach to me about family? You don't care about me, like Uncle Leon did. He taught me lots of stuff. If he were here right now, he'd put a bullet in your head instead of giving you a chance to talk."

"Trevor—he's not who you thought he was. He's a murderer!"

"SOOO! At least he had balls, unlike you!"

Pip hung his head. It was hopeless. He was not going to change his brother's mind. He was brain washed, and there was no changing that, but he'd die before he ever let him touch his wife. But how could he stop him?

"Trevor, I know you think Uncle Leon was the best, but I know differently. I know for a fact that he was the one that killed mom and dad."

"WHAT? No, he wasn't. Where did you get that from, you liar?" Trevor lowered the gun for a moment and stepped back, going over the new information. He shook his head and pursed his lips. "Prove it!"

"I can't prove it! You just have to trust me."

"Trust you? Ha! Not on your life. Not on your wife's life either," he shouted, aiming the gun at Dinah again. "How bout this? Since she's *family* and all, I won't mess around with her. That's all the mercy you're gonna get. I'll just put her out of her misery and shoot her right now!"

"*NO! Please! Trevor! I beg you! Don't!* Do you really want to live with this for the rest of your life? Do you really want this to be your legacy?"

"*Oh bah!* Do you know how ridiculous you sound right now? *Legacy?* As if I care about that. Where'd you get that word from anyway, the *BIBLE?*"

"No, but what you do will follow you. Your sins will follow you wherever you go. You can run, you can hide, but you can't escape your past unless you—"

"Unless I what? Repent? You sound like the old lady."

"Yeah, something like that." Pip mumbled, realizing he was at the end of his rope. There was nothing more he could say, nothing more he could do to prevent him from what he was obviously going to do. But there was one more thing he could try.

"Trevor, I'm sorry." He sniffled. "I'm sorry I haven't been a good brother. I'm sorry I got Uncle Leon killed. I'm sorry our family couldn't love each other like we should have. We were all screwed up. I should've been there for you."

"Yeah, you should have!"

"So, can I ask you one last favor? Shoot me, instead of her. *Please!*"

"Mmmm!" Dinah moaned loudly through the duct-tape, shaking her head violently.

"Well, by the looks of it, your wife doesn't agree with that. *So*—no can do. *Sorry!* Gotta keep the little wife happy. After all, a happy wife means a happy life. No, you can live Pipata. You can live with all the pain, like me!" Trevor cocked the trigger and aimed at Dinah. "And besides, I like to see you squirm."

"Trevor NOOOO!"

But it was too late. Pip heard the gun go off.

~~~~

The SWAT team charged in with semi-automatic weapons, just as the lifeless body keeled over. The officers sported riot gear, looking like a scene fresh out of a movie. They cautiously inched forward. "You alright?" One of them asked.

"Mmmm!" was the only answer.

As the SWAT members checked the bodies on the floor, it was evident they were professionals. They went about their business with skill and precision. "We got some live ones over here!" another said, calling for emergency Medi-Vac.

With the front door wide open, it was clear that a SWAT helicopter had landed. The beaming light from the huge machine was as bright as the sun.

Everything seemed to be running in slow motion when Dinah realized they were trying to help her. They ripped off the duct-tape from her mouth, cut off the rest of it, and then lifted her body to the sofa, examining her. *But she wasn't hurt, was she?* They shot Trevor just in time, hadn't they?

As the STARS Air Ambulance set down beside the other chopper, dispatching the EMS, the place sounded noisy with the swooshing of blades as they powered down. The medical staff rallied around, as they rolled a gurney in beside her.

Dinah wasn't exactly sure what was happening now. It was confusing with all the people examining the bodies. She recognized the defibrillator, as the EMT held out the paddles and counted, "One...two...three...Clear!"

But who was that for?

"Sinus rhythm?"

"No!"

"Do it again!"

Who were they working on? She couldn't see past the guy standing in front of her, or was he hovering over her. It didn't make sense. What was going on?

"One...two...three...Clear!"

But something was wrong, she could feel it. The EMS were shouting orders. Who were they working on? Was it her husband? The detective? Sadie? It wasn't clear, but Dinah didn't need clarity to understand the situation. She only needed her ears.

"Try it again!" came the final call.

Then another charge from the defibrillator.

"Anything?"

"*No!* We're losing her!"

Chapter 33

Chloe purchased all the necessary baby things at a twenty-four-hour Wal-Mart, after she cleaned up and traded vehicles at her house. She arrived back home again by early morning. As she walked in the door, her land line suddenly jumped to life. "Hello?"

It was the hospital, and they were calling for her. Her face went red as she set the baby carrier down on the kitchen floor, shaking for what she knew was coming next.

"I'm afraid it's your husband, he's been shot."

Without even listening to the rest, the phone slipped from her grasp and hit the floor. Her hands began to tremble, uncontrollably. *Stop it Chloe! Get it together!* It was her worst fear coming true; something a cop's wife dreaded the most. *The phone call.* For as much as she prepared herself for this moment, it hit her like a brick.

What was she going to do now?

Chloe took in a deep breath and looked at the sleeping infant slouched in her car seat. Would Grayson never be able to experience fatherhood? Would he never get to touch his new daughter's soft skin, or know what it feels like to feed her or change her? Why was this happening now when they were so close to being parents? But wait? She didn't know if he was alive or dead.

Chloe regained composure and picked up the phone again. She redialed the number to the hospital, and listened for the ring. Her heart pounded as she waited on the line. "Yes, I'd like to know the status of a patient."

"Just one moment, please."

And then she was put on hold while she listened to the droning music. What was she going to do if

Grayson was conscious? Would she bring him the baby and make up a story of where she had been? She hadn't thought that far ahead.

Panicking, Chloe hung up the phone immediately. This was all spinning out of control. If her husband was alive, that was the main priority. She could go to the hospital without the baby, just to see him. It wouldn't be that bad to wait until he got home to share the news of the adoption. But who would look after the baby? She scratched that idea immediately. Oh, what was she going to do?

Then the phone rang again, jolting her attention. Could it be the hospital again? But she wasn't ready for this. She wasn't ready to hear what they were about to tell her, or to face telling people about the baby. The phone continued to ring. *Answer it stupid!*

To avoid waking Lily, she realized there was only one option. "Hello?"

"Chloe?"

"Grayson!" It was her husband. He was alive. They would be a family, and get to enjoy their new little girl after all. He would be so pleased!

"After the nurse told me she called you at home, I couldn't believe it. I had to call for myself. Is it really you?"

"Of course it's me, sweetheart."

"Where've you been? We put out an amber alert on you and everything. We've been looking everywhere for you. What happened?"

Chloe didn't want to lie, but she had no choice. She wasn't ready to tell him about the baby yet. She needed to think about it some more, get her story straight, so he didn't doubt it. No, she'd have to leave out the important parts, for now. "I drove to the States, honey. I have a surprise for you."

"What do you mean, you drove to the States?"

212

Then, there was a long pause. Chloe didn't know what else to say, and she could hear the shock in her husband's tone. She needed to establish that she'd been out of the country, so the adoption would seem legit. It was legit. She paid for her fair and square, but her husband didn't have to know that part of it. "Like I said, I have a surprise for you."

"Honey—are you okay? You sound strange. I better send a squad car."

"No! I'm fine. I'm just tired." Chloe could hear her husband sighing, knowing full well he was worried. But he didn't have anything to worry about. He was going to be a daddy for the first time.

"Okay, well, I just wanted to let you know I'm okay. I just got a little banged up. The hospital automatically calls next of kin, but I'm fine. *Really!* And I'm glad you are too, honey. Just stay where you are, and I'll send a squad car to come get you."

"*NO!*"

"I'm not taking no, for an answer. He'll be there in about fifteen minutes." And then Grayson hung up. *Great!* Now what was she going to do? She had no choice but to bring the baby along, and try to explain as best as she could. *This was going to be interesting!*

~~~

Pip paced the floor in Grayson's hospital room.

Dinah was in surgery, and so was Sadie. At least Grayson was in good spirits. Apparently, his wife's disappearance had nothing to do with his daughter's kidnapping after all, because Grayson found his wife at home. Now he was happy, and teasing everyone while he lay there bandaged in his hospital bed. He'd gotten off easy. No surgery required.

But Dinah was lucky to be alive. When the SWAT team first arrived, they hadn't noticed Trevor's bullet had pierced her side. She'd lost a lot of blood because of it. And now they had to open her up again. But at least she wasn't as bad as Sadie. *She was in a coma.*

"Stop it Grayson!" Pip barked at the annoying detective. "You're not funny!" He was laughing and throwing paper spit balls at Pip, and generally driving him crazy. He realized it was mostly the pain medications they had him on, that were causing his foolish behavior. But still, if he didn't quit it, he was going to pace someplace else.

"I'm just trying to lighten the mood, kid. She'll be alright."

"How do you know that?"

"Because I know it! Now come sit down, and we'll play another round of twenty-one."

The card game was getting old, and Pip needed some fresh air anyway. If he didn't get out of there he was going to go nuts. His palms were sweaty and his hands wouldn't stop shaking. Surely he wasn't having another panic attack.

"Play solitaire or something, until your wife gets here. I'm done. I'll be back in about an hour. I need a breather!" Pip hoped he wouldn't take offense. It wasn't like he was abandoning Grayson completely—just for an hour. It would give him some time to collect himself, and get rid of the anxiety he was feeling. After all, he was absolutely not having another panic attack. Not now!

"Suit yourself." The detective giggled weirdly, throwing another spit ball.

Oh brother! Get me out of here!

~~~~

Chloe was led to Grayson's hospital room by a police officer. She wished he hadn't insisted on carrying the car seat for her, but at least Lily was sleeping now. She had given her a bottle on the way over.

"I'll take care of her for a few minutes, Chloe," the officer told her. "It'll give you and the old man some time alone."

Sure, he was willing to help, but could she trust him? "I—I guess." Chloe knew him for a few years now. He was harmless. And after all, she couldn't exactly spring the baby on her husband right away. She needed to do it gradually, and forewarn him first. Hopefully, he would be okay with the whole adoption thing. *Hopefully!*

"I'll stay in the waiting area, while you go tell Grayson the good news."

Chloe gulped hard and smiled. "Don't let her out of your sight!"

"I won't! Now go!"

Grayson was sleeping when she entered the shaded room. The blinds were closed, but she still saw all the bandages. Emotion erupted in her throat as she let out a sob and held his hand in hers. "Oh— I didn't mean to wake you."

"Mmmm—" Grayson moaned, fluttering his eyelids. "I fell asleep. They gave me a lot of good drugs." He grimaced against the pain, as he pulled himself up.

"It looks bad!"

"Nah! It's mostly bandages and pain. I don't know why they're making me stay. I can still get around and stuff."

"Yah—looks like it."

Grayson grinned, and gave her a hug and a kiss. "I was so worried, honey. I didn't know where you were. I thought you were with Rozelyn, and you were—"

"*Shhhh!*" Chloe cut him off. She knew what he was going to say, and she didn't want to go there. She had to focus on the baby. It was now or never. "Gray? I have a surprise."

"Yeah, and what exactly is this surprise?"

"Well, you know how we had that fight about adopting kids? Well, I found an adoption agency in..." She paused, not thinking it out clearly. Where should she say the adoption took place? It had to be somewhere that sounded credible, and close enough that he would believe it. "...Minneapolis. That's where I drove to. I was mad, and I just kept driving. I found this adoption agency online, and so I set up an appointment."

Grayson narrowed his eyes. "*In Minneapolis?*"

"Yes—*in Minneapolis!*" Chloe coughed. "Anyway, I set up an appointment, and I adopted a baby."

"YOU WHAT?!"

Just then, a screaming baby was brought into the room. The police officer Chloe entrusted Lily to, was holding the flailing child awkwardly in his arms. "I think she pooped!"

Chloe's face burned red, as she flew off the bed toward the child. "*Give her to me!*"

"I'm sorry, but she's leaking all over me!"

The least he could do was be discrete about it. And what a way to introduce a daughter to her father. She had to bite her tongue just to avoid swearing at the man. She had envisioned introducing her to Grayson in a much more pleasant way than that. *But it was done.* "Grayson, meet your daughter. Her name is Lily."

Grayson swallowed hard and didn't say anything at all. Did he hate her? Was he mad that she hadn't consulted him? "Well—say something!"

"*Honey*—*! What have you done?*"

"I didn't do *anything!* I adopted our child."

Grayson just dropped his head and shook it. His cheeks grew three shades of red, and he looked as if he was about to puke. She tried to hand him Lily, but he wouldn't take her. He kept shaking his head, and raking his hands through his hair.

"How much did you pay?"

"What? I told you I adopted him—*legally!*"

But he knew. She could see it in his eyes. She was not fooling him one bit. He'd always had the knack of seeing right through her. Maybe it was the cop in him, maybe it was because he was the witty one in the marriage, and she was not? She couldn't even tell a joke properly.

"Right—*In Minneapolis.*"

"*Right.*" But he gave her a look that made her feel as though the end of the world had come, and then the tears began to fall. Within seconds, a group gathered around her, as she tightly clung to the infant. A young native man stood beside her with tears in his eyes, as he observed the baby's features.

"She looks like me." He beamed.

"No she doesn't!" Chloe said defensively, turning her body against the crowd. She had a right to protect her own child. They were not going to take her away. *Never!*

"Chloe honey," her husband said. "Give this man the baby. She's his."

"No! She's not!" But two more police officers stood beside her. And the police officer that came with her, was standing there as well. *Traitor!* She felt as if she couldn't breathe, couldn't think. Why did they want to take her child away?

Grayson stood up, wincing against the pain. "Honey, let me hold her."

"No! *You hate her!* You never wanted children! *Admit it!*"

"That's not true."

"*Yes it is!* You wouldn't even let me adopt! *I hate you!* You don't know what it's like to be barren! None ·of you do!" And now she sounded like a crazy woman. They were all looking at her with wide eyes. Well, to heck with them! They were not going to take Lily. She was *hers!*

"Chloe, I just want to see her." Grayson inched forward.

Maybe he had a change of heart? Maybe? "If I do, then will you promise you'll let me keep her?"

"I can't promise you that!"

Tears flooded Chloe's eyes, blurring her vision. She didn't see her husband reach for Lily. He snatched her away before she had a chance to resist! "*Give her back!*" But the nausea hit again, as she backed toward the doorway. She had to get away from these people—had to escape the pain.

"Chloe?!" her husband called. "*Wait!*"

But she was gone before anyone could grab her. She took off running down the hall as fast as she could. She rubbed her tear-filled eyes, and stumbled near the stairwell like a klutz. *Get up! Run!* And so she ran down the stairs, through the front doors, and out into the parking lot. She bent over and vomited beside a pole where an elderly lady sat in her car. The lady left the vehicle to try and help, but Chloe did the only thing she could. She pushed her out of the way, and ran to the women's idling car. She jumped in the front seat, and squealed her tires out of there.

It wasn't fair! They had stolen her baby, and now she had stolen a car. She was going to run as far from the pain as she possibly could! *I hate you all!*

Chapter 34

"I don't care! I'm going after her, with or without your help!" Grayson argued with Jason, the police officer he sent to pick her up. He'd already sent the other two police officers after Chloe, and called in the cavalry. Rourke would handle that part.

"I'm staying here with my daughter," Pip told him.

Grayson nodded, and hobbled out of the room using Jason as a crutch.

"I wish you'd reconsider!" Jason sighed, trying to support the man.

"Shut up and give me the keys!"

"NO WAY, HOSAY! I'm driving!"

"Fine!" Grayson wasn't going to argue. He knew he was pushing it. Sure, he was going against the doctor's wishes by leaving the hospital, but what else was he supposed to do. She was his wife. She was hurting, and at the very least, she was a kidnapping suspect that needed to be apprehended. He hated thinking like that - *like a cop*.

She was his wife and that was the only thing that mattered. Besides, there was no way she would willingly kidnap a child. *No way!* There had to be a reasonable explanation for this. The look she gave him when he took the baby away, said it all. She really thought the baby was hers? *How horrible!* She was not only confused, but delusional. It brought on an overwhelming sadness, just thinking about it. *Oh Chloe! My sweet Chloe!*

As the two of them got into the squad car and sped off into the early morning dawn, Jason's led foot powered the vehicle at high speeds. *Good!* At least he was a man after his own heart. They were sure moving now! Grayson grabbed the radio and got a location on his wife. She was driving a 2004, Red Ford Focus.

He gulped hard when he realized she must have stolen it. That sent shivers up his spine. If she was capable of that, maybe she *was* capable of kidnapping. But Grayson didn't want to think that way. Not his Chloe. She was the poster child for goodness, and innocence. It was what attracted him to her in the first place. She was a good girl, the kind you wanted to marry and have a couple kids with. Yeah—*so much for that!*

He wanted to have children too! Why would she think he didn't? Man, he didn't realize how he had come across to her. Their arguments about adoption and the fertility treatments must have set her off. They argued about everything these days, especially the cost of IVF, and its effectiveness, even though they managed to scrape up enough to consider it. But, he was still willing to give it a shot—*for her!*

Grayson didn't realize he was giving off the vibe that he didn't want to be a father. He had to work on that. He had a lot of things to work on, he guessed. But first, he had to get his wife back and help her through this somehow. *God, don't let anything happen to her! Please!*

Jason put the siren on, and drifted around the next corner. According to the others, she had been spotted a couple blocks away. That would line them up directly in front of her. "There she is!"

"Careful! We don't want to spook her."

But then, roaring from around the corner, two cop cars blocked her way. She had no place to go but straight into some parked cars. She clipped the rear end of her vehicle on a black Cobalt, and then continued onward, finding an unexpected turnoff. "Go go go!"

"*I am!*"

"Well, go faster!" Grayson pounded the dash. "*We're losing her!*"

~~~~

Chloe was sweating buckets, and full of tears. She was never a good driver in the first place, and now she was fishtailing the car. *Steady!* She tried to even it out. It was hard enough to see through tears and bloodshot eyes, leave alone maneuver the vehicle properly. *Come on girl—get it straight!*

With a few sniffles, and a swipe of her forearm across her runny nose, she gripped the steering wheel and mustered the courage to regain control over the vehicle. *Now you're doing it!* She was getting away, away from them, away from all of it.

What made them think Lily belonged to that punk kid anyway? He barely looked old enough to be a father. It wasn't fair! *God wasn't fair!* Why was it so easy for everyone else to have a baby? What had she ever done to deserve infertility "*Ahhhhh!*" She let her frustrations out. She always pictured life as a mother. Now what was she supposed to do with herself?

And Grayson didn't care how she felt. If he did, he never would have ripped the child from her arms like he did. What a husband! *Good for nothing jerk!* She was leaving for good, and never coming back. Then he could live his life without her being a bother to him. It wouldn't cost him a dime! No fertility treatments, no IVF, no costly procedures. He could keep the stupid money they saved. But then, she spent it all, and there was nothing to show for it now. "*Ohhhhh!*" She wailed. *Everything was a mess.*

In the heat of the moment, Chloe lost control of the vehicle again. She sideswiped the brick buildings that lined the alley. What did she care? There was nothing worth living for anyway! *She might as well die!* Suddenly, she realized she was almost at the end of the alley, and a police car blocked the way. There was only one thing left to do—*RAM THEM!*

~~~~

Grayson got there just in time to see the Ford Focus catapult over the two police cars that blocked the alley. "*No!*" he cried.

But it was happening in front of him, and he had no control. The car looked like it was flying in slow motion, hovering there as if it held the balance between life and death. Visions of his life flashed before his eyes. His gentle loving wife was standing at the altar on their wedding day, beautiful as ever. He remembered that day with fondness. Her eyes sparkled the way they always did when she looked at him. *And now this.*

The car came careening down, tumbling end over end, buckling under the force of the crash. The roof crushed in, and the front windshield shattered to pieces. This was not good. *Not good!* In the blink of an eye, Grayson stopped short, and leapt out of the vehicle. He hobbled toward her as if to help somehow, but his comrades held him back. "It's too late!"

"*Let me go!*" Grayson swore at them, hyperventilating. She was his life, his very reason for being. How could this happen? Why her? He cried into the nearest shoulder. "*Noooo!*"

Almost immediately, the blaring sirens brought the ambulance and fire trucks to the scene. They went to work with the Jaws of Life, while everyone, including Grayson, hung in the balance. Could anyone survive a crash like that? *Not likely.* Yet, Grayson clung to the hope that his wife was still alive. He and all the bystanders watched in silence as the EMS crew worked quickly to remove the crushed roof of the car.

Then, a body became visible. His wife lay limp on the backboard, tightly bound in straps and a cervical collar. They lifted her to a gurney and moved her into the ambulance. "*Come on!*" Grayson finally spoke, waiting impatiently to be given the okay to see her. *It's taking too long!*

Finally, a familiar voice spoke. "Grayson, come with me." It was Rourke, his boss, coming to get him. He was bringing him through the crowd and over to the ambulance, where he would finally see his wife.

"Is she okay?" But nobody would answer his question. They just helped him into the ambulance to see for himself. It was not good—*definitely not good!*

Chapter 35

"How is she?" Grayson feared the worst, waiting for a response.

"Well...your wife suffered multiple fractures, and we don't know how she did it, but she's alive and awake now. Would you like to see her?"

"Seriously?"

"I'm quite serious. It appears the ambulance ride over, was the worst of it. She's stable now, and doing much better than expected. It seems like the big guy upstairs was watching over her. Most people in that kind of accident, don't even make it to the hospital."

Grayson couldn't believe it. He prayed and prayed, but never expected anything to come of it. Maybe there was something to this God stuff, after all? Pip was right.

The doctor led Grayson through the hallway to where Chloe lay, bandaged like a mummy. Didn't she look pretty. Her black and blue face and bandaged forehead fit right in, with the multiple casts she had to wear. Oh boy—and did she ever look ticked off. He wondered if he should even go in.

For a moment he paused, taking in everything that she was to him—the love of his life. Yes, he'd be there for her no matter what. She was his wife, after all, for better or worse. This was definitely the *worse* part, and that just made Grayson love her all the more. "Hey honey?"

"Go away!"

"I'm not going away!" Grayson wasn't letting her do that. He would force her to deal with this, and find a way to help her through, no matter what.

A nurse came in and smiled at both of them, moving a machine toward his wife. He was curious at first, wondering what that was for. But there were so many other things going on, he decided not to pay attention to it. More importantly, he needed to connect with his wife. "Honey, I'm sorry I hurt you. I'm sorry I had to take the baby away."

"You're not sorry!"

"I am too!"

Suddenly, he felt a group gather around them. It was a couple nurses and a doctor. One of them nodded to the other and smiled again. What was going on? "Ahem...Excuse me you two." The nurse with the machine interrupted. On behalf of the staff at the Royal University Hospital, we have something we've kept hidden from you." She turned, giggled, and motioned for the doctor to stand next to her.

What on earth was this?

"We'll just get this ready, and then we'll explain." Grayson watched as the nurse hooked a machine up beside Chloe and lifted her hospital gown, exposing her skin. Chloe didn't look impressed at the invasion of her privacy.

"What's wrong with me now?"

The nurse squeezed some blue gel on Chloe's abdomen and turned on the machine to a strange galloping horse sound.

"What's that?" Grayson furrowed his brow. Chloe looked disinterested, with a frown on her face.

The nurses giggled and turned to the doctor. "That's...a baby! —*Your baby!*"

"WHAT?" They both looked at each other with wide eyes, and busted out crying.

"You're a few months along, Chloe." The doctor informed her. "Yes, we were just as surprised as you, when we stumbled upon this little miracle. The baby is totally fine. Not affected in the least by this trauma. Must be a trouper."

"Like his daddy." Chloe sobbed.

"Or—her mama." Grayson winked, holding his wife's hand tightly. He couldn't believe this was happening now. After all the fighting and frustration over infertility, they had gotten pregnant naturally. *Wow!*

"We gathered you didn't know you were pregnant." One of the nurses spoke. "You see, I also work at the fertility clinic you visited. You probably don't remember me since it's been a while, but I kind of knew what you guys were going through, trying to conceive. I hope you don't mind that we presented your little bundle of joy the way we did."

"Not at all," Grayson told her. You have no idea how much we needed to hear this right now - *How much Chloe needed to hear this right now."* Then, Chloe burst into tears. "Honey? What's wrong?"

"You *know* what's wrong!"

And then Grayson remembered why they were there in the first place. It wasn't going to be easy to get Chloe off. They'd have to hire a good lawyer, but it was doable. "Honey," he spoke softly. He held his wife's hand. "Some things are out of our control. That much I know. A good friend once asked me if he could pray with me, and that made a world of difference. Now I'm going to do the same for you."

After all, this new-found curiosity in God made him realize that there was a bigger picture; bigger than him, bigger than their situation, bigger than crime and justice. Yes, it brought assurance to both of them as they prayed together in that little hospital room the day they realized God was in charge of it all.

Not only had Pip passed his friendship onto Grayson, but he passed on God's love as well. Now it was their turn. They were going to have a baby, and that was a blessing. Not only that, but it was an opportunity, a responsibility to be positive role models for a new generation. Yes, teaching this little one about God was definitely something they looked forward to.

And that is a legacy worth passing down!

Epilogue

A year later, Grayson picked up his giggling baby daughter and threw her in the air. The day she was born was the most amazing day of his life. His wife made it through the birth quite easily. No complications whatsoever. It was a blessing! Both of his girls were a blessing!

And now, as Chloe scurried around the house gathering the diaper bag and stuffing all the necessary things into it for her *Baby and Me* class, he realized how beautiful she was. She had recovered from the trauma of the car accident, and of being abducted, along with the other issues she faced with the fake adoption of the Eaglefeather baby. She was her happy self again. He was also glad Roz had miraculously pulled through. That played a huge part in his wife's recovery.

They all had to see a trauma councilor for quite some time, and that was very hard. But now, after the fact, everyone had made a full recovery—especially his wife. It helped that the charges were dropped as well. After a major investigation into the baby adoption scam, her testimony and co-operation with the police, led to numerous arrests connected with the scam.

Several people connected with Trevor Eaglefeather (a.k.a Trevor Standingontheroad) were running adoption scams just like his, in several different provinces. Grayson was just thankful for the children they were able to place back with their birth parents. He couldn't imagine what it would be like to have your child abducted.

As for Pip and Dinah, they were able to bond with their new little one, and make a full recovery from the trauma as well. They moved back home to Deep

Bay, when their little one was a couple months old. Pip told him it was to help take care of Sadie, but he knew it was where the boy's heart was.

Sadie miraculously came out of the coma, but was unfortunately paralyzed from the waist down. The woman was a fighter though, and the chair didn't stop her. She sprouted out *'Jesus'* to everyone she met, and didn't hesitate. She was a woman that completely deserved to have the Shining Star Lodge gifted to her by its owners.

Dinah became a published author, and writes murder mysteries underneath the evergreens that dot the horizon. Deep Bay is a place Grayson and Chloe have grown to love, also. They had the privilege of being invited up for Christmas for the first time, and all Grayson kept saying was, "*Breathtaking!*"

Since then, Grayson makes regular visits up there for work related issues. After all, Pip was still in training, and he was doing an incredible job. He was hired as the go-to guy for the Saskatoon Police Department, working from his virtual office as a researcher. And he's good at it too. He was much better than Grayson.

It suited the kid. He could work from home, enjoy the scenery, go fishing, be a tour guide, work maintenance, and be a full-time dad, all in the same breath. What guy wouldn't love to have that kind of job?

It was a thought that started Grayson's wheels turning as well. Why not move there? It would be good for everyone! But for now, he'd enjoy the many visits he and his family would have up there. The Eaglefeathers were becoming their most cherished friends, and he was thankful God put them together.

Grayson was thankful that he'd have these stories to share with his child when she grows up. He was thankful he met these lovely people, who were bold enough to share God with him. And Deep Bay, he was told, was a place of both beauty and *beast*, as Pip so cleverly put it. But even with that, they all realized that there were certain things in a person's life that they never want to remember. And then there were certain things that they never want to forget.

Our history is full of those kinds of things. But we all have a choice. We pick and choose which things we hold on to, and which things we don't. Every life-changing event molds and shapes us into the people we are today. It's our job to throw out the negative ones, and pass down the positive ones. If we can do that, the next generation will be able to live happy and healthy, without dysfunction and pain. The choice is ours—just like faith. Finding God was by far, the most profound life-changing event Grayson had ever experienced.

And that is a legacy worth passing down!

####

Afterward

I hope you enjoyed reading the final book of the Deep Bay series. If you haven't read any of the other books. Please consider reading book one: Deep Bay Vengeance. Please read a sample on the next page.

Deep Bay Vengeance - Prologue

Monday, January 30th - 3:58 p.m.

Screaming customers collapsed against a cold tile floor as the first gunshot ricocheted.

"The kid gets the next bullet if I don't get a key to the vault in five seconds," the masked man shouted as he yanked a teenage boy backward shoving a .357 Magnum to his lower jaw with a white gloved hand.

All doors to Chicago's largest National Bank suddenly locked simultaneously. Three more men appeared with Uzis, wearing black ski masks and white gloves. They shot out security cameras, shattering glass while customers covered their heads with their arms.

Silence.

"One...two...three...," the man shouted again, pushing the .357 Magnum further into the teenager's jaw. "Somebody better give me the key or I swear I'll blow this kid's head right off."

"Stop!" a woman cried with her hands up. "Please! Don't hurt my son! Let him go and take me instead. Please!"

"What?" the man retorted. "I don't care about your kid lady. I'll kill both of you if you don't shut up and get a key to the vault. Got it?"

The boy's mother shook her head, sobbing. "God help us!"

"Unless God has a key, you'd better shut up lady!"

"I'll shut her up," another masked man answered as he hit her on the back of the head from behind. She wailed as she dropped to the floor, holding her bloodied scalp.

"Wise up people!" the man shouted. "We mean business so don't try anything stupid. Now, get a key to the vault or I swear I'll shoot him!"

Nobody answered.

The masked man eyed the crowd and then the boy as he continued to choke, squeezing harder this time, pulling him backward while he struggled. "You guys are pathetic!"

Sobbing sounds filled the room as the man started counting again. "Let's see, where was I? Two? Three? No, it was four. Now four and a half, four and three quarters…Times up people."

"No...!" the boy's mother cried again. "Wait!"

"…Five!"

The gun pierced against the screaming cries as the teen's lifeless body dropped to the floor, speckling a bloody mess around him.

"Oh God! No!" his mother moaned, sobbing into her hands.

"Get up," the man kicked her head as he pulled her up by her black hair.

Screaming, she surrendered to his tight grip around her neck like a vice. "She's next if I don't get that key in five seconds. One…two…"

"Stop! Wait!" A small bald man from behind the counter rose with his arms up. "I know where the key is. I mean, I can get it for you."

"Well it's about time."

"B-but…I don't have it with me," the man smiled painfully. "I need to call someone first."

"Right and maybe I just need to skip to five."

"No! Really! See, the boss, he left early. He…he's the only one with the key."

The masked man smiled and slowly cocked his head to the side. "Well then, that's too bad for you now isn't it, baldy?"

The man's smile waned as he suddenly realized his fate. He collapsed immediately as a bullet perforated his sweaty forehead.

"Well this is your lucky day lady," the man grinned at the black-haired woman releasing his chokehold on her. "Seems as though baldy took your place."

She grabbed her throat with both hands and gasped for air, coughing as she crumpled to the ground beside a young woman in a pink business suit. Their eyes locked for a moment, sharing pain until the woman quickly darted hers away.

"On to plan B guys," the masked man grinned to his comrades. "We'll have to use the explosives. Come on Ruby. We need you babe."

The young woman in the pink business suit sheepishly looked around and slowly got up. All eyes met hers with shock and disbelief. She blushed against her long blonde hair and flipped it backward as if she didn't care what they thought. "I'm coming, Hun."

Moments seemed like hours as the hostages lay on the bank floor in wait. Suddenly a small explosion illuminated the hallway to the left where the vault was situated. Within minutes, the men ran out carrying bags, jostling machine guns over their shoulders.

"Hurry up, we set the silent alarm off," the woman in the pink business suit warned the others.

"Thanks Babe."

"What do we do with the hostages?" one asked.

"Shoot em!"

Cries filled the room as the men pulled off their ski masks, rubbing their matted hair. "On the count of five...One...Two...Three..."

The black-haired woman who lost her son lay her body down in surrender.

"Four...Five."

The compact submachine guns peppered the crowd as hostages scrambled on the floor screaming in terror. Some of them foolishly stood trying to run, only to fall like martyrs. The visual horror mirrored itself in the eyes of every victim as they cried for a mercy that would not come.

The grieving mother lay in wait. She peered through an opening between her arm and the floor. All four men wore smiles; their faces clearly etched in her mind forever. With a sudden jolt, a bullet pierced her arm, then her shoulder then...

Her eyelids fluttered, her breathing labored until a force beyond her control coaxed her to lay her heavy head down, relinquishing the fight, giving her the right of passage as her eyes glazed into a complete and utter darkness.

Chapter 1

One day earlier – Sunday, January 29th.

Loretta Lancaster hated her life.

If only she could turn the clock back twenty years. Being forty-five stunk. Who enjoyed watching her own body deteriorate anyway? Nothing seemed to fit anymore. Her saggy bulging stomach looked like white bread dough with too much yeast. It did nothing but expand every year, and the crow's feet only made her premature greying black hair appear even more pathetic. Thank the Lord for black hair dye. At least she could change that part of her looks without much trouble.

She dried her dripping hair upside down with a towel, her now jet-black locks without the grey, and flipped it up examining herself in the mirror. Her hair fell limp next to her pale dry aging skin, wrinkles creasing her forehead. She scowled at the pathetic reflection. Lord I know we're supposed to get old, but why must it be so difficult?

The phone rang, startling her. "Get the phone Bob!" she yelled from inside the steamy bathroom. "I'm doing my hair."

Loretta heard her husband pick up. She was relieved because she didn't want to talk to anyone anyway, not yet at least. First, she needed some time alone. After all, it was a special day for her, and she had to manifest a more youthful version of herself.

Sundays usually brought out a more cheery disposition in her, but today she couldn't seem to shake the depression. Today had crept up on her too fast. Ever since her fortieth birthday, time seemed to cheat her. Now at forty-five, Loretta was still stressed, still just a mom with numerous problems. Nothing ever changed. Her kids always needed something. If it wasn't money, it was her time. Everyone demanded her attention but never appreciated it, and her atheist husband was no better. In fact, he was the worst, taking her for granted, putting her faith down, and causing her tremendous suffering.

She wondered if life would ever get better for her. Part of her wished she never met her husband, never gave love away as if it came from an endless source. The fact was she had no more love to give. The well was dry.

For the longest time when the kids were young, she prayed for the day she could just have time for herself. But it didn't work out that way. Trudy started college two years ago and is still living at home, draining the family income. Tammy, the second youngest, is supposed to graduate from grade twelve this June, but wants to stay home too, and Jeremy, the baby of the family, apparently needs to sponge money from his mother even though his part-time job at McDonalds gives him plenty of spending money.

"What do you need twenty bucks for this time Jeremy?" she asked her son last night before he left for work.

"I need it for gas mom, what do you think? I told you my car is a gas-guzzler. If I had a new one, I wouldn't have to borrow so much money all the time."

"I told you we're not going to get you a new car Jeremy. It costs too much."

"Dad said I could."

Bob always handed the kids anything they wanted. It was an ongoing problem since birth. He always undermined her authority as a mother. Lately she found herself wishing she were anything but a mother and wife. After all, wasn't slavery against the law? She should be free to call herself, Loretta Lancaster, world-renowned Children's Book Illustrator.

What a joke. She ran her little art business from her home for nearly six years now, and not one decent book contract had come her way. Oh, she could draw beautifully, and the paintings she did were the finest quality, but to try to sell them, that was the problem. Nobody wanted to pay her. She always ended up giving her work away more than selling it. Nobody took her seriously, especially her husband. He told her to get a real job in the heat of an argument once, and he meant it. Everyone means it with their insulting remarks they make about her work being a good hobby. Didn't they understand? It wasn't supposed to be a hobby; it was supposed to be a job.

Loretta sighed; nobody respected her, not as a mother, a wife, or as an artist. Lord, when will things ever change for me?

As the morning lingered on and Loretta got herself dressed and ready for church, she gave herself a half-smile in the foggy mirror before she left the bathroom.

Jeremy complained when she got out, "Finally, you were in the bathroom for two hours. Are you going for lunch with the President or something?"

"Don't you talk to me that way young man, I am your mother."

Jeremy ignored her as he sauntered into the empty bathroom. "Whatever."

"I hope you're going to be ready for church on time young man," Loretta called after him as he slammed the bathroom door, grumbling. "I can't mom!" he yelled from behind the door. "I told you I gotta work at eleven."

Loretta sighed again, backing down like she usually did. *I give up.*

She worried about Jeremy's salvation. She didn't want him to turn out like Bob even though she was sure of his conversion when he was ten. But ever since he took the job at McDonalds, he missed church too often. At least he went to a good Christian school and Friday night Youth Group. She only hoped it was enough.

Maybe she should side with Bob and let him purchase the boy a new car after all, or perhaps one that just looked new. After all, Jeremy's car was a money pit, and it did consume most of his pay check. Maybe he wouldn't have to work so much then. Maybe he would be able to come to church more often.

"Bob," Loretta summoned her husband as he sat at the kitchen table eating breakfast. "I was thinking about Jeremy's car…"

Bob sat at the kitchen table still in his pajamas. He was a balding, fat, unattractive male chauvinist who seemed disconnected from Loretta most of the time. His bifocals sat at the end of his pointy nose as he read the paper without a hint of courtesy. He didn't even bother to look up at his wife. "Hugh?"

"Jeremy's car," she said with her hands on her hips.

Loretta hated his blatant disrespect for her. Was she really as repulsive to look at as her husband made her out to be? "Bob! Would you look at me please?"

Bob scowled, reluctantly looking sideways at her now. "What on earth do you want woman?"

"I'm speaking to you."

Her husband pulled off his glasses and shockingly looked his wife up and down. "What the heck are you all dressed up for?"

"Church."

Loretta's face grew red. "Not that you ever want to go?"

Bob shook his head, "Not on your life! Church is cancelled anyway. Someone called an hour ago to tell you but I wasn't about to interrupt your spa."

"What? Since when do they cancel church?" Loretta snapped.

"Since there's a winter storm warning," Bob grumbled and started reading his paper again. "You'd know that if you hadn't been in the bathroom primping for two bloody hours."

"Thanks a lot!"

Bob didn't look up. "Your welcome...By the way...Jeremy's old beater needs a new transmission. We could hunt another one down at the wreckers, but by the time we found one and put it in, it would cost a fortune. What he really needs is a new..."

"I know," Loretta reluctantly completed her husband's sentence, "a new car."

"Yah, I've been looking in the classifieds," he continued to read the paper, "and I found a good one in here for only ten-thousand."

"Ten-thousand?" Loretta shouted a little too loud. "We can't afford a ten- thousand-dollar vehicle!"

Jeremy came out of the bathroom then and casually walked bare-chested into the kitchen, grabbing a banana and peeling it. "Come on mom, don't be such a tightwad," he said, stuffing the fruit in his mouth and mumbling. "Trudy doesn't have to drive an old beater, and neither does Tammy."

Perhaps she was being a little stingy. If it would help him out so he didn't have to take so many shifts at McDonalds, it might be worth it. He could come to church more often. What was ten-thousand dollars compared to that? I'm outnumbered anyway.

"Fine."

Her husband circled the car advertisement and reached for the portable phone beside him. He punched in a phone number and talked to her before it connected. "You can go to the bank tomorrow and get the money can't you honey?"

Now you call me honey.

"No, if Jeremy wants a car for ten-thousand dollars, he's going to have to go to the bank with me and see just how much money that really is Bob."

"But mom," Jeremy whined, "I have to work after school, and..."

"Well you're just going to have to take some time out of your busy schedule to go with me to the bank if you want the money."

Bob groaned and rubbed his head. "Do what your mother says Jeremy."

His statement almost gave her a heart attack. Usually Bob told Jeremy the opposite. It was obvious he wanted to butter her up.

Loretta slumped down on the kitchen chair beside her husband and glared at her spoiled son still chomping on yet another banana. Sometimes she wished he'd get a little taste of reality just to push him to grow up for once. Adversity wouldn't hurt him one bit, it might actually do him some good.

Jeremy stomped away without saying a word.

Bob jabbered on the phone to someone about the vehicle he had found for his son. Loretta wondered why her husband would choose to use all of their savings to buy a car when part of that money was supposed to go for their summer vacation; the other part she assumed was going to be an investment for her art business. Bob had promised.

Why do I always have to give up my dreams for everyone else? And today of all days. Didn't anyone in this family even remember?

"So, I'm gonna run over and take a look at that car with Jeremy before he has to go to work Loretta," Bob informed her as he folded up the newspaper and pushed his chair away from the breakfast table. "At least Jeremy's beater is good for something: It starts no matter how cold it is, and it's as heavy as a tank on these icy roads."

"Be careful."

Bob rolled his eyes as he stood up. "Why don't you do something constructive instead of worrying about everything Loretta, like take that getup off?"

Loretta frowned. "Maybe we could go out for lunch when you get back?"

"Are you kidding, I'm not starting up our car in this weather."

No, but you'll take your son out in it.

Bob impolitely brushed past his wife. "Oh Loretta, don't pout so much, you'll give yourself more wrinkles. Why would you want to go out when they're forecasting a snowstorm anyway?"

Tears blurred Loretta's vision as she watched her son and husband slip their winter parkas on and slam the door behind them. Sobs turned to heavy weeping. Part of her wished her husband would never come back...and he could take that carbon-copy son of his with him for all she cared.

Oh, how she wished there had been church this morning. It was her only release, a time to decompress. At least God respected and valued her. He'd never turn his back on her, reject her, or abandon her like Bob and Jeremy always did. Why did you have to let the weather turn bad today Lord, today of all days?

What did she expect anyway; winter in Chicago was always like this.

Loretta stopped her pathetic weeping for a moment, sniffling as she listened to the creaking rafters of her empty home. Nothing but the brutal wind howled against her picture-framed walls. Jeremy's school picture hung there in a gold frame like royalty. Oh, how proud she was when she mounted it on the wall at the beginning of the school year. Now, she wondered why she even bothered to pine after his love.

Rejection was the only thing that lingered in the vacuum she lived in, constantly reminding her that her once happy home full of giggling children, noisy toys and bustling schedules, was empty now, just like her heart.

Empty was an understatement today. Trudy wasn't even home, she stayed overnight with a friend, and Tammy was still at a youth retreat. Bob and Jeremy's silly vehicle garbage had hurt her more this time than they even realized. But it didn't matter, nobody remembered anyway. She would just spend the day alone again.

"Well," she sniffled as she raised Bob's half-empty coffee mug as if to make a toast, "Happy birthday to me!"

Chapter 2

Present day, Thursday, June 29th.

Five extremely long and painful months lingered by since the robbery, and Loretta's arm still wasn't feeling up to par. The doctor said it would take a while, but at least the exercises were helping. She kept reminding herself that she really had nothing to complain about compared to the other victims. They were dead.

Loretta had been going to a shrink for a while. He wanted to help her with her "issues" as he put it. More like he wanted to take advantage of her situation. Some doctors would do and say almost anything just for a buck. It sickened her. It was bad enough she had to go through what she did, but to lose her son, and have someone make a profit off it: unbelievable. So, she gave her shrink the boot. He didn't make much sense anyway. He said she wasn't dealing with things. How could she not be dealing with things? It took her a week just to get up enough courage to talk about it. Did she finally do it? Yes. Did she talk to the police? Yes. She even went as far as working with a sketch artist to identify the four felons responsible for the heist. She never mentioned the bimbo in the pink though. That was her secret. Secret. Loretta herself was supposed to be a secret. The media reported that all the hostages had perished in the bank robbery. They didn't want anyone coming after Loretta.

"We know these four guys," the police told her when she was helping the sketch artist. "They're known felons."

But it didn't matter. They were long gone by the time their pictures surfaced on the news. It was her fault. She had taken too long to speak up, to identify them.

"They probably left the country by now Mrs. Lancaster." The police went on, "If you would have only co-operated sooner."

That statement still made her blood boil. Everybody blamed her, even Bob.

"Tell them what happened!" Bob shouted at her, as she lay wounded and speechless in the hospital bed. "Tell me what happened. I want to know what happened to my son!" He swore a string of swearwords at her but she didn't bat an eye.

Hospital security had to haul Bob out with his hysterical shouting and ranting. She heard him sobbing by the time the two officers escorted him down the hallway. But she couldn't do anything for the man. She had nothing left inside of her.

Bob never came back to visit her in the hospital again.

Jeremy's entire school had attended his funeral, everyone except his own mother. News excerpts showed distraught friends and family sobbing and hugging each other. Loretta, on the other hand, could not even cry. She still couldn't. She tried to, but for some reason, nothing came out at all.

Trudy moved out of the house the first week after Jeremy's death. Loretta received flowers at the hospital one day with a small white card that simply read, "Sorry mom, I can't deal with this. I moved out."

Tammy apparently graduated last week. Without a word, she took off to Europe with her friends. Her dad gave her money for the trip no doubt. At least she had the decency to send a postcard from Paris. Loretta wished she would have been able to go to the graduation but she knew she wasn't wanted there. Bob would have made a fuss.

Her husband finally got his wish. The divorce came through today. Loretta held the papers in her lap as she sat on her living-room sofa. At least Bob left her the house and Jeremy's old jalopy, though all it does is sit in the garage now, left as a shrine.

She never wanted the blasted divorce in the first place. In the beginning, she fought him tooth and nail. Then when he started dating all those younger women right in front of her nose, she didn't care anymore. He had wounded her heart beyond repair.

He spent most of his time drinking his sorrows away anyway. He moved in with some bimbo named Mandy, or Candy, or something like that. Apparently, she's supposed to be a beautiful twenty-six-year-old, and everything Loretta is not. Bob was old enough to be her father for heaven sake.

No loss though. She could have the old bald fool. Divorcing him was actually a relief. Life would be a lot more enjoyable without his put-downs anyway. But it was lonely. Sitting alone in a big house all day was the hard part. Old church members periodically popped by to visit even though she tried to give them the brush-off many times. She stopped attending church altogether after Jeremy died. Why should she pay homage to a God that seemed to be on a vacation when she needed Him the most? How cruel. If He didn't care about her, why should she care about Him?

Loretta set the divorce papers aside and moved over to the computer, her lifeline now, thankful for the second mortgage that helped her pay for the expensive thing. She'd borrowed against the house right after Bob told her she could have the "hideous thing" as he put it. The deed had never been in Bob's name. It had been her mother's beloved home up until she passed away. It was sixty years old, very small, and in desperate need of renovations, but it was home. She was glad Bob didn't fight her for it. He'd taken almost everything else.

The money from the house would be her soul source of income for a while until she figured something else out. Income. At least she had that now. She remembered her drawings...That silly business, never able to bring in a dime. Burning all her artwork was the best thing she could have ever done for herself. She had no talent anyway. But computers, this she could do, maybe even make a living from.

Playing around on the internet was how it all began, her brilliant idea that is. She typed in the names of the four felons one day, just to see what would pop up on the screen. From that, she obtained numerous amounts of pertinent information about them. Everyday she'd find out more. It was almost like a sickness. Finally, she came up with the perfect plan. If nobody else was going to find her son's murderer, she would. Luring those four goons to the most remote place she could find was easy.

Now she just had to get there.

Chapter 3

Friday, June 30th.

The morning was dreary and overcast when Loretta got up. She could smell the hint of rain in the air, odd for the end of June, yet somehow appropriate for the long over-due retribution that would soon follow.

"Come on," Loretta complained as she surveyed the empty parking space in front of her house. The taxicab she had called over an hour ago was late. Loretta checked her watch impatiently for the umpteenth time. It would be just her luck to miss the flight. She had to be at O'Hare at least two hours early.

Everything was ready, suitcases packed and waiting, every piece of pertinent information like her passport with that hideous photo, tucked away in her wallet. Loretta wished she would have been able to dye her hair already but that wasn't the plan. Her homely grey hair looked like a skunk because she hadn't bothered to dye it in the past five months. The top was grey and the ends were leftover black from January. She couldn't do anything about it now. She'd have to wait until she passed customs. It was very important that she follow her plans precisely. Every detail mattered, especially her hair. This time it would be a different color. She always wanted to be a redhead.

Moments later, a cab honked outside. "Finally!" she rolled her eyes as she glared out of the window. Loretta grabbed her two modest suitcases, and swung her combination laptop case-purse over her shoulder fumbling to open the front door. She set one suitcase down outside to pull the door closed and stood quietly on the step for a moment reflecting on how far she had come, how many pain staking hours of research and planning it had taken her to reach this point. She almost prayed for her plans to succeed. A dog barked in the distance, thankfully, nudging her mind from the thought. She didn't need God, and she was definitely going to prove it.

"Come on lady," the cabbie complained as he stood beside his open trunk.

"I'm coming."

Loretta lowered the two suitcases into the trunk and shimmied her way into the back seat of the cab swinging her laptop bag beside her.

"Where too lady?" the driver asked as he labored back into the vehicle. Speckles of rain began to dance across the windshield as the driver put the car into gear. She didn't answer him right away. Sadness seemed to linger, a sorrowful moment as she watched the rain dribble unevenly down the window, like mini streams not knowing which way to flow. The reflection troubled her. Perhaps it was last minute jitters, or maybe a little nausea. Whatever it was, Loretta didn't have time for it.

"Come on lady, where too?" the cabbie sighed impatiently.

She gulped hard, it was now or never, "...O'Hare International Airport please.

~~~~

"You've got to be kidding Harvey. Why would I want to go on a fishing trip?" the older woman chuckled. "Take one of your friends. You know I don't like to fish."

"Please Bertha! I told you Ben dropped out at the last minute, and he already paid for the non-refundable vacation package. There'll be an empty seat."

Harvey didn't really want to take his sister, but his options were running out. He had taken these sorts of trips with Ben ever since his wife died five years ago. But to face going alone? That was frightening. Lonely idle time meant idle thought, and idle thought meant him feeling sorry for himself, pining after his dead wife's memories. No. He had to find someone to take Ben's place, fast.

Since Harvey took an early retirement from the police force last year, he seemed disconnected from the people he worked with. He couldn't ask any of them to go. And friends were scarce since Rose passed away too. The only ones suiting that description these days happened to be Ben and his sixty-year-old big sister, and for some reason he couldn't picture Bertha roughing it out in the wild. Yet…as a last resort, he'd ask her one more time. "Please Bertha. I have nobody else."

It wasn't going to be a great July long weekend if she didn't say yes.

"No…and that's final." His sister scowled as she continued to stitch one of her monstrous Ladies-Aid quilts for charity. Bertha was a good companion when he needed a little company, but she sure could be cantankerous. His decision to move in with her after Rose passed was a blessing, but sometimes she could really get on his nerves. It wasn't as if he was asking her to give up a kidney. He just wanted a traveling companion. Ben sure left him in a bind.

"Why don't you ask someone from church?"

Harvey rolled his eyes…then contemplated it for a moment, "Maybe." He started leafing through the church directory. "Pastor Bill might want to come."

"Now there you go Harvey. All is not lost."

He picked up the phone with an impish grin and punched in the numbers. "Hi Pastor Bill, its Harvey Strong."

"And what can I do for you sir," the charismatic thirty-five-year-old preacher chided back.

"Well, I have a strange request…" Harvey noticed complete silence on the other end, not a good sign. "I was wondering what you were doing for the next few days."

"Well you know, it's funny you should ask…My wife just twisted my arm to clear my calendar for the weekend. Apparently, she wants to take the whole family across to the island for the July long weekend, see Butchart Gardens, Fable Cottage, and Sea Land. You know…the works."

"Is that right," Harvey frowned. "Well…you have a nice trip then."

"Oh, we will. We haven't been on a real family vacation in years, and since it's in our own backyard, we might as well," the pastor said. "But you wanted something?"

"Oh, it's nothing…nothing that can't wait anyway," he lied.

Harvey set down the phone with a sigh.

"Way to go chicken," his sister teased as she sat within earshot of the phone. "You're not going to get anyone that way, and your running out of time. Doesn't your plane leave soon?"

Yes mother, it does!

He had exactly four hours in which to convince someone to go with him on very short notice, and then make it to the Vancouver International Airport on time for his flight. Harvey exhaled through his puckered mouth and punched in another number. "Hi, is this Gale? This is Harvey…Harvey Strong.

Your husband wouldn't happen to be home this morning by any chance would he?"

"Oh...No Harvey," she said, "Martin's out of town this week. Is there something I can help you with?" Yah, maybe you'd like to go with me? Harvey scrapped that thought the minute it entered his mind. Now he was just being plain foolish.

"No. Just tell him I called."

Harvey placed the phone back on the receiver and blushed at his sister. She didn't have to be such a hawk, sitting there watching him with those carping eyes. "What?"

"I didn't say anything."

Thank the good Lord.

One more, Harvey thought to himself. He'd try one more number and that would be it. He punched in the numbers, turned his back to his sister, and plugged one ear with his finger. "Hi, is Pete there?"

"Speaking..."

Harvey's stomach started to hurt. "What are you doing this morning?"

The man on the other line answered, "Nothing."

"How would you like to take a vacation with me?"

"What?" the man replied with confusion.

"How would you like to take a fishing trip with me? I have an extra ticket and..."

The man interrupted rather annoyed, "...I can't go anywhere. Didn't you know my back was out again? Margaret put it on the prayer chain yesterday. Where've you been man?"

"Oh...I'm sorry..." Harvey blushed, apologizing like an idiot. "I didn't..."

Click. The phone hummed in his ear. The guy didn't just hang up on him did he? If that didn't beat all. Harvey slammed the receiver down, frustrated and enraged. He fingered his crumpled hanky in his pocket, yanked it out, and wiped his sweaty forehead. He didn't dare look at Bertha.

That's it...I'm going alone!

He marched down the hall to his bedroom and slammed the door. Rosey dear, I wish you were still here. You'd go with me I know you would. He sobbed, lifting a single dowdy brown leather suitcase to his bed. He popped it open and started heedlessly stuffing things into it. He was going on this vacation one way or the other, even if he had to go alone. And by George, he was going to have the time of his life too.

Bertha waved at him from the door as his taxi rolled away. He nodded at her as if he was about to explode. It wasn't her fault. It was nobody's fault. He would just have to endure this trip alone.

"Vancouver International Airport please," he told the driver, forcing a smile. "I'm going fishing!"

~~~~

Vicki Booth headed North on I-94 racing her vintage Harley Davidson Motor bike against the unfavorable weather. She'd picked a miserable day for riding with the on and off drizzle since this morning, a type of weather that made her think of Brighton England, her home where she grew up, where she and her sister were born.

She only found out that she had a sister when she was fifteen. Her drug-addicted mother had sent her sibling to a different orphanage in Chicago shortly after she was born. She lived there until she was twelve. Then, after a great deal of searching and persuading, Vicki finally managed to bring her sister home to England.

Now, after all those years, she still remembered the pain of watching her nineteen-year-old scrawny sister leave for the very place she rescued her from: Chicago. "It's much better than England," her little sister would boast, threatening to move back as soon as she was old enough, refusing to pick up the British accent like everyone else. "Talk right," she'd scold Vicki, embarrassed of her own heritage. It saddened her now.

Missing her sister more than words could say, Vicki said goodbye to her birthplace and followed her sister five years ago. It seemed as though she'd spent a lifetime tracking her down…and now again. A tear streamed down her already wet face as she thought of the only relative she had in the world.

Thunder cracked above her.

If she had been thinking clearly she never would have left the motel this morning. But she had to keep going, if she stopped for too long she might change her mind, and that was definitely not going to happen, not after everything she had been through.

"If your sister is missing Miss Booth, we have no leads at all and we can't spend any more time on the case. Chances are she doesn't want anyone to find her, or she's already dead. Aside from the last place she was, we don't know where else to look. If you want to hire a private detective, he would be more than willing to further the investigation. Other than that, there's nothing more we can do."

Vicki shook her dripping helmet head. Thanks for nothing! She had no use for a worthless police force that was too preoccupied to care, and why would she pay a P.I. to do something she could do herself? She knew her sister better than anyone else did, and if there was one thing she was definitely sure of, her sister wasn't dead. They were wrong. Her sister was alive; she could feel it

They were both women who had been around the block. They were flatmates for five years already, or "roommates" she was supposed to say. She knew her sister well enough to know she could fend for herself. No, if anything, her sister was just lost, wounded maybe, but not dead.

She floored the throttle with her black leather glove, and sped off toward Fargo, North Dakota. With any luck, she would reach the Canadian border by nightfall.

Chapter 4

Loretta was completely exhausted by the time her connecting flight from Minneapolis had arrived at the Saskatoon Airport. She gasped at the high temperatures reported over the intercom as they landed. She didn't know the weather in Saskatchewan could get up to thirty-six degrees Celsius. Actually, she didn't know much about Saskatchewan at all, or Canada for that matter. She never had a reason to until now. Her research informed her somewhat, but before that, she actually believed the rumors that they lived in igloos.

The first matter of utmost importance was to find a decent restroom, she thought to herself as she waited to exit the plane. Her bladder was completely full. She wondered for a moment if they even had modern facilities. Would she have to use an outhouse or something?

The modest contemporary terminal was buzzing with people. Loretta had underestimated what it would be like. She thought it would be old-fashioned and quiet. Instead, it was just like O'Hare, but a lot smaller. The business of the place struck her as a little odd. It was so noisy. Then she remembered the long weekend. This country had a holiday tomorrow. Why didn't they celebrate Independence Day on the forth like everyone else? But then, they did tend to do things a little backward. They celebrated Thanksgiving too early too.

Loretta shrugged her shoulders and headed for the bathroom, thinking how silly she was to assume she'd be using an outhouse. The extremely long line-up filled with women and children from all sorts of ethnic backgrounds. They waited with bags at hand and suitcases propped up against them. The wait was unbearable. For a moment, Loretta considered skipping it, but her bladder told her otherwise. She sighed as she gave into the hullabaloo, setting her own bag down on the floor against her leg to join the endless multitude.

~~~

The plane had been delayed two hours but Harvey didn't seem to mind. He was never one for schedules anyway, that was Rose's department, not his. He would rather be spontaneous anyway. As long as he got to Saskatoon some time tonight, it really didn't make much of a difference.

He ignored the crowd as he sat waiting for his luggage, chomping on the scrumptious baloney sandwich his sister had packed for him. He'd have to thank her after the trip. She must have snuck it in his bag unawares. What a doll.

The weather outside threatened a storm with its foreboding black clouds. Harvey missed that part of his old homeland the most. He hadn't been back in many years but he missed the unpredictable weather, this land of living skies where he grew up. It was like no other place, very different from the mountains. Prairie life always was. It seemed to have a certain charm to it, unlike the hectic fast-paced lifestyle of Vancouver. Yet, British Columbia was the place he met his beloved Rose. He stayed for her, and that was more than worth it. At times, he often thought of coming back here, but then he changed his mind, not bearing to leave her memory behind. He still had distant relatives here, but the last time he took Rose to visit them, she was young, vibrant, and cancer free.

Harvey pondered on that thought as he smeared a tear with his broad course thumb. No self-pity, remember? This was supposed to be an enjoyable trip and by golly, he was going to make it so. He checked his watch, wondering if he should bother looking up an old relative for the night or find a motel. He opted for the motel since he was practically a stranger to them now.

~~~

"Can I please have your attention everyone?" The voice interrupted on the loud speaker. "Environment Canada has just issued a severe weather warning as well as a tornado watch. This includes the city of Saskatoon and areas within a 60 km radius. Please be advised that all planes are grounded until further notice."

Loretta shook her dripping hands without drying them and quickly retreated from the confines of the bathroom. She shifted the weight of her shoulder bag, propelling her way through the crowd to the enormous glass windows facing north. Lightning bedazzled the onlookers, illuminating multi-level shades of ebony and emerald in the sky. It was like some ominous distant galaxy from a science fiction movie come to life. It was, to say the least, incredible, unlike anything Loretta had ever seen before.

It was time to move. Loretta turned around to locate the nearest pay phone. If she didn't hurry and call a cab soon, she might not get one before the storm hit. She'd manoeuvre her way to the luggage ramp first. Hers should be there by now. She'd pick it up first, call a cab, and then be on her way to the Prairie West Motel. It wasn't supposed to be far, just five minutes away, but she had to hustle her butt.

Suddenly…the lights went out.

The crowd began to scream.

Glass shattered and crashed to the ground.

Wind exploded through fragmented windows.

Loretta collapsed to the floor on instinct. The violent whirlwinds seemed to suck the air right out of her lungs. She couldn't breathe. Was she going to die? It was the bank all over again. She couldn't see the shots, but she definitely could hear them. Yes, someone was shooting at her. She could feel the bullet penetrate her shoulder again. This time she wouldn't make it. This time she would surely die.

~~~~

Harvey stumbled over a woman lying prostrate on the floor. At least he thought it was a woman. He couldn't really tell in the dark chaotic mayhem that danced around him. He knelt down, gripped her body in his arms, and started shaking her, but she didn't respond, she only palsied in his arms like a rag doll.

"Lady!" he hollered as loud as he could.

What was wrong with her? Did she get hurt? He wondered if the flying debris had pierced her body somewhere…but it was hard to tell in the shadows.

Suddenly…the wind died down as quickly as it started.

Lights flickered back on to a duller imitation, auxiliary lights that seemed to labor just the same. For the first time, Harvey surveyed the damage. Bloody lacerations marked the faces of panic-stricken people as they hobbled aimlessly about. The sight of it sickened him. Flashes of old images from days on the force, perpetuated through his troubled mind. Focus Harvey! Get a grip.

He closed his eyes and shook his head, remembering what he was doing in the first place. The woman...she still lay lifeless at his knees. He bent over to check for a pulse. It was pounding like a drum, calming Harvey with its rhythm.

"Wake up dear," he smiled as he patted her cheek, more confident now.

She gradually fluttered her eyelids until they opened. "What happened?"

"We went through a tornado dear." Harvey beamed, glad she was coherent now. "You must have passed out, but you're not hurt. Not like some of these people." He pointed to the destruction around them. "Mostly cuts and bruises, I hope. I don't think anyone got...I mean...I think the damage was minimal. Tornados are quite common in these parts. We're lucky; this one must have just clipped us..." He realized he was jabbering too much and suddenly stopped himself, blushing at the skunk-haired woman with beautiful green eyes. He cleared his throat, "Never mind."

The woman glared suspiciously at him.

"What's your name," Harvey asked her as he guided her to the nearest seat.

"Loretta," she crabbed, yanking an oversize carrying bag to her shoulder as if she was afraid someone was going to steal it.

"Is there something wrong?"

"No, I'm fine now...just leave me alone. Please."

Harvey's smile quickly turned to a frown. Way to go Romeo. He had been too forward. It was hard to gear what was appropriate and what was not, this day and age. He was definitely rough and out of practice when it came to women. He scratched his head confused. "I'm sorry...I just wanted to help. I could call you a cab or something."

"I can call my own cab."

Strike three…You are out buddy.

"All right then," Harvey mumbled as he walked away. He could take a hint. That's what he gets for being a Good Samaritan.

Chapter 5

Saturday, July 1st.

Loretta inspected her new reflection in the mirror as she wailed at the odd woman in front of her. "What the heck is this?" Something obviously went wrong during the processing. It wasn't supposed to look like...a cartoon orange. Luckily, she decided to dye her hair in her motel room instead of a public washroom, people might have thought she was a freak. She certainly resembled one now.

The sun hadn't even begun to rise when Loretta started dying her hair. Now as it rose, she pulled out the scissors from her bag and attempted to chop enormous chunks of it away. If she was going to look like a freak, she might as well go all out.

Hanks of the feathery orange stuff fell into the sink, clogging up the drain. She didn't care. It wasn't her sink; it just belonged to a dingy motel. If it had been her sink, she never would have permitted one of her girls to do this. But she was liberated now, free from responsibility, at least the old ones she used to have. Go free and fly...

Yet, for some reason, Loretta didn't look like a new liberated woman. She looked like something else...a clown, a punk rocker...or perhaps just a big fool. At least the new hairdo would conceal her age...or maybe not. The hideous wrinkles across her forehead that plagued her before were still there, her pasty white complexion with sunken eyes and gauntly cheeks still revealed her age...and those unsightly grey-black eyebrows, against the orange hair, were a clear ridiculous giveaway.

Loretta observed her complete body image as she stood in the mirror. She'd lost a lot of weight in the past five months, now her skin hung in places it shouldn't. And without makeup, she looked like a ghost. If only her skin wasn't so sensitive, she could at least apply some blush. She sighed at her homely appearance. The orange choppy mess didn't help matters much either. Bob would have disowned her had she done this when they were still married. She couldn't help but chuckle. At least she was unrecognizable, and that was a good thing. She'd top her ensemble off with a trendy pair of glasses.

As Loretta glanced at her watch, she realized she was out of time. She had one more stop to make before boarding the Greyhound bus. She hoped she wouldn't have a repeat of yesterday, with the tornado. To come out of it unscathed, was something else. There was no need for that old geezer to dote over her so much. It was embarrassing. Never had anyone fussed over her like that before. It was uncomfortable, odd. She didn't need anyone to take care of her.

~~~

Harvey handed the man his credit card as he waited for him to complete the rental agreement. He had chosen a candy-apple red Toyota Land Cruiser, hoping it was hardy enough for the trip. Ben would call him silly, but why not? He might as well go all out.

"Quite the storm we had last night, hey?" The man from behind the counter smiled, chatting while his back was turned.

Harvey grunted trying not to say much. Somehow, he had to get this fellow to move a little faster, or he wouldn't make it to La Ronge to connect with the floatplane.

"So where are you off too?" the man asked Harvey as he continued to chat.

"North...," Harvey sighed, fidgeting impatiently.

"North is a lot of places...Anywhere specific?"

Be nice Harvey...Do unto others, remember?

"I'm going fishing," Harvey said, hoping that would shut him up. It didn't.

"Oh...I got the perfect place. Tobin Lake, ever heard of it?"

The man droned on and on for fifteen excruciatingly painful minutes telling Harvey every detail about Tobin Lake, and about every trophy winning fish he ever caught: Northern Pike, Lake trout, Walleye, you name it. He went on about the cost of fishing licenses, about boat rentals, about how it was highway robbery the prices they charged these days. Apparently, that's why the man purchased his own 16.5 foot aluminum boat with a 30 hp Yamaha motor. Harvey forced a smile trying so hard not to be rude. He only nodded in agreement and hoped the guy would catch his drift and give him the keys some time before Christmas.

"So...are you off to Tobin Lake then?" the man asked again, waiting for the correct answer as if he needed confirmation.

"If I tell you will you give me the keys to the Toyota?

The man chuckled, "Oh, sorry about that pal. I get a little carried away when it comes to fishing...but yah. You tell me where you're going, and I'll give you the keys."

"Fine...Ever heard of a place called Reindeer Lake?"

"Have I ever! I haven't been lucky enough to go but that place is legendary. You can actually catch Arctic Grayling up there, and they're sneaky little buggers. You can't find them in most still water, but Reindeer Lake…Had a buddy of mine go up. He says there's this one place that's more than 700 feet deep."

Harvey beamed at the fellow's captivating response. Excitement washed over both their faces. "That's what the brochure says…I bought a vacation package and everything. It's a fly-in-fishing camp, one of the smaller ones on the north end of the lake. It's supposed to be a real secluded place."

"Well…I envy you man…Have fun."

Harvey felt sorry for the jovial car-rental attendant. His enthusiasm moved him with those round saucer eyes, mentally begging him to go along. For a moment, he almost invited him, knowing there was an empty seat available. Rose would have encouraged him to ask. She would have told him Jesus invited strangers. Yet, on this muggy sweltering morning, Harvey smiled; perplexed with his own paradoxical decision…He didn't want a companion. For some reason, as illogical as that sounded, he was looking forward to finishing this quest alone.

~~~~

Last night's storm affected Vicki more than she realized. She'd think twice before sleeping in a tent during a frightening storm next time, even if it did save her a few bucks. The radio announcer informed her this morning that a tornado touched down near the Saskatoon airport last night. No wonder there's nothing left of her tent. She trashed it shortly after the storm began, opting for a cold hard bench at the bus depot instead. Aside from a backache, sleeping there didn't bother her. She figured she could take care of herself if anyone tried to mug her while she slept. Her job at the truck stop prepared her for almost anything. Luckily, nobody bothered her. Aside from an occasional tourist gawking at her as she curled up with her leather jacket, the rest of the night was uneventful.

With morning, a sudden rush of travelers filled the bus depot, coaxing Vicki to move on. She swung her jacket over her shoulder and positioned her helmet under her arm, wrenching her back as she composed herself. With every inch of her body aching, not to mention her butt from the previous days ride, getting on that bike again did not look very appealing.

Vicki left the building with a sudden rush of heat wafting into her face; she realized it was going to be another scorcher. Straddling her mammoth bike, she jumped the motor to life, reminding herself why she was here in the first place. Her sister was missing and she'd never find her if she didn't get a move on. Stuffing her thick red curls into her metallic- black helmet, she tore out of the parking lot with a reverberation so loud it followed her long after she was gone.

Keep reading Deep Bay Vengeance by purchasing it on Amazon.com.

ABOUT THE AUTHOR

Award-winning author Kathleen Morris writes Christian fiction, mystery, suspense, and thrillers, to spread biblical truths around the world through her many flawed characters she creates. Her hope is to show that we all deserve God's unconditional love. Kathleen's debut novel titled Deep Bay Vengeance is her first in the Deep Bay Series, followed by Deep Bay Relic, with the third and final book in the series titled Deep Bay Legacy. Her latest novel is called The Prion Attachment, first book in the Blood War Series. Book two in the series, is called Blood Purge. When she's not writing, she enjoys spending time with her husband Barry and their three grown children at her home in Saskatchewan, Canada. For more on Kathleen Morris please check out her author page.

Other Books by Kathleen Morris

Deep Bay Vengeance (Book One)
Deep Bay Relic (Book Two)
Deep Bay Legacy (Book Three)

The Prion Attachment (Book One)
Blood Purge (Book Two)